W9-BXP-014

PARTING SHOT

PARTING

SHOT

JONATHAN
STONE

THOMAS DUNNE BOOKS
St. Martin's Minotaur
≈ New York

THOMAS DUNNE BOOKS.
An imprint of St. Martin's Press.

PARTING SHOT. Copyright © 2006 by Jonathan Stone. All rights reserved.
Printed in the United States of America. No part of this book may be
used or reproduced in any manner whatsoever without written permission
except in the case of brief quotations embodied in critical articles or
reviews. For information, address St. Martin's Press, 175 Fifth Avenue,
New York, N.Y. 10010.

www.minotaurbooks.com

LIBRARY OF CONGRESS CATALOGING-IN-PUBLICATION DATA

Stone, Jonathan, 1956–
   Parting shot : a thriller / Jonathan Stone.—1st ed.
    p. cm.
   ISBN-13: 978-0-312-35410-7
   ISBN-10: 0-312-35410-X
   1. Television journalists—Fiction.   2. Serial murderers—Fiction.
  3. Criminal snipers—Fiction.   I. Title
  PS3569.T64132P37   2006
  813'.54—dc22
                                                        2006040399

First Edition: June 2006

10   9   8   7   6   5   4   3   2   1

Michael Vines, fellow writer and best friend,
dangled the opening premise of this story over lunch
one day at Tuscan Square (51st St., just off 5th).

He let me run with it. He even waived his fee. What a guy.

Here's what I did with it, Michael.

To you. And to our friendship.

1

Another victim.

Sheryl Behar.

Fifty-four. (Though by now they know age doesn't matter.)

Another yellow pushpin in the county map. (Yellow for female. Blue for male. Red for child. Though by now they know gender and geography don't matter, either.)

Another news conference in the makeshift police briefing room at the far end of the station house's main hallway. A windowless, fluorescent-lit room of various former functions—temporary file storage, ad hoc staff meetings, end-of-shift surprise birthday parties for municipal employees—requisitioned now in the name of calamity.

Another occasion to pull open the tent flaps on the media circus. To crank up the calliope of local broadcasts and network feeds. The folding chairs and tables are jammed against one another haphazardly, as if violently broken from their original neat rows. Black, green, red, yellow cables wind along the floor like colorful, poisonous snakes.

The camera lights fill the briefing room with heat against

which three old ceiling fans turn uselessly. The lights flood the room with the blistering brightness of an interrogation, but in reverse: There's a cop in the halogen cross fire.

Another occasion for Webster County Sheriff William "Big Billy" Wyatt to get smaller. To continue performing his disappearing act. Diminishing before their eyes in some slight but detectable, physical way, with each announcement of each new victim.

Soon the media circus is in full swing, and Big Billy is the performing seal in the center ring—squawking, dancing, sadly amusing, pointlessly upbeat. The reporters are the circling lions and tigers, beasts of every stripe (baseball jackets over T-shirts, dark suits over sweat-stained oxford button-downs, the occasional tailored ensemble with pumps) growling and salivating and ready to pounce on the meaty, slow, well-lit prey. The long silver booms of the microphones are a herd of curious giraffes, insinuating their way from high up down into Billy Wyatt's face.

The victims: male, female, old, young, black, white, spinster aunt, bright-eyed teen—by now it's clear there is no pattern. By now it's clear that no pattern *is* the pattern. To make apparent the randomness. To strike fear and terror democratically, unilaterally.

Nothing new. Matches the same MO. Officers are swarming the area. The sniper will make a mistake. They always do.

Now the reporters are cormorants—squawking, shrieking as they swoop over a fresh corpse: What do I tell my readers? What do I say to my viewers? Stay inside? Avoid convenience stores? Avoid unnecessary errands? Keep the kids home from school? Don't travel alone?

A media circus. A frenzy of wires and cords and electronics and BlackBerries and cell phones and walkie-talkies and shouts and accusations and recriminations, tossed irritably and cynically toward the podium—the only conversational tone the reporters seem to know.

The bright, airless briefing room. A new and special circle of hell.

It's a chaotic, cheerless realm.

It's a grim, gruesome assignment.

And local TV reporter Sam Stevens would much rather be here than at home.

2

Whatever the sanitary term *failing marriage* might mean exactly, Sam Stevens knew his marriage was way past it. It was in free fall—separate rooms, petty revenges, combustible fury on simply beholding the opposing spouse. Fury like a flame—reliable, always flickering, always ready to ignite.

Her latest tactic was to ignore him. To turn away as if he weren't there. As if he were a ghost. Not just a ghost. An intensely annoying ghost.

They hid it skillfully. There, and only there, they were in sync. They presented the world with the ideal couple, the ideal family, so that to his television audience, he could remain trusted, well liked, and approved of. His high-visibility job was their meal ticket. But his job was also her trump card. Because high visibility also meant high vulnerability. She could at any moment, for instance, call another reporter—some "lifestyle" hack in thick pancake makeup, eager to land a scoop—and go on air to catalogue what a shit he was, a shitty husband and shitty father, and although the charges would be utterly groundless, it wouldn't matter, this being television. His all-important Q rating—the medium's measure of trustworthiness and likeability—would plummet, and his livelihood would be gone by the next evening news. The truth of it would be secondary—immaterial—amid the taint and whiff of scandal, and his employer would move swiftly on to someone squeakier clean.

Was she really capable of doing such a thing? Yes, more than capable. What had once been her impish sparkle, her playful unpredictability, had turned into a flamboyant recklessness. Yes. She could do it—or something like it that he hadn't sufficiently imagined yet. And the threat of that *something* was what let her stay out until three with her wildest and most unsavory friends while Sam fed their son, Tommy, and afterward helped him struggle through his homework. It was what let her fly off to Puerto Vallarta and Cabo San Lucas with who knew who to do who knew what, while he tucked in their son and reassured him that Mommy would be back very soon.

He had the job. He had the limelight. She had the power.

Sam drove home from the police briefing, keeping the radio news on, flipping between local stations, comparing the coverage. The excitement in the announcement of the latest victim was still in the live feeds and helped to distract him from his familiar dread about heading home.

What the victim had been doing. Who she was waiting for. Details of the victim's life. Brief on-the-scene exchanges first with neighbors. Then friends. Then with an uncle or cousin, the hastily appointed family spokesman. Finally, with the immediate family, who had initially refused to speak, but now—days or even mere hours later—was eagerly pouring forth. Despite the mantle of confusion, the story rolled out in a surprisingly orderly, predictable way, victim to victim. A ritualized dance of television culture. A Kabuki theater of disaster.

The sniper was out there somewhere. No one knew where he would strike next, but he almost certainly would. That was the tenor of the reports. That was the tone. That was how the radio stayed on in cars, in homes. Advice. Instruction. A voice in the dark. Don't go out alone. Don't go out unless absolutely necessary. Don't leave children unsupervised. Don't let them play in the yard.

Sam followed the familiar roads home—a route he could almost drive blindfolded.

In fact, it seemed there *were* fewer cars on the road. It felt like an off hour, a lull, although it was technically rush hour. There was still a sheen of normality if you turned off your radio. If you shut off your TV. That was your only chance to have any sheen of normality.

Sam was still a mile from home when he saw him.

He recognized the stride first. That bowlegged lurch that a lot of kids had with those heavy backpacks, but something distinctive in it, too. Then the mop of hair.

He'd been mildly disturbed to see a kid walking home alone.

He was shocked to discover it was his own.

Shuffling alone along the side on the road. That big blue backpack. A little soldier strolling through a war zone. The only kid out walking.

Jesus. Jesus Christ. Sam's face flushed with anger. His temples pulsed. He felt the heat in his chest.

He slowed, put the signal on, pulled the Toyota over to the side a few yards ahead of his son.

Tommy looked up from under his brown bangs and jumped back in fear, ready to run, until he saw it was his father.

Sam threw the passenger door open.

He was ready to scream at him. *What are you doing? Do you have any idea?*

But he saw Tommy's stricken face, the fear dancing in his eyes, the terror deep in there, probably present for the entire walk, probably surging with every passing car.

And then the next message of Tommy's look: *She didn't pick me up.*

"Get in. Right now," said Sam.

Tommy leaped into the safety of the Toyota's front seat. Sam saw the gush of relief on him.

"What the hell . . ."

"I had Chess Club." Tommy looked down at his blue backpack. "She didn't come get me." He played with the zipper of his parka absently. "I guess she forgot."

One kid. One precious son. And she forgot.

A maniac loose. And she forgot.

The ball of rage, the knot of fury, gathers up in him, almost chokes Sam Stevens.

Cunt. Selfish cunt. Selfish, out-to-lunch cunt.

Sam looks over at his son. He is relaxing now, the tension leaving his young frame, in the presence of his father.

Tommy looks up at his dad. A look Sam sees more and more as the boy grows older and observes the world and observes his place in it. A forlorn look. Sam recognizes it—recoils to recognize it—as an echo of his own haunted look, his own posture of guardedness and weariness—the withered garland of his marriage.

Now, at last, written plainly on his own son.

She's his mother, all right.

3

He waits until Tommy is settled in front of the television with a snack, then follows the scent of her cigarette, bounding up the stairs on the energy of his rage and into the open master bedroom, slamming the door behind him, unleashing.

"Where the hell were you?"

"What business is it of yours?" She is thoroughly ready for him; drily unflappable.

"Do you know what's going on out there?"

"He could have waited. He *should* have waited."

"He *would* have waited if he thought you were going to show. But he's not stupid. He knew you wouldn't. Your record is atrocious. *That's* why he was walking!"

"Jesus Christ. He was *fine*. You're overreacting. You're all caught up in this thing. Naturally." Dismissive. Mocking. Not even trying to suppress her superior smirk.

"Don't you care, you piece of shit? Don't you even care?" he screams at her.

It's about this—about leaving Tommy to walk home—but it's not about this at all. It's about this, but about everything. *Don't you even care?* She looks at him, and only after a calculating silence, answers. "He's ten. He's not a baby anymore." Sam thinks it's only a reference to Tommy being able to think for himself and make judgments, but it turns out it's not that at all. It turns out it's something more startling and brazen.

"I see you in him," she says. "Your walk. The sound, the inflections of your voice." She takes a drag from her cigarette. "Maybe that's why I didn't pick him up," she says, the smoke from her cigarette hanging as if with bitter speculation.

Her seeing Sam in their son, Tommy. Sam should have been able to experience it as a moment of pleasure. A moment of satisfaction in the miracle of generations, of genes, of family. She turns it, instead, to a fault. To a failure. To something, indeed, horrifying—a multiplication, a reproduction of the beast in front of her.

She says it, he knows, to startle him, to shut him up. Using shock to get him off her back. Out of the bedroom.

It works. He is silenced. He is indeed driven out of the bedroom—though not before a hamper is kicked over. Not before the still-undone laundry is tossed across the floor. Not before a decorative plate shatters against the baby-blue wall.

As he heads back down the stairs, across the back edge of the TV corner, out from under his blind rage, he can see his boy, escaping into the universe of a hundred channels. From down here, TV blaring, could Tommy hear what emanated from the master bedroom?

When their fights punctured the night, Tommy cowered in his own bedroom, Sam knew. It was always Sam who went to him. She never did. Maybe she was embarrassed at what the boy might have heard her say. She never went to Tommy. And now, at least, she had explained why.

4

The next morning, Darryl Jenkins struts around bare-chested in his loose-fitting pajama bottoms. He is potbellied, pasty white, greasy haired, and balding—so perhaps it isn't strutting but nonchalance.

Darryl smiles gently, formally—shows an exaggerated courtliness toward his guests and their queries.

Sam has rarely seen a man so comfortable, so at ease, with the lights and camera trained on him. Maybe it comes from Darryl's familiarity with his surroundings. But the ease, the zen peacefulness still strikes Sam as remarkable, since his surroundings are a small cell in a maximum-security facility. The cell that has been Darryl Jenkins's home for twenty years. That will be Darryl Jenkins's home until he dies.

It is a series Sam has been doing, trying to fill airtime with stand-ups and live segments of any relatedness at all, while he and the other reporters wait for the next grim news, hoping like foolish gamblers for a scoop or a break.

Inside the Mind of a Serial Killer. It's an embarrassingly blunt, particularly odorous slice of journalistic tripe. He started it as a way to eat up time, but it has found an audience. It has turned into a nice little piece of broadcast equity. A nice little point of advantage.

He knows he has Darryl Jenkins to thank. Darryl's odd serenity. His bizarre, infinitely mutable philosophy. His strange aphorisms. His seedy appearance. His beady coal-black smiling eyes.

For the past few minutes, Darryl has been talking technique. (*God forgive me*, thinks Sam.) Choking. Suffocation. The human torso's infinitely vulnerable anatomy. But Darryl's discourse on technique is tapped out. Technique has given Sam all the shock value it's going to. Much of this he can't use anyway—it's over the line for local broadcast, even for him. Sam signals to Darryl—as if to an actor—to wrap it up, move to a new subject.

"I know that's *how* you can do it, Mr. Jenkins," Sam says sonorously, tossing in an amusing little barb, he thinks, with the respectful honorific *Mr.*—"but, well, how *can* you do it?"

Darryl smiles in recognition and appreciation of the turn of meaning, the efficient little verbal twist, and then—as easy, as dreamy, as relaxed as always—the murderer rocks gently on his ancient stool and takes his cue.

"It's like anythin'," he says in his down-home drawl. "Like learnin' to swallow a pill, ride a scooter, anythin'. Somethin' you can be taught, I guess, but mostly you teach yourself." He twinkles, revels, in the self-evidence of it. "It's exactly what you think," Darryl informs the audience. "Exactly what you expect. Surprise of it is, it ain't no surprise at all."

He picks with concentration at a cuticle. "First one is the hardest, 'course. Oh, you retch. You puke. You shake. You blink over and over, uncontrollable, like some part of your brain cain't really believe it." A little shrug—almost delicate. "But then you get used to the idea." He shifts on the little stool in the cell, frowns for a moment. "And after that, it gets easier. After that, you start watchin' closer. You start payin' attention." He pauses. He focuses for a moment on a spot on the cement floor. "You start to get good."

He looks up. "You either want to do it to see what it's like, or you have to do it, 'cause you got no choice. That's the only two categories of everything we do in life, in't? Things you want to do or things you have to. But this falls right in the middle, don't it?"

He stares at Sam, the reporter, and smiles impishly, displaying a set of teeth that obviously had never known dental care before his arrival into the auspices of the state. "That's the dirty little secret of it," he says. "The dirty little secret you only discover if you actually do it. That it's just like anything else." His trademark gap-toothed punctuating smile disappears abruptly. There's only the frank stare of the coal-black eyes.

Sam Stevens has been listening so intently, he isn't even sure if the cameras are still rolling.

5

Sheriff Big Billy Wyatt pulls out a high-powered rifle from behind the lectern.

The gun produces a general stirring among the reporters, an increased alertness, but no gasps, no ducking for cover, no greater reaction than that.

He holds it up high with both hands, displaying it for them like a priest with a sacred object. "This, ladies and gentlemen, is a U.S. Marine Corps M40A3," he proclaims.

Sam and the young radio reporter who has been sitting next to him all week—Jim Needham, a carrottopped kid with ears like biplane wings, which would probably keep him in radio—look sidelong at each other. Both shake their heads at the fast-approaching embarrassment. The latest reason to cringe.

It's the morning briefing, and the sheriff and his department are obviously borrowing a page from the television reporters' playbooks—maybe even Sam's, as well as the national reporters' far slicker productions. Taking a lesson from the coverage that has encircled them like whooping Indians around a mud-stuck covered wagon.

They're starting to do their own stand-ups.

Oh, sweet Jesus.

Wyatt grips the rifle now with paramilitary correctness. He has the big frame of an aging athlete—of a star college linebacker or a forward or a rangy fastballer twenty years past his prime— the spry, joyful athlete, the tuned body, still lurking in there somewhere, beneath the weight and the years hanging off him now. "The M40A3. Individually manufactured in Quantico since 1996 for Special Ops sharpshooters. Seventy-millimeter scope furnished by U.S. Optics. High-powered, high-velocity tactical weapon that delivers better than point-oh-five minute-of-angle—which means extremely and consistently accurate, at seven hundred meters and even above. One shot, and that's that—whether you're the killer or the victim," he quips.

The sheriff starting, apparently, to enjoy the element of theater. Something to entertain the reporters with, to distract them from the fact that the Webster County Police Department is nowhere. Has nothing.

It was a strange dance between the media and the police. After all, if there was enough of a lull between murders, the crime reporters would all head back home. But as long as the story seemed like a live one, the reporters hung around, killing time, waiting, each making a professional guess on when the next murder would be. Should they head to the airport or to the hotel?

And in all their downtime, how do you keep these restless, congenitally irritable out-of-town visitors amused? How do you keep them from rutting around your quaint little village, your mediocre little police department, digging for more stories just to mark time? How do you appropriately play host to such a gruesome local attraction?

Both police and media knew that while an arrest would be news of some sort at least, another murder would be infinitely better as far as news value—and news careers. The story building. Arcing toward some promising crescendo, still fertile in the public imagination. Some of the more wantonly ambitious privately hoping, praying, it isn't solved too quickly.

An ordinary and unremarkable exurban county had been turned into a war zone, and the correspondents were here with their war-zone mentality.

"This weapon—or something like it—is a part of his MO that I can share with you at this point," says Wyatt.

"What's the part he can't share?" whispers carrottopped Jim Needham.

"The part about all shots fired from approximately one hundred yards," mutters the crusty gray eminence of crime coverage who usually sat in front of them—arrogant, superior, not bothering to whisper. "Perfect distance to maximize accuracy with chances of getting away unseen. Gun nuts all know those stats and algorithms. So do weathered old crime reporters." The old reporter smiles.

"Now let me introduce Paul Greeley, associate professor of criminology at Webster State," intones Big Billy Wyatt from the podium.

Wyatt gestures to a small man in a bright cardigan sweater stepping up beside him. The man seems to welcome the limelight. Probably a lecturer. A man who clearly relishes an audience. A new actor in Wyatt's theater.

"Associate professor at a local campus," mutters the old reporter sarcastically, leaning back toward Sam. The old crime beat reporter sighs loudly, shakes his head again at these pathetic attempts.

"This is a crime of modernity," the professor begins.

Oh, Christ—get off it, thinks Sam. A crime *theorist*—one step less practical; one step further away from solving it.

"Today's perfect crime. No victim's blood on the killer, no hairs, no fibers, no contact. No social network or network of interaction to trace from victim to killer. This is the crime of our anomie. Symptomatic, axiomatic of our society. Professional. This is crime using technology maximally—a high-powered scope, a high-powered rifle, an efficient single round applied with apparently surgical precision. No apparent social connections, so a trail that never even begins, much less ends anywhere, probably through the careful management, control, and manipulation of personal information via the Internet and computer systems, I'm willing to bet. It's like the killer is taunting us with our own modernity. With not only the crime's perfection, but with our construction of a world that allows this perverse perfection. This perfect and ultimate and momentary connection of killer to victim, and then utter disconnection—"

"Sheriff Bill," says one of the national reporters, interrupting the professor easily with his familiar, powerful, national-television voice—bored, condescending, demeaning, making clear that he wasn't falling for these little diversions. "A name, a face, a suspect—that would make much better theater."

"You're at six, Sheriff Bill," another reporter calls out. Six victims so far.

"Six . . . and in a fix," someone else shouts out, anonymously and gleefully inane, from the back of the briefing room.

The predators circle; the calliope wheezes joyously; the circus is in full swing.

The professor, alas, had only been summarizing. *Those who can't, teach.* But it does let Sam realize something new. Something startling.

The precision, the rigor of each attack, had already led the profilers to quickly assume and quickly agree that they were dealing with someone highly trained, someone paramilitary, with some connection to the military at some point in life. Or else someone who only wanted it to look that way. The absence of any error, any trail or lead, tended to confirm that. The sniper's choice of hollowpoint bullets, fired at that high velocity, it has been explained to them, tend to shatter on impact against the skull, leaving little chance of tracing a slug to a particular weapon; leaving in fact, little slug to examine at all.

If it was a professional of some sort—well, the fact was, professionals often *didn't* get caught. In plenty of cases, the pros were never identified, never found out, whether they performed a single hit or two dozen. Unless they wanted to be. Unless they turned themselves in. Scraped and missing serial numbers. Customized weapons. Customized rounds. These things were their stock in trade. Child's play.

The lack of any apparent human connection, the perfect phantom quality of each attack, suggested someone with the ability to closely manage and even erase his own official and electronic existence. The precision, the accuracy, the rigor, the absence, was part of the terror—and part of the very intent of the terror. It was something even colder and crueler than a professional hit—because worse than merciless, it was meaningless. If there was rage attached to it, it was global rage. Ceaseless, relentless rage, uncompromised by any other emotion.

A one-man crime wave. (The *one* and the *man* only presumed, of course.) A homicide tsunami. Putting little Webster County on the map as no previous college sports star or minor actress with a big American smile ever did or ever could.

Sitting and listening to the preening professor, Sam has realized—sensing it slowly, listening to Wyatt and his experts, gathering it with increasing conviction—what no one has said aloud in any of the briefings. What no seasoned reporter has leaned over to mutter to the wannabes.

Maybe, what no one has dared to say.

Surely some of them—some of the most seasoned reporters— had to be thinking it, based on this profile, based on this MO.

That this one was different.

This was the one they'd known was coming for a while.

This was one that might not get solved.

This was a killer who might never be caught.

Sometimes the world changed, and its busy, blindered inhabitants noticed only later. The human species had reached the point where a device in a backpack could render New York City uninhabitable for centuries. Where a soldier's handheld technology could locate a target of just inches from hundreds of miles away. And where a sniper who had the motivation and intelligence and training not to be caught also had the means not to be. If he really wanted to get away with it—if that was really the primary point of his enterprise—well, he could.

You're at six . . . and in a fix.

Sheriff Billy Wyatt glared.

Despite his size and normally dominating presence, he had recognized that his standing at the lectern alone delivering the meager updates wasn't enough to placate the media maw. Hence the rifle. Hence the expert. Hence an attempt to provide them something more. Yet this was their reception. Cynicism. Sarcasm. Unregenerate dissatisfaction.

They were pushing him, Billy Wyatt knew. Goading him. Hoping for a mistake. Hoping to force a misstep in his painfully methodical, earnest approach. It's what they did, the media mob, the lawless rambunctious Fourth Estate. It was their own subtle, crafty M.O.

Because a mistake, a misstep, an investigative blooper—now *that* would be theater. That would be ratings. Tune ins. Extra column inches.

Come on, Wyatt. Give it to us.

6

Inside the Mind of a Serial Killer. Last in a Series.

The ratings have been excellent. But Darryl Jenkins has had his moment, has run his course. You're talking about the banality of evil, after all, Sam knows. It's nothing, nothing at all, Darryl has told the audience frankly. And in a broader sense, too—in murder's lack of any hidden meaning, its absence of anything instructive—Sam knows what Darryl said is certainly true.

In this final segment, Sam begins by touring an empty cell identical to Darryl's. Showing what life is like physically, literally, daily on death row. Now, to conclude both the segment and his little series, he's back with Jenkins himself, one final time, one final adieu.

"Anything more to say, Mr. Jenkins? Any parting words of wisdom or advice?" Sam hopes his facetiousness is loud and clear. He prays no one thinks he's actually seeking life wisdom from a serial killer. He hopes his audience understands there is irony at work here. But you never know. It's a big world. The lowest common denominator is always lower than you think.

Darryl cocks his head at Sam Stevens. Shrugs. "Don't know what else I can tell you," he says to Sam. "Taught you everything

I know," he says mockingly, proving himself equal to Sam's face-tiousness. "It's your turn now, son. Go out and do me proud."

Darryl gives a little sly smile and settles back onto his hard bunk.

The cameras go off. The bright lights are extinguished. The cell block is returned to its customary weighty shadows and echoing quiet. It is a moment of suspension, of an eerie intermezzo between television and life.

Sam Stevens looks evenly at Darryl Jenkins, who, from the bunk, is looking—still smiling—back at Sam.

Darryl's familiar smile is different, now, Sam notices. Subtly shifted. It's a smile of . . . inquisitiveness. After all of Darryl's showy languor, all his riveting indifference, Darryl's expression is one of genuine curiosity.

7

"Rounds taken from a new box of cartridges are machined to tolerances within thousandths of a millimeter. For all practical purposes, they're identical," says Dr. Leon Eggers, national and celebrated forensic expert, taking a bullet from a box, holding it up. "But that same round, once fired, can become as distinctive as a fingerprint."

Sheriff Wyatt stands beside Eggers. The sheriff has wised up a little, Sam sees. Recognizing that a local criminology professor long on philosophy isn't much of an attraction for the national circus, he has imported a more experienced and more credible cast, one with more stage credits, even some stars. The Billy Wyatt Theater has had an upgrade.

"A bullet's trip through wood or plaster or cartilage and bone can deform it severely, of course, but that's not the distinctiveness I'm talking about. I'm talking about the first leg of its journey—through the barrel of a gun."

Eggers looks out at the audience. "Every gun barrel has a rifling pattern—the arrangement of spiral grooves that runs along the inside of the barrel that every manufacturer designs specifically for every model. Now a bullet, of course, is made primarily of lead, a material that softens when exposed to heat. That property of softening with heat is, indeed, the very quality that lets the bullet travel through the snug rifle barrel so predictably in the first place. In its high-temperature, high-pressure, high-velocity trip through the barrel, the lead softens enough to actually pick up and imprint its own version—a kind of echo—of that particular gun's rifling pattern."

Sam can see that some of the national reporters already know much of this. But it is something, at least—some effort, some regrouping from the overwhelmed Wyatt, and Sam appreciates that.

The projector beside Eggers clicks. The slide shows what is clearly a fired bullet, magnified significantly, with—indeed—a tightly packed series of parallel lines and markings running laterally across it. "Think of these markings and striations you see as a miniature map of the bullet's journey. A diary entry of its extremely brief trip." He looks over his bifocals at them. "A fossil record written in lead. An inverse record, incidentally. Because the grooves from the barrel show up on the fired slug as microscopically raised markings, called 'lands.' While the barrel's 'lands'—its raised portions—show up on the slug as grooves." Eggers clearly relishes the parallelism, the logic of it.

"A fired slug's unique fingerprint of striations—once we factor in caliber and/or gauge, and once we check it against the two FBI databases established for exactly this purpose—lets forensic scientists say definitively what model of gun the bullet came from, often streamlining an investigation substantially and providing a route to the shooter's identity." Dr. Eggers is a tall, stooped man, whose scoliosis makes him look as if he has spent his life bent over a microscope—which probably he has. But here he stands up straighter for a moment, as if with some measure of pride. "Meaning also, that a forensic scientist can connect any bullet—at a courtroom standard of evidence—to the weapon that fired it." Eggers now looks out at them and smiles meagerly. "Usually," he says. "Because everything I've said so far is, in this case, irrelevant."

Click. Another slide appears. A gleaming unfired bullet, its conical head of lead jutting above its copper sheathing, the very tip of its lead sheared flat. "Our boy is firing semijacketed, hollowpoint rounds. For now, I've been instructed not to characterize the rounds any more closely than that. Semijacketed hollowpoints are a typical enough choice for a high-powered tactical weapon. Now, when a semijacketed hollowpoint from a high-powered rifle strikes something hard—like steel or bone—there's a fair chance the round will literally shatter or crumple on impact, leaving the forensic scientist without those telltale striations, without that fossil map in lead. Hollowpoints, being hollow, are inherently weaker and specifically designed to shatter and splinter. That's their purpose, after all"—he shrugs at the obviousness—"maximal stopping power through maximal internal damage.

"The shooter in this case has consistently, unerringly, hit cranial bones—his victims' skulls—so that no slug has remained intact enough to provide any striations. But I believe the purpose of semijacketed hollowpoints in this case isn't primarily to inflict extra damage to the *victim*. It's to inflict extra damage to the *round*. A shattered, fragmented round can't lead us to a particular make or model of weapon. It doesn't lead us to much of anything." Eggers says it, Sam notices, with an unmistakable measure of admiration. Eggers regards the room somberly. "The seemingly intentional broad range of victims, you'll notice, has not included any infants, whose skulls are soft and would leave a slug intact enough to be useful."

This observation seems to stir even the jaded veteran in front of Sam to the edges of visible disgust. Eggers senses it. "Sorry," he mumbles from the lectern, "I'm a scientist. I have to look at everything."

He turns off the projector.

"He's playing a high-risk game. Relying on his choice of ammunition and perfect marksmanship. On the other hand, he's winning the game so far." The forensic expert goes a degree quieter, hushed and nearly worshipful for a moment. "It's almost as if he's taunting us with his choices and abilities. With this high-wire firearms act of his." He shakes his head. "But that's assigning state of mind, which is not my arena, after all."

Eggers goes on to explain the differences between the more rugged military tactical weapons for Army Rangers and Special Ops and the lighter precision weapons for police SWAT sharpshooters, speculating about how the shooter's background might influence his choice or how he might consciously try to cover that background up.

But Sam is hearing it all from a strange distance now. From somewhere removed. He is alert to every word, he is absorbing it all, but from some shaded, unaccustomed place inside him.

"Sam? Hey, Sam? . . ."

It takes Sam an instant to focus. The briefing is over, Sam realizes. He turns. It's Jim Needham. Carrottop. "Feel like gettin' a beer?"

"I'd love to," Sam says, "but I promised my wife I'd pick up my kid at Chess Club."

He'd told Denise he'd be there. Not that she cared, one way or the other. But he figured it was easier. Avoid another incident. The path of least resistance.

"You're a good dad."

"I could be better."

"Next time, then," says Needham.

"We know there's gonna be one," says Sam, with a fatalistic shrug.

8

Adam Katz.

Seventeen years old.

Coming out of a supermarket, running a quick errand for Mom. Apples and lemons for a recipe. A chance to drive the car with his new license.

Katz. Hate crime? Bias attack? The words don't even fly half-heartedly. They know it is random. Democratic. Equal opportunity. Fair and balanced.

Another colored pin goes onto the map. Blue for male or red for child? The pattern is no more illuminating either way.

Fresh bedlam in the briefing room. The glare and buzz of the lights. The whir of the cameras.

Adam Katz. Seventeen years old.

Number seven.

Sam's got the home-field advantage over the national guys, and he's not afraid to use it to the fullest.

Thanks to the mayhem, his career is going from good to great. While his marriage has traveled a similar distance from bad to worse.

He had seen it there in their bedroom that night—the night she drove him out with her spite for their own son. *I see you in him. Your walk. The sound, the inflections of your voice. Maybe that's why I didn't pick him up at Chess Club.* He had been too stunned in the moment to process it—at some level could not believe he'd seen it, had not wanted to see it—but after leaving the bedroom, in the hours and days following, he had come to recognize and accept what his eyes had caught. He is a reporter, he knows what he saw. There, in the ashtray, as if luxuriating amid the harem of her thin, white, stubbed-out cigarettes, was a fat, half-burned cigar.

But more than the object itself—the arrogance, the insouciance, the brazenness of it. The finality of it. Yes, maybe just the super, making a repair. There was a toilet to fix, a thermostat that needed attention, and he noticed they'd been taken care of. Sam wouldn't put it past her that the cigar was there only to taunt him, to enrage him. Maybe just the super; maybe not.

Yet just as hurtful to Sam Stevens—just as damaging and painful and revealing in the night's aftermath—was the comment at breakfast that he'd overheard, that he was even intended to overhear, he assumed, as she could not have missed Sam's footsteps coming down the noisy hardwood stairs. "Your dad said he'd pick you up at Chess Club, Tommy. He told me he'd be there. I'm sorry about the confusion, honey." Further confirmation of the petty lies in passing, the accruing moments of belittlement, snideness, and outright fabrication behind his back—their offhand delivery somehow adding to their authority, their capacity to convince. Altering, steadily eroding, his own son's perception of him.

It burns, it sears, like a half-smoked cigar.

For some time now, he has been sleeping alone at the cabin, more than an hour and a half away. The one they bought together. Their former love nest. Hah. Now they can't even stand to be in the same house.

No one else knows his marriage's true state. No one is aware of it. Certainly Tommy doesn't understand the depth, the extent of the crumbling. How could he? Their child.

"Scott? Scott Bayer?"

"You got him."

"Sam Stevens, WWBS Television."

Scott smiles. "Seein' a lot of you lately," he says.

"I'd like to see a little of you, Scott."

"Meaning what?" Cold. Suspicious.

"Hear me out," says Sam. "Here's my thought. See what you think."

Scott Bayer was a cop. Still is. Sort of. Scott Bayer was on the street three years ago, and it was night in the ghetto in an alley (practically scripted, thinks Sam) and Scott was too quick on the trigger, and a black teenager lay dead on the pavement. Although the kid was armed, it turned out it was a Swiss army knife flashing, not a gun, and Officer Bayer, after all, was far out of knife-swinging range. The dead kid turned out to be not a small malnourished twenty-one-year-old specimen of unremitting trouble but a big thirteen-year-old with good grades and hardworking parents. The black community came out in force, marched on several Sunday mornings, got an audience in city hall, and the media was all over it, which is where Sam got to know Scott. Sheriff Wyatt, to his credit, defended his department strongly, which made the issue even more a cause célèbre, and the mayor and the department ultimately compromised, not firing Scott Bayer but disciplining him, sanctioning him, taking him off the street and putting him in a backwater, a departmental limbo, a dank, dusty police purgatory.

Scott was in Evidence. Sat out his daily shift at a wooden table behind a grate, overseeing long, crowded aisles of cartons, metal trays, and sealed containers stretching out behind him.

A clerk, a nonentity, though pension intact. But Sam Stevens had not forgotten him—the earnest young officer at the center of a firestorm.

He'd become old, Sam saw. Had aged in the dim bowels of Evidence with no one looking. A kid in his late twenties whose hair had gone white. The stress of a desk. The stress of the utter quiet. The stress of no stress. If ever there was a kid meant to be a street cop, it was Scott Bayer. And the department, with its wisdom and fine intentions, had managed to concoct the ultimate hell for him. Evidence. Windowless, airless, companionless. A living death.

Sam could tell that Scott was both pleased and embarrassed to see him. Officer Bayer still wore a badge, Sam saw, pinned to his white short-sleeve button-down shirt. Sam wondered if it was a departmental requirement, or did Scott pin it on every morning to feel a little better? Just vestigial habit? Or did he do it only to torture himself?

"I'm surprised you remember me, tell you the truth," Scott said modestly through the grating. Sam realized it wasn't just psychological prison. The protective bars at the entrance to Evidence made it actually seem like jail—jail for ten hours a day. Perfect, cynics on the disciplinary committee must have said. A perfect sentence.

"I'd ask you how it is in here, but I think I know," said Sam, starting to restore the rapport he'd once had with this kid.

"Ain't that bad. Quiet. Safe. And I can't get myself into too much trouble, at least," he said, smiling.

"You see my pieces with Darryl Jenkins?" asked Sam.

"Sure did," said Scott.

"Well, I'll tell you frankly what that's all about. At WWBS, we want to stay one step ahead of the national guys. And we're doing it. We're on a roll." He smiled at Scott. "So my thought was, let's give viewers a tour of Evidence. You know, show them the system, the evidence boxes and bags. Maybe a quick flash of one of the victims' clothes. Build the drama. Show 'em, you know, how it all comes down to this." Gesturing to the dim universe surrounding Officer Bayer.

The ensuing silence was draped in Sam's eager tone. A tone of optimism, of expectation.

Sam wasn't aware of any rule prohibiting it. But it was, ultimately, Scott's call.

"Let me think about it," said Scott cautiously, after a few seconds.

"Don't think too long," Sam said. "When they catch this asshole, the story's over."

After the hand searches of all the camera equipment and its black carrying cases, (the aluminum and steel-bodied cameras and equipment have to go around the metal detectors, of course), after the patting down of clothing and pockets—all of it punctuated by good-natured banter, but searches nonetheless—the gate to Evidence finally swings open. Sam and his cameraman hustle in, determined, wordless, weighted with the equipment, as if they are criminals themselves, about to pull a well-rehearsed job.

It hadn't taken Scott long. Sam wondered what made him agree to it. Was it wanting to talk back to the system that had destroyed him, show it that he still had some power, some autonomy over it all? Or was it just Scott's missing the limelight, his time in the glare? Had Scott checked with anyone or simply gone ahead? Was this the same impulsiveness that had shown itself in that dark alley three years ago? Sam would never know and didn't much care. He was in. That was all that mattered.

They have moved quickly, smoothly, through their earlier camera setups, their easy manner and jokes and professionalism putting

Scott more and more at ease, bringing them to this point. The camera and lights are aimed forward and down, trained on the old metal container—rectangular and shallow like a painting tray—and focused tightly on the dozen or so spent rounds in small plastic evidence bags within it.

The technician switches on the video camera, and in a moment, after checking metered light readings and lens apertures, nods to Sam, and Sam begins the final part of his commentary. Formal, but intimate. Casual and matter-of-fact, but urgent and intense. He is a master of the modulation for this kind of piece. He is a broadcast natural, born to the medium.

"Here are all the sniper's rounds. They form a kind of forensic family, these rounds. Because under the microscope, each is unique, and yet, under that same microscope, they're all clearly . . . closely . . . related," Sam utters with portent.

He reaches a hand into the tray and lifts a bag. Just beyond the lights, he can see Officer Bayer shift a little uncomfortably at an unofficial hand in the tray but grudgingly accept it, not wanting to interrupt the taping, patient with, going along with, the drama himself. "Each plastic bag, as you can see"—Sam holds a bag at the perfect angle to minimize glare—"is marked in a consistent and simple way, with the date of the evidence handwritten in black on the bag."

He puts the bag down and can almost sense Bayer's relief. Sam gestures with the same hand to all the bags together. "Here are the sniper's rounds—death, gathered up as if into a macabre collection. Collected, catalogued, contained. Is the perpetrator, still at large, some kind of collector, too?" Sam says ominously.

Then Sam nods to the cameraman, and in a previously arranged moment of fairly conventional and predictable ambush journalism, the cameraman spins the camera and its bright light around onto Officer Bayer.

"Meet Officer Scott Bayer," intones Sam.

Officer Bayer is momentary blinded by the camera light. The

cameraman is occupied looking through the lens at Officer Bayer, checking the new framing and focus. Behind the glare of the light now trained on Officer Bayer, Sam Stevens lifts the evidence bag once more, moves it momentarily behind the open steel camera case, where—with his other hand—he slides out of the spare battery pack not the expected nickel cadmium battery but instead a deformed thirty-millimeter slug that he slipped into the battery pack an hour before.

In a moment, the deformed slug is in the plastic evidence bag, back in the tray, and the actual spent round from Evidence is deep in Sam's pocket. To the stray eye glancing over, trying to squint past the glaring camera light, it is nothing more than Sam's quick fussing with some camera equipment, the specifics hidden by the open steel camera case.

This is a crime of modernity.

He does it all nearly without looking. He's practiced with Baggies in pitch dark at home for four nights straight. Practiced it by feel only, looking straight ahead of him into the dark, never down. It takes him only seconds. Officer Bayer is still blinking in adjustment to the camera light.

It is two adjacent worlds, Sam has come to see. The world of light in front of the camera, the world of shadow behind it. This notion, this metaphor, of two adjacent worlds—abutting, interweaving, the seen and the unseen, the exposed and the hidden—has been turning in him with increasing power and reverberation ever since he began his broadcasting career, ever since he noticed himself moving fluidly and professionally between the two. Which world is more real and which less real, he couldn't say, although there is a heightened illumination and clarity to the world in front of the camera—a place, after all, from which the news illuminates, explains, the darker, wider, unlit world beyond it. Yet the heightened reality of the world lit by the camera lights is—officially, conventionally—never classified as "real."

The notion of these two adjacent worlds has given him the energy and conviction to practice the maneuver with the bullet at home in the dark, in the shadows; to rehearse and observe his own motions over and over into smooth second nature.

If his little exchange is discovered, of course, he'll be finished. The local reporter whose eagerness for a scoop, whose hunger for headlines, overtook him, they'd say. The local reporter who saw his big chance—his big story at last—and couldn't control himself. A guy who'd do anything for ratings. Anything to beat the competition. Who fantasized about personally breaking the story open. Who apparently even believed he could get further than the local police. *Hubris. Unbridled ambition. You could see it in his stand-up pieces.* They'd say all of it. They'd be right, of course, about ambition. About hubris. About a reporter who saw his big chance.

But it isn't going to be discovered. All possible ballistic work has already been done on all the slugs, Sam knows. As a local crime reporter, he knows the inner workings of Webster County Police forensics. The slug is here, because it's no longer needed elsewhere. It has already told its meager tale, said all it's going to say. It's now—like its victim—just a number. A statistic. A fragment consigned to a plastic bag.

"This is the officer in charge of Evidence," Sam intones portentously in the next moment, not missing a beat, just off camera, the lens still trained on Scott. "It is located in the bowels of the police department, but it is as important in the courtroom as anything that happens in a car chase or a helicopter or in the world of cops and criminals above us. Explain, if you would, Officer Bayer, the crucial role evidence could play in *this* case."

Bayer blinks, but does not protest. Does not ask that the camera be turned off. He answers succinctly, professionally, and proudly. He beams as he begins to explain. It's as if he fully expected such an ambush. As if he welcomes it. It is his moment in the sun, at last. As Sam knew it would be. Sam knows the hunger for the limelight when he sees it. The unquenched hunger—he recognizes it well.

9

E stelle Saunders. Seventy-three.

Churchgoing. God-fearing. Topping off the old Buick Electra after morning services. As she did every week.

Dressed in her finest, as it turned out, to enter the Kingdom of Heaven.

Sunday midday.

Broad daylight.

As if making sure random has a capital *R*.

Estelle Saunders.

Eighteen great grandchildren.

"Weemee" to her friends, for as long as any of them can remember.

After seventy-three years, she has a new nickname:

Number Eight.

It is three in the morning; in Sam Stevens's townhouse basement, Tommy is asleep. Denise is out for the night. Won't say where. Won't say with whom. An aggressive muteness, he knows, primarily intended to infuriate him. No discussion of her plans. No ne-

gotiation about scheduling. They're long past discussion or nego-
tiation. While he's trying to cover the biggest story of his
career—*because* it's the biggest story of his career, it seems—she
heads out wordlessly, without explanation or apology, into the
night.

Which, tonight, is perfect.

The microscope is a high school model they have stored in
their basement, alongside old textbooks and model rockets that
should have been tossed years ago. Sam was saving the microscope for Tommy, who hasn't really been interested yet. Though
ancient and outdated, the microscope is still adequate for his purposes, so he doesn't have to buy one somewhere. Good. A microscope would be a fairly noticeable purchase.

The thirty-millimeter rounds are, oddly, not nearly so noticeable. Easy to come by, in a nation of gun nuts. A nation of
firearms fans. Out near their cabin, after all, the gun store is not
so far away from the pharmacy—geographically or psychologically. Out near their cabin—beautiful rolling bluegrass hills, unbroken fields, and miles of woods—picking up a box of shells at
the strip mall is still akin to picking up deodorant.

But Sam is a local television personality, and Sam is not a fool.
One of the kids on the crew, an intern trying a semester in the
real world, drove out into the country to pick up boxes of shells
for one of Sam's earlier "Serial Killer" pieces. Picked up several
boxes, per Sam's instructions—conventional, semijacketed, full-
jacketed, lead, lead alloy, standard, and hollowpoint—a boxful of
everything. Sam hoped to convey comprehensiveness and impressive scholarship in his on-air piece, and didn't know much at
that point about the differences between them, or exactly how his
on-air piece would go. It wasn't very much money per box, so
Sam is fairly sure—with the intern back at school now—that nobody at WWBS knows exactly how many boxes—or much cares.

He slides open the box of semijackets—like a box of bluestick
safety matches or woodscrews—and takes out a shell. Dense,

shiny, perfect, machined, like hardware—a certain piece of hardware you've been looking all over for—and he sets it on the clear microscope slide carefully, holding it there with a little piece of the craft gum he uses to put Tommy's artwork and posters on his son's bedroom wall.

Now, more carefully, he takes a crumpled plastic Baggie out of his pocket—his own informal evidence bag, holding and hiding the spent slug. He carefully removes the slug, looking closely at it now, under the desk light, at last with the luxury of a little privacy and time.

The slug's base is the only part of it that still resembles its original form. The rest of it is crunched into a tiny metal mushroom—a severely sheared mushroom at that. He inspects the deformations, marks, and scars—a tiny, torturous landscape.

With a second piece of gum, he places the slug next to the pristine shell on the slide. They're side by side now on the microscope slide—the shell from its box, fresh and shiny and reflective in the harsh directed desk light, and this one from Evidence, that had sliced its way through muscle and organ and shattered against bone, in its millisecond, brutal, corporeal journey, in its own fast, brief life.

The deformed slug he'd left in the tray as a replacement had never actually been fired. It had instead been manually plied from its casing, its primer and propellant powder carefully removed from its base; then it had been pounded and hammered and misshaped here in this basement to approximate one of the real ones. The real slugs had already been put through all the standard tests, so no one was going to know this was a hammered imposter, a piece of sculpted stagecraft.

So what is it? What is it that Sheriff Wyatt has asked Dr. Eggers not to mention in his little lecture? It has to be some aspect of the slug, some more narrow identifying feature that would help Wyatt separate the sniper's slug from another—that of a potential copycat, for instance. And probably something Wyatt didn't want the sniper to know he knew. In the endless forced courtship of law enforcement and the media, there was the time-tested, time-honored practice of the police holding back at least some piece of critical information for precisely those kinds of reasons.

It might have to do with range, as Sam had gleaned from the jaded expert who sat in front of him. It couldn't be shape, certainly, considering how deformed and unrecognizable all the slugs presumably were. So what exactly?

He adjusts the focus on the microscope and squints into the eyepiece.

He sees nothing. Could it *be* nothing? Merely a stance that Wyatt has taken to give the impression, at least, of competence, of forward motion? To make the media believe he has something?

That kind of stunt doesn't seem like Wyatt. Not the Wyatt Sam has come to know, covering local crime. Billy Wyatt may actually have the intelligence and wiliness for that—despite the hastily formed opinions of the more cynical guests in the briefing room—but Wyatt has always been a straight shooter.

Sam adjusts the slug manually up and down beneath the microscope, looking for something, anything.

He sees nothing.

He feels desolation and anxiety rubbing together in him strangely.

He goes to put the slug back into the Baggie, and as he does, he notices the black residue on his fingers.

I'm a scientist. I have to look at everything. The stooped doctor's awkward apology comes back to him.

He crosses the basement to his little workbench, grabs a rag from the top of a pile of paints and painting supplies, leftover from when they would paint together—preparing Tommy's nursery, envisioning a home together, a future together. The paints, all but forgotten now, consigned to basement shelves.

He takes the slug from Evidence, and now—not so careful

with it anymore—begins to rub the tiny base of it with the old painting rag.

A coating of black starts to come off the slug's base easily.

The gun barrel's oil and grease and powder from the fired round have left the slug coated with residue, he realizes, which a forensics team probably doesn't concern itself with, searching for more important residues: tissue, blood, internal organ . . .

He rubs at the coating some more, expecting to see some hint of the copper coloring of the jacket.

But he doesn't.

He goes back to the pile of rags and the basement paints and pulls out a nearly empty can of thinner that is still with the paints.

He dabs some on the rag, rubs the slug some more.

The base of the slug is relatively clean now, but it still doesn't resemble the copper jacket of the fresh round next to it or the gleaming copper coloring of the bullets in Eggers's slides.

He knows by now—after doing his on-air piece—about the astonishing variety of materials that ammunition is composed of and available in. Brass, bronze, copper, steel, lead, lead alloys, tin—even gold and silver bullets are marketed, should you have to stop a vampire.

Jesus. Wait a second.

He bounds up the basement stairs, sits down at the kitchen computer, and goes online into another America that operates vibrantly and boisterously in cyberspace. He checks a handful of ammunition-sales sites—*Backyard Ballistics; American Armageddon; Buddy's Warrior Supply*—all of which quickly confirm it.

With this caliber of high-powered round, the majority of jackets are copper.

This one is steel.

Is a steel jacket—of this particular brand at least—structurally weaker than copper? Manufactured a little thinner? More ready to crumple and deform? Given the price of copper, he bets they're cheaper, at least. . . .

Jesus. It isn't much, he thinks. Copper is more typical, but steel is hardly unheard-of. But it's at least something, he supposes, for poor Wyatt. Maybe as much for Wyatt's own sanity as for any evidentiary usefulness. Wyatt would probably take anything.

He knows that one of the boxes the intern bought is steel semijackets. Hell, the intern might have grabbed them based only on cost.

His breath catches for a moment as he realizes.

Weighing odds and geography and coincidence, he can't avoid it, can't dodge the possibility: The sniper's shells might easily have come from the same location where the intern bought the boxes of shells.

Does Sam have a responsibility to inform the police?

Could informing the police lead to that dealer, who might remember something or someone? Certainly the police have already interviewed all the local gun dealers. But would this information lead to a second, more intense and focused interview, which might yield something more?

Could this little bit of information, in fact, bring an end to all this killing?

Well, there's a scoop, Sam Stevens. There's a break in the case. You'd be a hero, wouldn't you?

Yet Sam knows he can't. He's tampered with evidence. Informing the police is out of the question.

And if it's true about the ammunition—and even if it isn't—he can't help but notice . . .

He's moved—in psychology, in activity, bent over ammunition at three in the morning—one step closer to the sniper.

10

D amien Agnew.

Fifty-six.

Silver haired. Handsome. Getting out of his Audi in the huge parking lot at the aerospace company, where he has worked for thirty years.

Divisional director. There early as always. Always one of the first in.

Stock options, annual bonuses. He'd ridden out the lean times; now he was enjoying the good.

Nice blue suit, crisp white shirt, black shoes.

Shoes still polished, pointing upward.

Blue suit horizontal.

White shirt pink from collar to chest.

An easy shot from the tree line, across the immaculate mani-cured grounds, across the lot, into Damien's left temple.

Golf handicap, four.

Son in med school. Daughter practicing environmental law.

Enfranchised. Insider. Achiever. Winner. One of the lucky. Until that very moment.

Random.
Still utterly random.
Number nine.
The pace is accelerating.

They had bought the cabin together when they first got married. It was an act of faith, given that they had had no money at all. They borrowed for the down payment, took out two mortgages. Even then, all they could afford was something modest, something way out here. They hadn't improved it much; it was still pretty rustic and primitive, and the second-home frenzy had never really caught on this far out. Only a few friends even knew they owned it. He'd been the only one to come out here in months.

It needed a ton of work.

Right now, it was perfect.

Sam Stevens stood by the trunk of his car, looked out at the empty acreage around him—some of it beautiful, much of it scrub—and lifted the rifle in its soft black cover out of the trunk.

The intern was supposed to have returned it after the televised piece. Sam knew; he'd heard one of the producers give the directive to the kid.

But the intern couldn't find it, of course, and Sam had given him more pressing assignments. Sam was the on-air personality, his needs came first—and then, a week later, the kid was back at school.

The staff assuming the gun was returned, if they even thought about it at all.

The intern assuming someone on the staff eventually returned it, if he even thought about it at all.

Sam slid the black cover off the rifle, and regarded it. A lean, lithe, elegant, no-nonsense stranger.

Time for a little research.

How far out was their cabin? Far enough out into America that you heard the report of a weapon now and then, and it was natural, part of the landscape, part of the American birthright. You heard a shot every so often, at dawn or at nightfall, and you thought, pheasant. You thought, deer. You thought, hawk. You thought, badger. You thought, coyote.

You never knew exactly where a shot came from. Its echo bounced around the woods, the sharp high hills, without direction, without origin. But that's what his neighbors would certainly think—pheasant, hawk, badger—if they even heard anything at all. Because Sam had the feeling—given the gulch his property was in, given the distance from even his nearest neighbors, given the hillock between them, given his neighbors' erratic presence, in residence even less than himself—that the shots wouldn't even be heard. If anyone heard them, it would only be him.

His neighbors know who he is, of course, but they've always respected his privacy. They know that he comes out here specifically to escape the glare, get away from the lights, dodge the crowd and the recognition, to find a little peace and quiet and solace, and they respect that. They admire themselves for leaving him alone.

The cabin was perfect.

How far out was their cabin? Far, but then, not far at all. Because now, nothing was far, everything was near, everything was everywhere. Although the rugged topography blocked cell-phone reception, he was always reachable on the landline for any breaking news, for another attack, for anything that required him. The cabin was far. But close enough, too.

. . .

A few hundred yards from the cabin, at a particularly sorry edge of the property, an ancient oak tree was dying.

He had never fired a gun growing up. He had never even been near one.

But he now at least knew what to expect. Because the only gun he had ever held, that he had ever fired, was this one. And the only place he had ever fired it was on television.

One bullet. Into a target on the police firing range. *Special Segment—Up Close: The Sniper's Weapon of Choice.* With a little live demonstration, of course.

To look good on television, he had been shown how to hold it, how to aim, how to squeeze slowly. He was alarmed at how close the telescoping sight drew you to your target, pulled you intimately into another realm hundreds of yards away. With computer-assisted optics, marksmanship, it seemed, was idiot's work, if not exactly child's play. The computer-enhanced scope drew you out of your own world, into the world of your victim, so that you could forget yourself, your humanness, as you were made part of the machinery. He experienced instantly—in a single sighting down the barrel—how an assassin becomes disassociated from his all-too-human prey. How the machine is the master, the operator merely the obedient servant, and not the other way around.

He'd felt and absorbed the kick against his shoulder, just as he knew he would.

The segment had required only one take.

Looking through the computer-enhanced scope was, well, a little like watching TV.

Now he fires, for the first time, off camera. Fires, for the first time, into the real world. Fires into a living object, in fact. Living, but dying. That ancient oak.

He squeezes the trigger. There is everything at once. The mechanical harmony—the smooth machined click of the trigger, initiating the chain of micro-events inside. The firing pin striking the bullet casing's rim. The highly contained and directed ignition of black powder and primer and propellant. The kick against his shoulder. The gun's celebratory spurt, and the barrel's uncontrollable rise. The low thud of the first bullet against the oak. All of it occurring in the space of a moment too short to appear on a watch face.

Deer. Hawk. Pheasant. Badger.

With a piece of chalk from Tommy's old chalkboard (he remembers Tommy's primitive cars and airplanes and happy families in chalk) he draws a small square on the tree.

From a hundred yards back, the powerful scope takes him intimately into the ridges and folds of the bark. The tree's flesh and skin. Another channel. Another world.

He begins to fire at the square—careful, deliberate each time, collecting the brass shell casing after each shot, keeping count— and soon he is hitting inside the square consistently.

He pulls the trigger once inadvertently, a second too early, when he hasn't quite settled and aimed. He hears the round strike somewhere behind the ancient oak. It's a good little lesson, a safe little lesson in attentiveness, in humility.

A half hour later, he draws a square half the size just above the first one.

He's hitting within the smaller square fairly consistently a half hour after that.

It's some sort of base plate from an old refrigerator. It was in the corner of the cellar crawl space when they bought the place. It must be at least thirty pounds. He hefts it up the bulkhead stairs, over the open scrub and brush, and sets it against the bottom of the dying oak.

He moves back to his hundred-yard position.

For the first time, he takes out one of the steel-jacket rounds.

He catches a glint of his red work shirt in the round's reflective surface.

He loads the round into the chamber.

Bolts. Cocks.

Crouches. Aims. Pulls the trigger. Squints and hunches self-protectively. He has no idea if the shot will ricochet dangerously, flying straight at him or veering away uncontrollably to disappear into the woods.

He sets the rifle down carefully. Trots across the low scrub and up to the thick base plate.

There it is. Embedded in the plate. A metal mushroom. A wild mushroom, grown out here in the woods in the blink of an eye.

Doing just what it was supposed to.

He heads into the deep woods behind the cabin. He knows he will not have to look long. He has seen it out here before, hiking in here just weeks ago. He remembers exactly where it was. It's not something you forget. And the part he needs is exactly the part that will still be there, untouched. The one part not stripped by the original predator or the opportunistic scavengers who shortly followed.

He walks purposefully through the slanted, fading light.

In just minutes, sure enough, there it is.

Exactly where he remembered it.

Exactly as he expected it.

The skeleton of a huge buck.

In the weeks since he saw it out here, the various parts of its skeleton, though all still there, have detached from one another.

He has brought a knife with him, but he won't need it.

He approaches the skeleton. The buck's stature is still impressive, even in this desiccated state. He stands humbly over the big skeleton a moment, before bending down, and picking up the heavy skull.

It is almost thoroughly cleaned—by scavengers, by the elements.

It is ready for him.

As if he has been expected. As if it is meant to be.

He carries the skull back through the woods, inhabiting, moving through, a world of dead and dying things. An old tree. A deer carcass. A marriage.

All dead already, he ruminates. He is merely formalizing their ending. Finishing them off.

He carries the heavy skull as the itemized rage bounces around his own:

Pages of billing from a four-star spa in San Diego. Three-hundred-dollar bottles of wine ordered from around the world. New wardrobe piling up mockingly, unworn, a fabric mountain in the bedroom from which he's been banished.

His finding precisely zero in the checking account. The entire balance having been purposefully, accurately removed, and shifted to God knows where.

The phone number of his WWBS boss, scrawled casually but prominently in her day planner. *I have his number. I can dial it anytime. Say anything anytime.* An elaborate threat in a mere seven digits.

The scent of cigar suddenly permeating the kitchen. As if not to exclude any of his senses from the generalized assault. He suspects she has simply relit it there, puffed on it only to taunt him, literally to ignite his paranoia and his jealousy, make them dance madly with each other.

And always, Tommy as leverage. Always finding ways to remind Sam of that leverage. "Mom told me you want me to quit the Chess Club!" "Mom told me you don't like my friend Jerry." The boy's pained, tremulous expression of silent suffering. Of bottomless defeat. Sam doesn't know how much longer he can bear witnessing the pain in that expression.

His own skull is weighed down with it all. All so relentless, obvious, screaming itself out. All so focused, aimed like an arrow at him. A sum of cruelties large and small, as if to signal the inexorable nature of it, the ceaseless variety of it yet to come.

It is his last experiment. The light is almost gone. As if the natural world is sending him a message that his grim self-education, his rites of initiation, must now draw to a close.

The natural world seems to send him one final sign.

The steel-coated semijacketed hollowpoint crumples completely against the buck's heavy skull.

It's going to work.

If he wants it to.

He lies there, alone, in the double bed they found at a garage sale. The furniture is all secondhand, assembled at local garage sales, castoffs that roommates and friends were getting rid of. Though they have redone their town house a half dozen times—reinventing their tastes, reinventing themselves—the cabin has remained untouched. As if to mock him with memory—the memory of each piece stumbled on together, tossed into the back of their old pickup with a sense of irony and playfulness, with a sense of love and romance and possibility. The town house—modern, mirrored, furnished, decorated by hired designers—perfectly represents their mirrored, polished, inauthentic, smooth-surfaced selves. Identities shed and assumed like snakeskins, with each redecoration. But out here, he must inhabit, confront, their shared dreams. Out here, he must stare at their lost sense of wonder and possibility, face their lost sense of themselves.

Tonight, he is past such losses. He is beyond such a consideration of his marriage and his past. He lies there, staring at the ceiling, thinking nothing. Aware of nothing. In the moments before sleep, thinking only of his son.

He sets the alarm for 4:00 A.M. He'll get dressed in the dark, drive back into town and to the town house. Have breakfast with her and Tommy—he and his wife pretending nothing is wrong. Both keeping up the façade. A devil's pact if ever there was one. For the sake of his job—he knows, she knows—the source of income for both of them. His fairy-tale pretty wife is part of the fantasy, part of his image, an unspoken clause of his employment contract. A necessary accessory to his appearance as family man, everyman, friendly, approachable American. He'll have breakfast with her and Tommy, then take Tommy to the school bus. Making sure he *gets* to the school bus. Protecting Tommy from her. And he'll be seen saying good-bye to his wife. And seen leaving for work from their pretty home.

Who will blink first? He doesn't know. He knows if he tries anything with his son—tries to take him from her, tries to turn him from her, tries to poison him against her—she will play her trump card. She will cry it out to the media, play the martyr to perfect pitch. Her theater background, her failed theater career, will suddenly know its first stunning success. Even when it turns out— months later—that the charges can't be substantiated, the damage will be done. His own career will be irremediably tarnished, his life will be forever altered. Those are the rules in the halogen glow of the media circus—and no one knows them better than a reporter's wife.

The dutiful, put-upon spouse, silently abused by her celebrity husband, keeping quiet for her husband's and little family's sake, until she can't take it anymore, and cries out for justice, for the justice she deserves. That's what she is holding over him, holding the boy hostage, knowing that his son is what he wants most, is all that is left for him from the marriage. She doesn't love the boy, but she keeps him, because the boy is the source of her power over him. She knows that's what tortures Sam most.

She was born to this game, Sam can see, Sam can feel. The way she keeps her various flings utterly discreet, the way she begs and wins the boy's forgiveness every time, reasserts and manages her love for him to keep him tethered to her. She is a master of the game, Sam is a poor neophyte, and the escape from this dreadful, cruel, unspoken game has narrowed and narrowed and narrowed for him to nearly nothing. To a narrow slice of light slanting in past the door. To one final roll of the dice. To this.

Soon, he'll gas up his chain saw, take down the faithful but rotted old oak, burn it, tossing the latex gloves he's been wearing for all this practice into the fire, watching them flare as the flame finds them.

The wail of a chain saw, the smoke from someone burning something on their property—both are as common out here, as unremarkable, as the discharge of a rifle.

He'll toss out the spent shell casings and the refrigerator base plate along with the broken lawn mower and lawn chairs and other junk he's been meaning to get rid of.

There'll be no evidence of his practicing, no trace elements from the fired rounds.

He realizes that when the moment comes, even if he misses, it will still be the first intact slug. It will simply appear that the high-risk sniper has finally missed.

The sniper—arranging it for him. The sniper—inviting him in.

It's like anythin', Darryl said. *Like learnin' to swallow a pill, ride a scooter, anythin'. . . . That's the dirty little secret of it. . . . That it's just like anything else.*

The 4:00 A.M. alarm awakens him to news radio, alerting him even in half sleep, in semiconsciousness, to any developments.

The 4:00 A.M. alarm begins the charade anew.

But now, he feels energy. He is not tired. He is outside tiredness, already somewhat outside his previous patterns, his previous human cycles and previous emotions.

Just like Darryl said. Jesus. It's just like Darryl said.

11

Big Billy Wyatt looks even worse than usual at this morning's briefing. A new level of haggard. A new pain and pinch in his eyes.

Sam Stevens knows the look. It is the look of pressure.

Of feeling the Feds at the back of your neck. The pressure of the *federales*, wanting, pushing, to take over.

For the last two briefings, an extremely well-groomed, impassive bureaucrat in a crisp white shirt and blue suit has sat in a folding chair behind Wyatt. Wyatt dutily and hurriedly introduced him as Carl Brady with the FBI, advising us in the investigation, providing us extra resources and support.

Breathing over my shoulder is what Wyatt meant, Sam knew. Breathing short and impatient, waiting for me to stumble, waiting to step in, waiting for their chance.

There's been a lively pool going on precisely that, among the reporters. The national guys started it, figuring they had the inside track, having seen it all before. When will Wyatt turn it over, when will he fold, when will he swallow his pride? Maybe the rumor of the pool has even reached Big Billy himself—not a real strong confidence builder.

Sam watched him start out sure, cocky, smart. With the confidence of his conviction, with the resources of police technology, of guileless science, with the silver hammer of justice clanging proudly behind him.

But they are dealing with an assassin. They are dealing with a phantasm—a professional who clearly has looked forward to this, who has planned for this all his sick dark shadowy deceitful life, who, God knows, may have picked Billy Wyatt's jurisdiction with the express purpose of torturing him, breaking him, making a big man finally weep like a baby with impotence, with powerlessness, with defeat.

Whatever each one of the reporters is betting—a day, three days, a week more left for Wyatt at the helm—they're nevertheless all pulling for him. Because that's where the color is. That's where the excitement of the professional fumble and the human foible will be. Once the Feds take over, it's all the fun of watching a machine in a factory. Fascinating for a few moments in its precision, and then deadly dull.

The *federales* will undoubtedly solve it faster and bring the show to a close.

If nothing gives, if nothing breaks, it's going federal.

The clock is ticking.

12

Sam knows where she goes at night. Who she hangs out with. He knows the clubs. Places of glossy surfaces, places glimmering with false smiles and frothy with the promise of consensual sex.

He knows where she goes.

He's pretty sure she knows that he knows.

He's pretty sure she even knows that he has sometimes followed her.

For her, it must be just another facet, another means of torturing him. To let him see her on barstools with her girlfriends, talking to men, leaning forward, flirting.

He knows she's glad to torture him further. To demean and belittle him another notch. To turn him into a puppy, following senselessly. A sniveling, whimpering puppy.

But she would never imagine this from him. He can barely even think it himself. So how could she?

He could have hired someone, of course. That is the conventional, salaried white guy's white-collar way. Particularly for someone in the public eye. But the obviousness of doing it that way would make it more predictable in an investigation, it seemed, and therefore less desirable. Even beyond that, the problem with hiring someone was always the same: if someone else was involved, it was one less element you controlled. You never knew if they'd eventually talk. He knew firsthand how people loved to talk. How most people couldn't resist. It was how he made his living after all. People talking. And he couldn't be sure that a hired hand could follow the MO as precisely as he himself would. Follow the protocol to the letter. He would never be able to count on the intelligence or exacting care of hired help. No, this way, there was only yourself to trust. Or to fail.

She will never know, of course. That would be impossible—too far from the MO. He has to match the MO. He's sorry he can't have the satisfaction of her shocked expression. A satisfaction that could accompany him for a lifetime. That he could smile at perennially from his Caribbean paradise or from his prison cell. That he could take with him to his own grave. But we can't have everything we want. Even as we are arranging to have everything we want.

It is a beautiful night. A night of vibrant stars, thanks to a mere sliver of moon. A fragrant, quiet, windless, cool, lovely Tuesday night.

The last few Tuesdays, she's gone drinking with brassy, foul-mouthed Nell Anderson at a club called Dominique's. After which, she's stopped—alone—for a coffee to go at the coffee shop on Fourth, on her way home.

He's considered the mornings, too, of course. When she is smoking in bed. Lounging in the living room. Snacking in the kitchen. On the phone in front of the bay window. Mornings, when the cigar's owner might have made, might still be making, his cocksure, arrogant appearance. But daytime is too dangerous. Neighbors close by. Traffic. Busy. Sam needs to be in the briefing room during the day, covering the story.

It's the nights, nights like this, when he can roam free, come and go. When everyone assumes he's at home, and she's the only person who knows he isn't. (Tommy, too, knows his father isn't at home, but Sam knows that isn't going to matter.) He needs the night, he needs the darkness, for this.

At midnight, he drives through the Dominique's parking lot. It's dimly lit, across the street from the club itself.

There is her green Audi—*their* green Audi, their good car. The car he gave her gladly, ungrudgingly. The life he gave her gladly, ungrudgingly.

A moment later, he glides back out of the Dominique's lot in their other car, their old Corolla, silent, catlike, back onto the two-lane highway.

Following her. Following her as he has on countless other nights. Following her thoughtlessly, automatically. Absorbing her routine. Is this night really any different?

At two, he is looking around the coffee shop counter. At the stacked cups, at the containers full of green coffee stirrers, at the rack of easy-listening CDs for sale. He is looking at the menu. At the two Pakistani clerks. He is looking at the clock on the wall—coffee cups instead of numerals. He is looking around the whole bright shop. He is there in the coffee shop with them, but he is not, of course, because he is looking through the powerful scope of the rifle, slumped down in his Corolla, at the curb of the little urban park across the street from the shop.

There are no pedestrians strolling here at night, no secret courting lovers; no one. He has checked it. He has been careful.

He has checked and rechecked the gun.

He has planned minutely, incessantly.

To do it without mistakes, yes.

But more, perhaps, to give it the force of inevitability.

To make it like a thing already done. Already executed in the mind. Already experienced in the bones. As if now there is just the minor matter of actually doing it.

But is he really going to?

That was the question at the outset, when the notion first slithered into his consciousness—insinuated itself into some primitive part of his brain, burrowing in there firmly, stubbornly—and it is no less the brute, blunt question now, at this moment.

Is he really going to?

While he ponders exactly that—no closer to an answer, no further from one—she appears in the scope sight.

Through the high-powered scope, close enough to talk to, close enough to smile at, to flirt with, to sucker punch, close enough to kiss. Close enough to see the smudges of her makeup, her bloodshot eyes.

Close enough to be married to.

Is he really going to?

Or is this only the culmination of an elaborate fantasy—the occasional, passing fantasy of a million spouses in a million loveless marriages. A fantasy that the current stresses of Sam's job (the once-in-a-lifetime news story) and his life (a marriage crumbling beneath him) have set in motion for him. A fantasy that—with a rifle left inadvertently in his office, with his investigative fervor for the correct ammunition—he has been able to play out particularly fully, far further than most. A *useful* fantasy, providing him some sense of control over a life careening wildly out of it; offering him some measure of psychological release.

And now it's time to rein it in; to pull back from the precipice.

The young, eager Pakistani clerk smiles generously at her, but she doesn't smile back. She orders expressionlessly and turns toward the window and the street, looks this way, toward Sam—an unconscious dare, an unwitting challenge.

He feels nothing, he notices. Nothing now, except his finger, hot—strangely, searingly hot—against the cold trigger.

She pays, puts away her wallet, takes a sip, steps out of the coffee shop and off the curb, which in the telescopic sight, translates to a looming, startling move toward him.

She pauses for a moment to look out at the cool, fragrant, sliver-moon night and to take another sip.

She is about to bend down to get back into the green Audi.

The X of the scope's crosshairs brushes back and forth against her temple. The weapon's idle massage. The drifting crosshairs, a kind of contemplation, of indecision . . .

Is he really going to?

Despite the endless hours, the endless days of preparation—preparation practical, psychological, and philosophical—the question is as strong at this crosshair moment as it was when the thought first snuck in on him, invaded him, lodged in him like a bullet itself.

Is he really going to?

But how can he not?

It is both an ending and a beginning. It is swirling, skimming thought and no thought at all. It is a moment that harnesses all emotion, some emotional analogue of a high-mass stellar explosion, and yet a moment devoid of emotion. He isn't there, somehow, at the precise moment; he is absented from it, but, of course, he is there, utterly and entirely. He will dwell on these dichotomies, these mysterious oppositions and juxtapositions, in the flattened, complex time to come.

He squeezes.

He blinks at the flash.

She is down. She is crumpled at the curb, partly obscured by her car.

He wants to fire again, itches to fire again, to be sure. But he can't. That's not the MO. One shot, one hundred yards. (If the crusty crime reporter in front of him was right.) The killer doesn't miss, doesn't take second shots. So he can't either.

But down doesn't mean dead.

Is she dead or not?

He has thought of everything, but he hasn't thought of this. Undoubtedly because in some way it was impossible to think about. No, he realizes glancingly, tellingly, he hasn't even considered her surviving . . .

In moments, his own body has attacked him from every angle. His heart. His stomach. His legs. His throat. The vomit rises. He swallows it; it rises again. His stomach burns. His own temples pound, hot. His leg is jittery against the gas pedal. But the task is to drive. To pull far from the event, to let the event retreat behind him physiologically, just as surely as it does geographically.

In the car, his whole body shaking as he had expected, shivering as he had predicted, he turns on the radio to try to calm himself in some way, to put himself in some small degree back into a world he knows.

But the radio announcement propels him into some far-off, unmoored, incomprehensible place. A world he has never imagined.

"... There's been an arrest in the serial sniper case gripping Webster County. We go live to Amanda Steele. ..."

Noisy. Anxious. Breathless. "This is Amanda Steele. Police brought in a suspect just hours ago, officials here have just announced. ..."

The cell phone on Sam's belt beeps. He fumbles for it thoughtlessly.

"Yes?"

"Sam, you hearing this?" His producer, breathless, too.

"Yes."

"You've got to get down here right now. They're going to make an announcement."

"Already on my way." The words are somehow there, floating in front of him, barely his.

"You are? Jesus, Sam, you were up listening at two A.M.? My God. Impressive." A giggle. "Or nuts."

Five minutes later, the police, the sirens, the rushing squad cars, bunched like a pack of frantic two-ton hounds, race the other way past Sam's Toyota, two big white boxy ambulances close behind them, all searing the night red.

Sam drives automatically, unthinking, arms clamped to the steering wheel, body paralyzed in the driver's seat, mind frozen around the fact.

Denise Stevens was killed while the serial murder suspect was in custody.

So the suspect in custody could not have committed Denise Stevens's murder.

Probably it was someone she knew, then. Most murders are. Probably a family member. Most murders are.

He turns it over like that—outside himself. He can bring it no closer. It is as inarguable as it is incomprehensible.

He'd been working as fast as he could.

Which turned out to be exactly the wrong speed.

A little faster, he'd have pulled it off.

A little slower, he'd have called it off.

As a crime reporter, he knows how the police work. He knows the methodology, the dogged laborious steps, of Sheriff Billy Wyatt's department. They were processing the suspect. Putting the facts together. Assembling the case. All told, it might take several days. Then, they'd turn their full attention—methodically, separately, just as doggedly—to the matter of Denise Stevens's murder.

He probably had just days. Not days of freedom. Days of crushing weight. Days of suspension. Days of burden.

He had pulled the trigger and would now pay the price.

Fate, it seemed, had for once bound itself efficiently to justice.

Fate had descended upon Sam Stevens in the lowly guise of poor timing.

Wyatt has been roused from bed, and has arrived at the station house at midnight, to personally supervise the processing, to make sure there are no mistakes.

He is exhausted. Elated, but exhausted. He checks his watch: 2:45 A.M.

"Sheriff?"

"What is it, Jimmy?" Wyatt asks his deputy impatiently. Big Billy Wyatt is about to make a formal but brief announcement to the press. There's only a handful of them out there—graveyard shift, backup crew—but he refuses to be accused of sitting on information.

"Hate to spoil everything, sir." Wyatt looks at Jimmy. Jimmy's lips are pressed together, as if to keep himself from saying something. He wears an uncomfortable, shifting expression, as if he wishes he could be somewhere else.

"What is it?" demands Wyatt.

"Another victim was just hit."

"When?"

"Few minutes ago, I think."

"Found a few minutes ago or hit a few minutes ago?"

"Hit a few minutes ago."

And Chief Wyatt, whether still in the elation of the arrest, or in appreciation of the irony, cannot completely suppress his smile. "Well, we've had our guy here for hours now. Which means we got us a copycat with terrible timing. Which means we got us someone new to catch. Kind of a twofer, eh Jimmy?" says Wyatt, still smiling.

"I guess," says Jimmy.

Wyatt will wonder, hours from now, if it was the wave of elation that kept him from understanding the full weight of Jimmy's news.

Sam Stevens tiptoes in at 4:00 A.M., passes the foldout couch and Patricia, the professional babysitter they call in emergencies, curled up on it. ("Pat, it's Sam. Denise is out with a friend tonight, and I've got a work emergency.")

He gently pushes open the bedroom door, looks in on his boy—asleep, soundless, angelic.

Sam turns to go.

"Daddy?"

He turns back, smiles. "Hi, son."

"What time is it?"

"Early, sweetie. You sleep. I was just checking on you."

"Where's Mommy?" Tommy asks. He knows his parents sleep in separate places, even when his dad is here. But he doesn't know any more than that.

"Mommy? I don't know," Sam says.

He *doesn't* know. The morgue? The operating table? The police station?

He doesn't know what the police and ambulances have found. Still alive? Conscious? Paralyzed? Life support? Able to communicate? Nothing was said at the briefing. Sorry. No details available yet. The story was still the sniper's arrest, and there was no other. He had been watching for any telltale flurry of activity on the sides, any whispering in the wings. He half-expected, was half-ready, to see a note handed to Wyatt; to see Wyatt look up at him; to have an officer tap him tentatively, somberly on the shoulder, ask him to step outside, tell him that they have some unfortunate information for him. They haven't yet processed who she is beyond name and address, obviously, haven't processed her relationship to him. She went out at night without her wallet, just cash, to avoid any chance of being connected to him, to protect them both. The registration on the Audi was still in her maiden name, the address was their rental apartment before the town house—it didn't necessarily lead immediately to Sam. And if they suspected him already, if he had already been placed in the suspect pool, they may choose not to "inform" him yet. They may organize for an hour or two, prepare for their first encounter with him. They did that sometimes, he knew. As a crime reporter, he knew that.

Or maybe she is still in the OR, still hanging between life and death. And the worst reckoning to come won't be the one with the police. But he won't risk calling the hospital to see. Not even anonymously. Phone records can be checked.

"I'm glad you're here, Daddy," Tommy says. Meaning, Sam knows, so much more: I haven't seen much of you; I wish I could see more. I don't know what's happening between you and Mommy.

"I'm glad, too," Sam says. "You sleep."

"Don't wake Mom in the morning," Tommy advises his dad, fear of her moods ingrained in his thinking already. "She likes to sleep," he says.

"I won't wake her," Sam tells him. "I promise."

She can sleep as long as she likes, Tommy.
Let's let her sleep.

He is here with his boy.

It's the two of them now.

And if she is dead? He knows it. He feels it. It is absolutely the right thing he has done. The absolute wrong, absolute right thing.

Denise Stevens was killed while the suspect was in custody.

With just one rifle shot, Tommy has lost his mother and will now lose his father. The single shot has found one parent, but will leave him without either one. What an efficient shot. What a poor shot. The single shot has exacted its own justice, has orphaned his only son.

Will the police come take him in the morning? In the afternoon? In a week? In a month?

He can only play his role. He will play it perfectly. He is a crime reporter. He has seen the process close up a hundred times; he knows better than anyone how to play it. And he will see.

The boy falls back asleep.

Sam sits on the floor of his son's bedroom, watching him sleep, feeling the silence and the darkness pressing up against them.

13

The police come to the door at dawn. Three patrolmen. No sirens. A loud, firm rap on the wood.

Like Eastern Europe or South America. Here to escort him roughly to the Gulag. Here to put a pistol to his head above a ditch at the edge of the cold woods.

Sam opens the door. "Where is she?" he says—exhausted, anxious, frustrated, disturbed.

The tallest one stoops as he speaks, like a gangly awkward kid embarrassed into confessing something. "Mr. Stevens . . ." he says.

"Where is she?" Sam demands sharply.

"She's dead, Mr. Stevens."

Sam shakes his head, keeps shaking it—wordless, stupid, repetitive, senseless. "I wondered," he says softly, head still shaking. "I wondered."

He knew the tears would be in his eyes. He knew his body would shake. He was still jittery, jaggy, emotional, overwrought, still awake from the killing just hours ago, and all he had to do was suppress all that emotion for the first few moments the cops stood in the doorway and then let it unleash in front of them, give it free rein. He knew he could count on the trauma, the shock, of his own actions—his physical sickness, his inevitable natural reactions to killing his own wife. It washes over him in a fresh wave, a pulsing emotional echo, that anyone, that everyone, could see.

I wondered. Why she didn't call. Where she was. The perfect phrase of mute confusion. Of grim prescience. Of half knowledge.

"It's not possible," Sam says. "It's not possible."

Denial. Classic first symptom. Classic first stage.

He looks at them, close to sick. So close to sick he is sure they can see it. "Is it because? . . ." and he lets the thought drop, but his meaning is obvious. *Is it because I'm covering the story?*

"That's what we're wondering, too, of course," says one of the cops.

"Oh, God," says Sam. Clearly realizing the possibility of complicity. Of an inadvertent role. Horrified that he might somehow be at fault.

"Sorry to have to bring you this," says the oldest of the three, and Sam suddenly has the sense the older officer has delivered this kind of news before.

And suddenly, there is Tommy, standing behind his father at the threshold of the front door. Holding a hand up against the harsh dawn light—and the blinding harshness to come.

"What's going on, Dad?"

Sam looks at the cops, and the cops look at Sam.

Sam will never be able to thank Tommy enough for waking up. For coming to the door. For asking, wide-eyed.

Because Sam knows that telling his son that his mother is dead will tear Sam apart. Will make Sam break down. Tommy will cry or scream or collapse—and Sam, having to tell him, will be close to that, too.

"Tommy," he says, grabbing him protectively, holding him close against whatever reaction he will have—knees buckling, falling dead away, screaming . . . exploding.

"Tommy . . . she's dead."

It is a moment of suspension. Of cessation. The world goes soundless, timeless, as the cops and Sam, watch, listen, witness the boy in front of them.

He shakes his head slowly, side to side.

Then a bursting, howling, strange syllable punctures the dawn.

Then a wail—soaring, searing—descending in a moment into a thick, strangled sobbing.

Sam moans involuntarily in sympathy. Tears stream down his face.

Thank you, Tommy, for being here. Thank you.

14

At 8:00 A.M., Big Billy Wyatt sat in the big beat-up leather chair of his big bright office and hung his head.

The speech he'd been prepared to make this morning—the more extensive, detailed, glorious follow-up to last night's brief announcement—now dangled uselessly from one of his immense hands, in scrawled note cards.

His deputies surrounded him, leaning uncomfortably against the paneling, perched cross-armed on the edge of his oversized desk, watching him, like he was a dying beast, unable to help him and unsure what to do.

Down the hall, the reporters' briefing room was exploding with anticipation. Big Billy and his forlorn deputies could hear the stirring all the way up here.

He'd been proud of the speech. Concise, modest, it conveyed satisfaction in the arrest itself, and not in the recounting of it. He'd scribbled it on note cards as soon as the suspect had come in, and it came naturally, fluently, and he'd been as eager to give it as the reporters and the local citizenry and much of the nation was to hear it.

He crumpled the note cards, tossed them for now into his desk's top drawer.

The suspect was in a holding cell downstairs. The basement's most interior cell, watched by ten officers, all told.

He was exactly what the high-paid profilers had said. And exactly what Big Billy's instincts had told him from the second killing on.

Special Forces operative and alumnus. Weapons and tactical specialist. Marine-trained marksman. In the service for fifteen years. Computer consulting now. On the road a lot. Home was a rented apartment outside of Phoenix, Arizona, where no one ever saw him, and neighbors assumed it was a vacation rental for him. Ray Fine was his name. Ray Fine. Hah.

The facts about Ray Fine beyond those were thin so far— extremely thin for eight hours later. Records had been expunged. Data had been transferred. Which all tended to confirm the kind of past, the kind of existence, that this kind of military operative often lived.

He'd said nothing. No bragging. No explanation, no cause, no words at all. A couple of the deputies had been furious with that, but it was exactly as Big Billy Wyatt had expected. Just a confirmation of who he was.

The deputy, the county, the state, the nation, the world, were looking for why. Billy Wyatt understood immediately that there might not be a why. Might be no why at all, and if there was, they'd probably never learn it or comprehend it.

"Ain't he gonna say anythin' ever?" asked Dwight in frustration.

Wyatt shook his head. "Prob'ly not. Part of their code, these types. This way, they feel they can still be fighting you and still have the upper hand, even from their jail cells. It's power. They got somethin' you want, and they're not givin' it. But hey, it just helps tell me we got the right guy."

Of course, having him was one thing. Keeping him was another.

The problem was twofold.

First, they couldn't find any weapons. Not a trace. Already, in just the last two hours, cooperating police forces across the country had searched Ray Fine's rental apartment in Arizona, were searching the trail of his motel rooms, searched his rental cars, searched his cross-country route, reconstructed from eyewitnesses and sales receipts.

The absence of any weapons might not have been a problem in and of itself. They'd just begun, after all. The guy was smart. They might very well find them with a little more time. There was a little arsenal, somewhere. Wyatt was sure of it.

The bigger problem was the other killing that had just taken place with precisely the same MO. On its own, it wouldn't be a problem. On its own, it was fascinating—classic copycat stuff, of course.

Except there were details not officially released to the press, details to it that would presumably be known only by Wyatt and his department—maybe picked up by a particularly alert and experienced reporter here or there, but that would be it—details that perfectly matched the details of the previous killings.

Details like a hundred yards, almost eerily close to that, every time. The maximally effective distance, those who had been trained in the death arts knew. Maximal intersection of accuracy and stealth for a professional or proto-professional.

Details about the sniper's exit strategies—clearly thought through, rehearsed, well planned. So that while the victims themselves had seemed thoroughly random—up to now, anyway—the setting and time and circumstance of each attack had certainly not been random.

Although Wyatt knows in his heart and in his bones this is the right guy, he now also has to question it, and *that*—more than the seething briefing room, more than the humiliating, equivocating speech to come, more than anything—is driving him crazy.

Because whatever Wyatt might know in his heart, all the reporters were going to know was that another killing took place after an arrest was already made. So how useful, how reassuring an arrest is it? Not very.

He knew the reporters by now. He knew they would make the matter of the latest killing—with a suspect already in custody— into the story. He couldn't blame them. You had to admit, that *was* the story.

If you've got no weapons, and another killing just took place with the same MO, an MO whose details aren't widely known . . .

The victory speech, the resolution, his moment in the sun—it would all have to wait for ballistics.

A lot would depend on that.

It had also turned out that this latest victim was a local reporter's wife. Denise Stevens. Wife of Sam Stevens. When they finally ID'd the body and brought him the news, Wyatt stood before his deputies and shook his head mournfully.

Another name. Another victim. Another tragedy.

Random killing goes on long enough, thought Big Billy Wyatt, it eventually, inevitably, gets beyond random, just by the odds. Even in an area as large as a county, it eventually gets to someone you all know, someone you love.

Of course, there was also the chance that it wasn't random at all.

She was the wife of the local reporter who'd been covering the story, after all.

And that indicated something different. A modified MO? A new MO? Something not random at all?

What if, when the ballistics analysis came back, the round that killed the reporter's wife was a match? While a suspect was in custody?

Big Billy Wyatt held his big head in his big hands.

The clamor is deafening. The jockeying for position is a sport with no rules, a classroom with no control.

"Sheriff!"

"Sheriff Wyatt!"

"We have a suspect in custody," says Wyatt steadily. Flat. No modulation. Revealing nothing further by the tone of his voice. "I'm not free to give you much beyond that at this time. I need to protect the suspect's identity and the circumstances of his capture for the time being."

Because it's entirely circumstantial, and I don't know how this is going to go. I don't want to say or do anything that will aid his defense, and I don't want this guy suing us and bringing down everything I've built.

"I'll take just a couple of questions."

Throwing open the floodgates.

It was bedlam. He could barely make out individual voices.

"Has the suspect said anything?"

"Not a word," said Wyatt.

"Can you show us a picture?"

"Absolutely not."

"Is it true there have been no weapons found yet?"

Man, their sources were fast. He looked at the reporter lugubriously. "Yes, that is true." *It's early yet—just hold your horses.* But it was no use saying that to a reporter.

"Is it true that Denise Stevens, Sam Stevens's wife, is the latest murder victim?"

"Yes—although we can't say with any certainty at this point that she is a victim of the same killer."

"But didn't her murder take place well after the suspect was in custody?"

Jesus Christ. "Yes, indications are she was murdered after the suspect was in custody, but establishing time of death and a time line is a matter for the coroner."

A wave of questions, an interrogative roar. He squinted into the glare.

"Has anyone in your department spoken to Sam Stevens?"

"We have spoken with him briefly. As you can imagine, he is in a state of shock and grief, and we are trying to respect that, but we will be speaking to him extensively; don't you worry 'bout that."

There is a lawyer in Ray Fine's cell by midmorning. Ray has, since his arrest, deigned to utter only two sentences, the first one direct, the second full of braggadocio and arrogance and evident knowledge of his surprisingly strong position. "Get me a lawyer," he has said. Adding, with a thin, smug smile, "Any lawyer."

So the state has assigned—with no awareness of the irony of the name, presumably—Andrew Feingard. Wyatt knows Andy Feingard isn't the world's most powerful or passionate or knowledgeable defense attorney, but Wyatt figures he doesn't have to be.

Feingard asks the deputies, in a reasonable, flat tone, what the entire department, what the entire county, what every reporter, what the entire nation has been asking.

From Feingard, of course, the question has greater import. It isn't just rhetorical; it's highly actionable.

"So, where's the weapon?" he says.

"We're looking."

"That's fine," says Feingard, "but let me ask it again"—he holds open his palms in supplication—"where's the weapon?"

Meaning: *Where is* any *reason you are holding my client at all?*

The deputies are glumly silent this time.

"You can hold him twenty-four hours," Feingard announces loudly. "Which gives you about eighteen to go. I'm setting my wife's kitchen timer."

"What makes you think I did this?" Ray Fine says suddenly, just above a whisper. His third sentence in six hours. An even, flat, forgettable American voice. The deputies and clerks surrounding him have never heard him speak. There is a stunned, fascinated silence.

He shakes his head in mock offense at the accusation. Then, insolently, he smiles.

Ray Fine had been pulled over at a random alcohol and seat-belt checkpoint, and his Arizona license, Chicago rental car, and general evasiveness had felt funny and creepy to a nervous, alert, overly ambitious young cop. All the patrolmen were on edge; they had been for weeks. To defuse the suspicion, no doubt, Ray Fine had begun to chat a little with the other middle-aged cop about the military—finding a point of bonding, seeking the unspoken *I'm okay*. The nervous young cop listened to the conversation and then, insisted—over the objections of his older partner—on checking Ray's story with their on-board wireless access. They couldn't find any military record. They checked him against their profile. He kept fitting the profile, kept fitting it point by point. They asked him if he would step out of the car, please.

When the young, nervous, ambitious cop climbed into the rental car himself, he smelled a lot of fast food, although the plastic and paper bags and refuse, he saw, had been fastidiously emptied out. He got a strong impression of an endless stream of meals eaten in the rental car, smelled lots of human presence, someone living in the car, spending hour on hour there. Beyond that, stronger and more distinctive than that, he swore he smelled gunpowder, the residue of someone firing from the car. He couldn't really trust his own overeager nose, of course, but he was sure that when they got a trained dog into the car, it would start barking up a storm, proclaiming the moment the animal had been trained for.

They were soon—excitedly, pulses pounding—dealing with several different driver's licenses, which would peel the top layers off several half identities, origins of which all seemed to be Ray Fine.

Billy Wyatt had heard the whole story several times now—the

last couple of times at his own request, to get it into the record, to imprint it permanently in his memory and imagination, come what certainly would of trials, retrials, interviews, reconstructions, etc.

But what *does* make them think Ray Fine did it?

A profile. A style. A lot of night driving, based on the night bugs on the windshield. Mileage on the rental car. Gasoline stops. Times on surveillance cameras at all-night food marts.

All excellent, diligent police work.

All merely circumstantial.

Where is the weapon? Where are any of the weapons that belong to the weapons expert, the weapons freak? Where is anything, for that matter? Any usable evidence at all?

15

When Sam opens the door to Tommy's room, Tommy is sitting on his bed, staring out.

He is dry-eyed. As if he has just awakened and is looking out at a new day.

There could be none newer, thinks Sam.

Sam walks over and sits on the bed next to him silently.

She was the boy's mother. Yes, unreliable. A lush. Unpredictable. Manic. Bitter. Depressed. But his mother, after all. A ten-year-old boy's mother.

"It's going to be okay," Sam says. Hoping that Tommy somehow, somewhere, already knows it.

And then the boy stops his staring out and turns to look at Sam. In his look is something apart from fear of the unknown, something apart from what Sam fully expects to see in the face of a ten-year-old, a face Sam knows so well.

There is a calm there. A knowledge. And, Sam is sure, the faintest sense of accusation.

The boy knows. Sam senses it. Tommy knows.

It should be inconceivable for a child. A child should be largely protected from such knowledge by its very inconceivability. But Tommy was the only person in the world who knew any-thing of the war between them. Who not only knew, but felt the depth of their animosity, felt its heat and simmer.

The boy knows. Maybe not even consciously. Maybe just the preconscious sense that Sam has been the architect, the engineer of this.

This is the second thing Sam hasn't thought of. The second thing he hasn't thoroughly planned for. First, that she might fall but not be dead (but that is resolved.) And now, this. This is something he will have to take as it comes. Play it as it lays.

Sam knows, of course, it could be only his own guilt, playing on him, angling at him, insinuating itself, since conventional paths of guilt obviously haven't held him in check.

He knows it will likely never be spoken of between them. Not even when Sam is sitting in some prison visiting room, and Tommy is across the glass. It will, Sam suspects, remain a silence forever, so that Sam will never know for sure.

Oh, maybe he will come to know. Maybe they will both come to understand. Maybe Tommy is thanking him already, in his un-conscious ten-year-old way.

Sam smiles at Tommy.

You're welcome, Tommy.

16

A re you ready?" asks the coroner.

Sam nods mutely.

The coroner gestures to his big assistant to stand next to Sam, the assistant's hand at Sam's elbow. Sam knows why: in case Sam goes down.

They pull the sheet off Denise Stevens.

Sam looks. Looks along her body, regards her familiar limbs and curves a long time, shielding his own view with one hand, psychologically preparing, before he can bring himself to look up near the gunshot in her left temple, where he knows it will be.

Part of her face is blown away. But not enough.

He nods mutely. Yes, that's her.

In a moment, the room whirls, and he feels last night's dinner in his throat, and his knees crumple.

The coroner's assistant misses Sam's arm. Sam hits his lip on the table as he goes down.

That's good, he thinks, sitting outside fifteen minutes later, the spinning and nausea now stopped. The bloody, puffy lip— that's very good.

. . .

Big Billy Wyatt sat across the holding cell from Ray Fine.
It was the only thing he could think to do.
Feingard's kitchen timer was ticking. The hours were sliding
by. And they were nowhere.
Four of Wyatt's deputies sat outside the cell.
It was quiet here, silent, and the silence was a relief from the
noise and pandemonium of the briefing room upstairs and the relentless phone calls in his office. Over the weeks, the briefing
room had become like an animal's cage. Papers and trash scat-
tered everywhere, though it was cleaned every night. An odor
hung over it permanently now, a stale smell of clustered human-
ity, of sweat magnified by the heat of the lights and cameras. He
wondered if his own office had that same stale, over-occupied
smell. The ripe scent of Billy Wyatt, nervous, sweating. The
scent of pressure.

He knew he could count on the silence here. Because he knew
the monster across from him would stay silent. Because this was a
stealthy, self-contained monster, as everything had indicated
from the first killings on.

Sheriff Billy Wyatt looked at Ray Fine. Fine had what Wyatt
thought of as that Special-Ops wiriness, that leanness attained
while learning to live off bugs and roots and reptiles. The white,
translucent skin of night-ops—of a night owl, a sleeper, a
watcher. This guy, Ray, didn't look as physically tough as some of
the others. He seemed to be all eyes and hands—a weapons specialist right down to his build. No wonder he fit in so well as a
computer consultant. He looked enough like you expected a computer geek to look.

He and Ray Fine were the two opposing paramilitary types,
thought Billy. Opposite styles, both drawn to the paramilitary
professions. Billy was big, gregarious, extroverted, loved the

companionship and guys-together aspects of police work, loved being out in the community and the different neighborhoods with their different unspoken customs and rules and the after-shift softball and bowling leagues. He loved the interaction of it, loved the easy pace of it, and the hours and the practical jokes and the playfulness—all of them the inevitable result of men together, together forever, a result you could count on. While the Ray Fine type, he knew, was drawn to the order, the discipline, a place to belong, a place to not stand out in your strangeness. The Ray Fine type was drawn to the fact that it would counteract, interrupt, the instincts and life of a loner. It let a loner feel like part of a group, part of things, for a change. And the power, of course. The automatic power to reduce, to disguise, to slowly melt away, the sense of inadequacy.

Generally, the silent, beady-eyed little Ray Fines resented the big bluff Billy Wyatts, and generally the Billy Wyatts never even thought about the Ray Fines—until a moment like this.

No weapons found. The trail of Ray Fine's life had now been trampled, like a physical and electronic and psychological path dug behind him, dug deep behind his movements and his life for the past month, and they had found nothing—not a shell casing, nothing.

The clock was ticking. The hours were sweeping by.

As Ray Fine's profile became clearer, one of the forensic psychiatrists on the case, a Dr. Davis—guy in Levi's and a white blazer over a Hawaiian shirt—had insisted on pulling Wyatt aside to make some rather urgent observations about the Ray Fines of the world. About these Special-Ops types who had spent a lifetime working utterly alone, silent, erasing their own identities, being relentlessly and occupationally close to death and destruction and torture, inhabiting a Caravaggesque world for years on end. Such a career, such an existence, Davis said, could cause a psychotic break—dissociation, multiple personality disorder, all kinds of unfamiliar effects of the human mind overwhelmed by stress yet at the same time unaware of and undefended against it. The psychiatrist emphasized that it was not even that uncommon, although these psychotic breaks could take unique, individualized forms. It was well documented in the literature. Wyatt had listened politely, had heard what the shrink had to say. But the shrink hadn't stared into the eyes of Ray Fine. The shrink hadn't seen Ray's thin smile. This was no psychotic break. This was no split intelligence, no multi-personality. From what Billy Wyatt could see, this was just evil—self-knowing, self-aware, highly cognizant.

He knew it was Ray Fine. From thirty years of police work, from the moment he saw him, merely from the look in Ray Fine's eyes, he knew it was Ray Fine, and Ray Fine knew he knew, Wyatt could see.

In a few hours, Feingard would be back, Ray Fine would have to be released, and these Special-Ops guys were experts at disappearing—that was the easiest part of what they knew how to do.

Billy Wyatt looked at him. Ray Fine returned the look—smug, arrogant, proud, eyes brimming with amusement and mirth.

What would happen if they did find a weapon? A trial—long, twisting, changes of venue, grandstanding attorneys, technicalities, false starts, retrials, books, movies—and through it all, that smug look.

Wyatt could make it all so much more efficient. He could reach across the little table between them and take that windpipe in his huge hands and crush it and be done with it. Save the state countless millions. Save nine families bottomless suffering. Everyone would shake their heads, condemn his unprofessionalism, and silently, wordlessly, thank him. Only the networks would be annoyed with him—for cutting the story short.

Reach across, grab that windpipe, before Ray or the four deputies standing outside even processed what was happening. Reduce justice from years to a minute or so.

Ray Fine was going to walk out of here, and Billy Wyatt would be through, he knew. Forced to take early retirement. A national moment of embarrassment the local powers couldn't abide. That didn't bother him. He didn't care about any of that, really. He didn't really care how he looked to millions on their TV sets. It was the smugness—the smugness of a sniper who knew exactly what he was doing. That's what was eating at him.

Wyatt breaks the silence.

"You ain't gonna say anythin'. I know that."

But Wyatt heard it—too late—as a little power play between him and Ray, where Ray's silence could prove Billy's point, could prove Billy right—and Ray heard it, too.

"You know that, huh?" says Ray. Proving Billy wrong—and saying, in effect, *You don't know shit.*

Wyatt hadn't slept well in a month. Victims danced before him like sheep—sheep that had exactly the opposite effect on his sleep than they were supposed to.

He wished the preliminary ballistics results could have been here already. It was driving him crazy with impatience. The local coroner, Neil Tarsin, couldn't assemble his autopsy team at two-thirty in the morning, of course, so it had had to wait until 8:00 A.M. this morning. And given the glare of national attention, Tarsin was being doubly sure not to make any procedural mistakes, so he was taking extra care and extra time with every portion, including the extraction of the round. Wyatt was itching to at least know the round type and caliber, the basics of a ballistics match, but under the pressure and scrutiny, Tarsin had to do everything by the book. Plus, their local ballistics lab was not certified, so once the round was in ballistics, they would be repeating each of their tests, taking extra precautions, not wanting to be challenged or reversed if or when the round had to go to a certified lab in D.C. This was probably wise on everyone's part, given the disputability surrounding ballistics findings. Preliminary and final findings, independent of each other, would give the result more standing in court, should the need someday arise.

It all meant, though, that Feingard's kitchen timer would ring, and that Ray Fine might have to be released, before any forensic ballistics results were back. Wyatt had called for any topline result hours ago. He had pleaded. He had bullied. But in the national glare of the case, everyone seemed to fear for their licenses and their livelihoods. They wouldn't do it any way but by the book. Just a couple more hours, Sheriff Wyatt. Hang in there.

He felt the ticking of Feingard's kitchen timer.

He felt the *federales* at his back.

He felt the pressure, the tightness in his chest, at the back of his neck. The phone calls, the questions, the noise . . .

He felt this latest murder . . . cutting a fresh swath through him . . .

He'd been here since midnight. He hadn't slept.

That little white windpipe in his two big hands . . .

Wyatt had grown up on a farm, wrangling livestock. He'd had more than his share of fights. He knew bodies. He knew it wouldn't take much.

And suddenly, Big Billy Wyatt is across the little table, on top of Ray Fine, and Billy Wyatt's hands are on that white windpipe, and the holding cell's silence is broken by the clatter of chairs, by the shouts of the deputies as they tumble into the cell, by a generalized alarm and panic and hysteria.

The deputies pull Wyatt off him. It takes all four of them, but they pull him off.

And Billy knows immediately—by his thirty-plus years' experience—the depth and difficulty of the situation he's just created.

He's made it political. It's as if he's handed Feingard live ammunition. Now they won't be able to extend holding Ray Fine uncharged for a minute more than Feingard has given them. There were legitimate pretexts, earnest pleas, and rational arguments to be made that a judge would now look on with little sympathy. Now they'll be forced to let Ray Fine go that much faster, if nothing more concrete turns up in these last few hours. My client's safety, Feingard can say. The untrustworthiness of the local justice system. Billy has given Feingard—or any defense lawyer—all the fodder he or she could want. Powerful artillery for the media. A powerful negotiating position. Billy knows how it goes.

And it is all for nothing, because even lying there on the holding cell floor, the smugness never leaves Ray Fine's eyes.

Billy would have settled for that: for the smugness, just for a moment, leaving those eyes.

17

Denise Stevens.

Thirty-five.

Coming home from drinks with a girlfriend. Stopping off for coffee.

The shot comes from the street. A car pulls out, heads away. No one sees it. No one can identify it. No one knows if the shot came from the car.

Straight to the temple. Down onto the pavement. Gone before she even hit it, according to the coroner.

Upper middle class. Nice looking. Nice life.

Ten-year-old son.

Denise Stevens.

Wife of local newsman Sam Stevens, who had been reporting the story.

Random? Not random?

Number ten.

In his cell, Darryl Jenkins is watching the news on the fuzzy TV high in the corner of the cell, a privilege he has earned after eighteen years of incarceration without incident.

He smiles. "Jesus Christ," he says aloud to no one, and shakes his head and feels mirthful all the way from his rotting gums to his curled up bony toes. "Jesus H. Christ."

Sam opened the front door of his town house to the glare of the lights and the frenzy of the cameras. As he walked out among them, they formed a semicircle around him, a clumsy frantic broadcasters' ballet on the town house's little front lawn. As he moved, they moved. When he stopped, they stopped.

Like his kid's soccer game, thought Sam, with all the players angling toward Sam, the ball.

This was, of course, a glare he knew well. A glare he lived in and was comfortable in, was ready for and understood. He would never admit it aloud, but he felt more at home in the glare of the lights than anywhere else. He felt more in control in this familiar blinding brightness than in the dark alone. He felt calmer, more secure here, surrounded by cameras and reporters and microphones, than he felt inside his own home behind him, alone with his ten-year-old son. He knew what was here; he knew exactly what was going to come, what the questions would be. But in the dark alone, he didn't know what the questions would be.

"Sam, what was your first reaction?"

"Sam, do you think the sniper knew?"

"Sam, had there been any contact, any warning?"

"Were you working on a certain angle? Had you gotten too close, do you think?"

They were his colleagues, his competitors, who were still, nevertheless, his friends.

This frankness, this familiarity—they were clearly trying to take advantage of it to get more. To get something unique. Sam understood and accepted that. There was no sense in pretending otherwise: Sam was a victim—an indirect victim—but he was also a reporter.

Sam held up his hands genially, gently, and they quieted down. He took a breath.

"As you can imagine, it's very strange to be here, instead of out there, with you. It's strange ... more than strange ... to be forced into the story." He looked out at them. "You should all pray, every one of you, that you are never up here with me." He felt the tears well up. He let them. The emotion, the turmoil, the tension of the past twenty-four hours, was under the surface—reliable, ready to summon.

"I'm going to say just a few things. . . . I'm going to try to say just enough to get you all off my lawn." There were a few appreciative smiles, but Sam was not smiling. "First of all, there is nothing like this. There is nothing comparable in life; it defies our description, and now that I understand that firsthand, I am never going to ask anyone about it on-camera again."

"Second, my son is in there, and all I am thinking about is him, and everything I am doing or will do or say will be through the filter of helping him."

"Third, I do not know Ray Fine. I first heard his name at the same moment you all did."

But it was as if he never said any of it. Just as he knew it would be. The questions flew, and he answered them the best he could.

"What was your wife doing out at that hour?"

"Having a drink with a friend."

"Wasn't that late to be out for a drink?"

"Yeah, it was late."

"She'd had a lot more than one drink, according to the coroner."

Sam looked at the reporter with disbelief. It was someone Sam didn't know. "Apparently, you're not too sober yourself," says Sam, with irritation.

Ask another question like that and you'll be horizontal, and every-one'll cheer it, thinks Sam. *Don't disparage the behavior of my sainted wife.*

"Do you know Ray Fine?"

"I already told you. I have no idea who Ray Fine is. I'd never heard of him before my producer called."

"Could he have a grudge of some sort over your broadcasts?"

"I don't see how or why, but we're not talking about rational behavior here."

"Do you believe in the death penalty?"

"Do you want the death penalty for Ray Fine?"

"I want justice," said Sam.

"Do you have any message for Ray Fine?"

"Do you want to meet him? Do you want to look in his eyes?"

Sam looked into the glare of the cameras. Into the lights.

"That's all I can handle for now," he said, his eyes wet, turning his face away.

Drenched with the drama of what he had done.

He turned and headed back into the town house.

18

The coroner's report and the ballistics report arrive by early afternoon, within minutes of each other.

The coroner's report confirms Denise Stevens's time of death: between 2:00 and 2:45 A.M. Which was merely formal but essential confirmation of the Pakistani coffee clerk's police statement and the incident report of the first officer on the scene.

Time of Ray Fine's arrest: 11:45 P.M. More than two hours earlier.

The preliminary ballistics report on Denise Stevens is unequivocal. The single slug removed from the left lateral anterior lobe of the deceased offers multiple and significant points of ballistic intersection with the previous crimes. Semijacket lead hollowpoint. Jacket material not copper but steel. Entrance-wound burn pattern indicates round was fired by a high-powered weapon. Entrance-wound burn pattern further indicates firing distance consistent with previous cases. Entrance-wound location consistent with previous cases. Cranial deformation of round prevents further verification via rifling pattern. Caliber and type are a match.

Feingard is back in the station, asking for the lab report.

Wyatt watches the lawyer's posture and stance literally change as he reads it.

Either Feingard suddenly realizes he's going to be a hero, or he thinks—with a growing astonishment and renewed passion and zeal—that his client may actually be innocent.

Feingard looks up and asks for copies, unable to modulate his excitement. Figuring he'll never be believed unless he has the report in his hands.

They've had two attorneys from the prosecutor's office working on it all morning, petitioning judges, pointing to precedent, suggesting loopholes, to no avail. Turns out you can't alter the Bill of Rights. Not if you're a county DA, anyway.

It's almost time to let Ray Fine go.

"Feeling a little calmer, are we, Sheriff?" Feingard inquires mock-politely upon seeing Wyatt again, referring pointedly and purposefully to Wyatt's holding-cell escapade. They both know that Feingard might not be dealing with Billy Wyatt much anymore. Probably one of the deputies—Dwight Martin, most likely—will be appointed to serve as an interim contact.

"We've been patient," says Feingard. "More than patient. It's time to turn my boy loose. That means no surveillance, and it means no tails. Trust me, Mr. Fine is a man who will be well aware of either."

And able to shake either one anyway, thinks Wyatt.

Billy Wyatt had been shocked to see the report. It seemed impossible.

And he had to ask himself: Was he wrong? Were his instincts wrong?

Had he lost control for the first time, embarrassing the department and himself?

Had he looked into those dead-dance eyes, found all the confirmation and certainty he had ever needed, yet had been proved mistaken? Proved blind?

Had he leaped across the table and tried to strangle an innocent man?

In which case, his coming dismissal—disguised as retirement, no doubt—was deserved and justified and well timed. In which case, it was high time he stepped aside.

He regrets the leap across the little table, the leap for the white windpipe, because he knew his deputies weren't going to stand there and watch him do it. This wasn't a department in the Deep South in the thirties; these guys actually liked him and weren't about to let him destroy himself. He'd thought that whatever happened, whatever followed, he'd always have the momentary satisfaction of that leap. But now he only regrets it.

There is a little service exit in the back of the police station. Billy Wyatt is surprised that none of the press, in their weeks camped out here, has discovered it yet.

To keep anyone from knowing, to fool the crowd, they restrict the process to the bare minimum—Wyatt, one deputy, Feingard, and his client Ray Fine.

Feingard stands with his arms crossed as the deputy removes the handcuffs.

No one says a word.

Wyatt gestures vaguely to the exit door.

Ray Fine looks at none of them—makes no eye contact at all—and, unhesitatingly, unceremoniously, presses down the horizontal bar and slips through the institutional door.

With as much talent for non-presence, for invisibility, as had led him to nine victims in the first place, Wyatt thought.

Wyatt was sick to his stomach. He felt like he might vomit.

He knew it was Ray Fine and that the latest killing was a copycat.

But, of course, he didn't know it at all.

He hoped, he prayed, he even expected they'd eventually get Ray Fine.

But until then, more would die.

Wyatt turned his big frame to head up to the briefing room. To take center ring at the circus once more. To inform them that they'd had to let the suspect go.

Media lynching was the official term.

A performing seal on his way to the lions.

19

Ray Fine walked out into the harsh sunshine of the little parking lot behind the police station and began to stroll down the sidewalk toward the commercial zone.

The dream continued.

The seamless dream.

He was floating. He was dumbstruck. He was an angel. He was a god.

Elation filled his chest. Amusement tingled improbably in his fingers and toes.

The sense of exhilaration danced across the dark borders of his mind.

What do you know, Joe! What do you know!

We've got a way to go, Joe! We've got a way to go!

The blackness in his brain, the dark, wild stage that no one suspected, the shadowy proscenium that he had performed from since he was a child, was oddly, unaccountably, flooding with light, flooding with action.

He understood Billy Wyatt. He understood him very well. It hadn't required Billy Wyatt's thick hands on his windpipe to understand Billy Wyatt, he had felt close enough to him without that.

So he knew that Billy Wyatt would hardly be leaving him alone now, despite Feingard's warnings. He knew he'd have to watch behind him, he knew this freedom could be short-lived if he weren't extremely careful. But he *was* extremely careful. That was the thing. You couldn't predict an overalert, high-IQ, earnest do-gooding paranoid nut like that eager-beaver cop, but on the whole, Ray was very, very careful.

When the reporter's wife had been killed, he had been initially shocked. Was it someone angling to take credit? Someone, with one cowardly shot, threatening to recalibrate everything? To have the whole thing tally up differently?

He also understood that whoever it was had actually saved him. Inadvertently, unintentionally saved him. Because it was obviously supposed to look like the sniper—trying to slip one in for the sniper, let the sniper get the credit, add one to the sniper's total, but clearly, the guy's timing was awful. And Ray's timing, it appeared, was consequently brilliant.

So who was it?

Ray knew exactly who.

He could see it over the TV, for Christ's sake. How could you not? The information was beamed at him directly into his rental's little living room, express, no stopping at go, like a free service add-on of the local cable company. He knew how minds worked. It was that reporter, Sam Stevens. In one of the most conventional and common and cowardly and uninspired crimes of modernity—killing your bitch wife.

Ray had watched the coverage of the murders, of course. He had watched that reporter and that reporter's stories and that reporter's growing fascination. He couldn't understand how everyone didn't see it, but people were idiots.

Sam Stevens. The reporter who had freed him.

Freed him temporarily, at least. Because he couldn't live the rest of his life with Wyatt's clumsy bloodhounds panting and lolling their tongues behind him.

So when he could, he'd arrange a little visit with that reporter. Not to thank him, exactly.

No, something more involved than that.

But for now, Ray Fine walked out into the sun, into the morning he thought he'd never see.

The powerful, terrifying, strange dream was fated to continue.

He pictured the huge sheriff looming over him. Felt the thick clammy fingers. Smelled the clammy breath. Smelled his sloppiness.

The dream continued.

You don't know Joe, he thought to himself, with satisfaction that rode the crisp clear morning.

There you go, Joe.

The Joe they don't know.

20

"Sheriff William Wyatt of Webster County announced in a briefing moments ago that a suspect in the serial sniper case was just released on lack of evidence. This is surely unwelcome news for Webster County residents. We go live to reporter Amanda Steele. . . ."

Sam looked at the radio, uncomprehending. He must have heard the newscaster wrong. He must have imagined it, hallucinated it.

Amanda Steele repeated the lead, as if to clarify exclusively for Sam.

His mind went momentarily blank. Then erupted, exploded: questions and emotions colliding against one another in a fission of possibility. Elation and confusion, ecstasy and anxiety, singing a contrapuntal symphony.

Had they bought into the matching MO? The hollowpoint must have shattered. The slug must have mushroomed. He'd planned minutely and risked everything and won the bet, for now. It required opposite attributes, he saw—meticulous planning and utter recklessness.

But it couldn't be the matching MO alone. The detectives

would be alert to the prospect of copycat killings, after all—to any case where the external pattern matched. No, it must be they had no evidence to tie the suspect to the murders. And ultimately—with all their legal maneuvers and jurisprudential vamping played out—they must have had to let him go.

Yet Sam had seen Wyatt operate. He had seen Wyatt's plodding, deliberate process, his own meticulous care. So there must have been, Sam figured, substantial cause to bring in the suspect in the first place. Then again, maybe they were just panicky, reactive, with a high-pressure, monster case like this, and they had brought in the wrong guy, whoever he was, who probably fit the profile but hadn't done anything. A guy in the wrong place at the wrong time. Wrong résumé. Wrong responses to police questioning. And then the panic and the politics: They didn't want another Richard Jewell on their hands—the guy accused of the Atlanta Olympic Games bombings, a security guard who fit the profile perfectly, but hadn't done anything, and made the authorities look far more foolish and incompetent than they otherwise would have. Wyatt wouldn't want to cost Webster County a legal settlement in the millions and incalculable embarrassment.

So Wyatt and company had released this poor guy from his Kafka nightmare, and the real sniper was still out there.

Sam is giddy, dizzy, spinning. . . .

He falls back on the couch, spread-eagled, collapsing in joy, covered in elation.

He'd thought he might have just days at best.

But now, out of nowhere, he's been handed a chance.

He feels special. Chosen, somehow. He knows that's ridiculous, foolish, and yet he can't help feeling it. The fates have intervened for him. How? Why? It doesn't matter; they simply have. He feels the power of that. He is surprised to feel that power—the power of possibility, the power of new life—but there it is, strong and undeniable.

Will the sniper—the real sniper—continue to kill?

Sam can't deny that dark hope. He sees it purely tactically, separate from any feeling about it. It will help him. It will help immeasurably to tuck Denise's name into an ever-growing list of victims. To fade into that list, to soften and smudge into a number, a mere statistic. No longer Denise Stevens. Merely victim ten. Caught in the general horror of a local war.

Of course, the *sniper* presumably knows that he didn't kill Denise Stevens. Only the sniper knows for sure it's a copycat killing. Is the sniper flattered? Or infuriated? Would the sniper, once caught, reveal that to the police? *She wasn't mine.* Would the police believe him? Would the sniper ever be caught?

Sam will still be questioned, he knows. There will still be the arduous process. But obviously there's a chance now. A real chance. To pull it off. To be with Tommy. To have a life.

21

Sam Stevens sits across the desk from Billy Wyatt in Wyatt's big disorganized office.

At bottom, they were the two locals, thought Wyatt. The two locals caught up in a national story, a big bucking bronco of a story that each had hoped to ride to the next level of their respective professions, that each had hoped to rope and wrestle into submission, but the story had tossed both of them to the dirt. At first, it had only been Wyatt buffeted and humbled and brought low by it, but now there was this reporter, Sam Stevens, who had joined him. Joined him in the spotlight after standing so close, too close, to center stage.

He had never cared much for what he'd seen of Sam Stevens. The man's obvious and preening ambition was written all over everything he said and did in his sensationalizing broadcasts—and Wyatt thought it was this same obvious and preening ambition that would probably keep Stevens forever in this local market.

But he pushed these thoughts aside for now. Sam was a nice-looking guy, and his wife—everyone who had met her agreed—had been a quiet stunner. A dark-haired beauty, a private person by all accounts, who, if you did notice her, was obviously something special.

The funeral had been predictably gut-wrenching. Wyatt had attended it, as he had all of them. This little family, just starting out, decimated, reduced by a third. The little boy standing there at the graveside, silent, stunned. Wyatt saw it was a small family even beyond the marriage—a couple of white-haired parents still alive, a couple of aunts and uncles, and that was it. The wind blew fiercely. The trees shivered. The dark, massive clouds looked heavy with dissatisfaction, as if they were sending Wyatt an angry, irritated message.

His guys had done a good job of keeping the cameras out. His guys knew all the crews by now, could identify the reporters and their support staff, so the usual tricks of miniature cameras and switching camera operators didn't work so easily anymore. The reporters were kept confined to their cordoned area. Although with their fancy lenses, they had been able to roll tape from there, and had gotten dramatic, beautiful long shots of lone silhouettes against the morning sky—the boy's, the husband's, the casket, the neighboring headstones—which in the end might have made their videos pieces more effective anyway. It was tough to beat the cameras. Tough to conquer the news.

"I'm sorry about your loss, Sam," Wyatt said now, as he shook Stevens's hand. Despite his other feelings about Sam, he genuinely was sorry.

"Thanks," said Sam. A shy smile.

The two locals. They both knew they shared that, though both deemed it too obvious for either of them to say anything about it.

"Thanks for comin' in," said Wyatt.

Sam shrugged: *of course.*

They had given Sam Stevens a couple of days, but they couldn't give him any more. Ray Fine had walked out into the sunshine, and Wyatt didn't know how long it would be until Fine discovered and shook the surveillance.

"I'm asking your forgiveness in advance, Sam. These are the standard questions, and they've got to be asked, and that's all there is to it. So let's get to it and get it over with, if we can."

If Sam was any kind of reporter, he would know it was highly unusual that these questions were being asked by the sheriff. If he was any kind of reporter, he would surmise that it was because the sheriff himself wanted to see, to gauge the reactions, to look in the man's eyes and judge for himself. If he were any kind of reporter, he would realize that he had actually answered these questions, subtly, to various officers before, and obviously they hadn't been entirely comfortable with what they'd heard.

Billy Wyatt looked at Sam. He had to assume Sam was the kind of reporter who did understand all that.

"Your public life was very public. Your private life was very private," commented Wyatt.

"That's how Denise liked it," said Sam.

Wyatt smiled as he said it. "And where were you on the night of October seventeenth?"

"Home. Home with my son. Until the news came about the arrest of your suspect. And then, as you know, I was here."

Wyatt leans his big frame forward. "So if we have a couple of witnesses who say they saw you earlier out in your car—caught sight of the local celebrity reporter out in his beat-up Toyota—we should just dismiss that? Is that what you're tellin' me?"

Sam wasn't that stupid. He understood that Wyatt hadn't actually said he *had* such witnesses. He knew this game. Wyatt must know Sam knew it. He had the sense that Wyatt was simply going through the motions. Of course, it was possible that he was seen. Of course, he had to consider that. Seen driving, though, if anything. Nothing else.

"Well," Sam shrugged, "I did drive home from work. They could have seen me then."

Wyatt nods. Doesn't ask him about time line, Sam notices. Doesn't ask him if he could have been driving home at midnight, which is when he cruised through the Dominique's parking lot, the most likely place he would have been noticed. Wyatt doesn't pursue that at all—which could confirm that Wyatt doesn't know anything about relative times, but makes Sam wonder if Wyatt really *does* have witnesses, and he's holding them in reserve.

"Home with your son."

"Yes," says Sam, as if it is self-evident.

"Of course, a ten-year-old boy won't be much good corroborating that," says Wyatt. "They can get their nights confused. Which, as the father of a ten-year-old, I'm sure you know very well." Wyatt looked out the big window. "Of course, we could figure out the night by what TV show he was watching or which homework assignment he was doing"—Wyatt smiled slimly— "but it doesn't matter. If that was all we had, we couldn't get it to rise to the level of testimony, which, as a reporter, you know very well. And then there's the natural ten-year-old boy's impulse of wanting to protect the only parent he has. Of being receptive, therefore, to his dad's version of events, to his dad's coaching." Wyatt hasn't looked at Sam for any of it. He is looking out the window, as if merely watching the small downtown events of the October day. "Of course, it cuts both ways, doesn't it? Because if you were really home, a ten-year-old doesn't give you as much corroboration as you could use."

Sam Stevens manages to look a little stunned by this. Not offended—that would be the wrong tactic. Stunned. Which, luckily, he somewhat is.

Wyatt smiles wearily. Sam senses futility. Sam senses Wyatt going through the motions, knowing that this is for form only, a dead end.

"We're going to chat with Tommy, if that's okay," says Wyatt pleasantly.

Sam knows he has the legal right to be with Tommy when the questions are asked. He knows Wyatt will be listening for that self-protective response and knows what Wyatt will think it indicates.

So now it's his turn to surprise Wyatt.

"Of course," says Sam. "Just treat him right," says Sam. "He's been through a lot. He is a boy."

The interview with Tommy Stevens took place first thing the next morning.

Sam waited on a bench outside in the hall.

Tommy had been nervous. He didn't know what to expect. Sam said to just be yourself, and answer the questions; they were only expecting a ten-year-old boy to be a ten-year-old boy, and not a criminal, and not a superhero.

When Tommy emerged from the room twenty minutes later, he hugged his dad and said nothing.

As they drove off down the street in the tan Corolla (the green Audi had been returned to him, but Sam felt it would look unseemly to drive it just yet), having dodged the couple of enterprising reporters who'd managed to figure things out and catch them at the car, Tommy turned to his dad.

"Don't worry, Dad," he said. "I didn't tell them." He looked up at his dad for approval, for acknowledgment, for anything.

Sam's chest seized. His breath caught in his throat.

He knows.

Sam pictures Billy Wyatt. The big, bumbling, angry, shrewd Billy Wyatt.

You didn't tell them, Tommy? Or do you only think *you didn't?*

Sam feels Tommy looking at him. Sam keeps his eyes on the road in front of him. He is afraid to look over at his son.

22

Denise Stevens was in the ground.

A thousand, ten thousand, a hundred thousand tears had been shed. By Sam and Denise's neighbors and acquaintances. By Sam's WWBS colleagues. By shocked, empathetic strangers sucked into a story in the news.

And now, a week later, reporter Sam Stevens—as he knew he would, as he had always imagined, as the only practical choice he had to support himself and his son—returned to the newsroom.

Of course, he was asked if he wanted off the sniper case. Of course, it was assumed he'd say yes.

No, he said. *Don't take me off it. I want to stay with it.*

I want to see it through to the end.

The word went around.

He wants to see justice.

He wants to be there to stare the truth in the face.

Now that was a real reporter.

The national media—right there in the briefing room, after all—seized the story eagerly, proudly. One of their own. A representative of their guts, their instincts. "Reporter Back in Briefing

Room"—a significant sidebar to the main story. Bigger, in fact, at a moment when there was a temporary quiet to the main event.

No, don't take me off it.
   I need to be there.
   I need to monitor the situation.
   I need to be close to the investigation. See where it's going.
   I need to stay one step ahead.

Don't worry, Dad. I didn't tell them.
   Tommy knew.
   Of course, he didn't *know.* He couldn't *know.* Not to a certainty, not to the standard of testimony. But his pure little ten-year-old instincts were right, of course. His unencumbered pure gut sense.
   Sam was amazed to discover that instead of this knowledge separating them, being a wedge that drove them apart, it actually seemed to be drawing them closer. It began to make them a world unto themselves, he and his son, Tommy and Sam. The new connectedness and closeness between them was certainly one that the wider world—interpreting it more generously and sympathetically—would understand and encourage and even help protect. How nice.
   This new closeness, through the unspoken secret they shared.

Breakfast became a ritual of quiet connection. Sam took liberties with his schedule, which was readily accepted. His staff and the station were happy to work around him if it meant not losing their epic, tragic, new media star.
   He dropped Tommy at school the next few mornings and was

instantly aware of the pretty young mothers looking at him with something new, something transparently wistful in their regard. More than tragedy and sorrow hung irresistibly over his story, he knew. Handsome, a good provider, a good father, a television personality, and now alone. They were skilled, these young mothers, in domesticity, in nurturing. They could bring their skills, they knew, to his needs. To all his needs. These skilled, educated, still shapely and gym-buffed suburban moms who hungered for purpose. Who hungered for a project. He was both.

He and Tommy formed a picture—going for an ice cream after dark, strolling down the street with their cones. The following weekend, he watched from the stands as Tommy played baseball, and Tommy's singles and catches as a first baseman were all events now, worth heartier cheers and claps and smiles than before—from Sam, from the other parents in the stands around him. Contained in all those smiles was relief that Tommy's life was going on, a sense that goodness, that life, would prevail.

They occupied a golden bubble—watched and respected and admired from afar.

It was like starting over. It was exactly the starting over that Sam had wished and dreamed. And maybe some pretty and sexy young widow would make her way into the golden bubble eventually, or maybe one wouldn't. Right now, either way was okay with Sam.

It was everything he'd hoped it would be.

Now, he only needed it to last.

23

ay Fine was aware of the surveillance immediately.

It was a white Toyota Camry that he was supposed to take for a rental car, but Christ, the plates weren't rental car plates. Hertz had Fords, Avis and National had GM cars, and all three had some Toyotas, everyone knew that, especially car renters like himself, but those just weren't rental-car plates. Typical dumbshit police-department move. Typical dumbshit police work. It could be seen as insulting, if it weren't so amusing . . . and so sorry. It made him wonder if they *wanted* him to see them, to know he was being followed, so don't try anything—if that was their tactic. But he knew that wasn't it. They were simply incompetent.

And the *nerve* of them, the arrogance—tailing him, watching him like this, an innocent man, a victim of the justice system like himself. He could call Feingard, a card-carrying and vocal member of the ACLU, he knew. Feingard would be eager to charge harassment, make a stink, establish a perimeter, and that might give Ray a little more room to move. Ray would call in that card—if he needed to.

Ray Fine only had to glance at the surveillance once to recognize it, and he wouldn't look up again until he was pretty certain they weren't going to be there. No sense in risking their knowing he knew; he was gathering in, storing, as many advantages as possible. You never knew when you'd need them. That was how to play the game.

He had taken his own rental car out for a drive that morning. Just a pleasant little aimless drive around, just to flush out the surveillance, see who it was, and judge by their driving technique how competent they were. He had gotten his answers on all these questions in less than an hour.

You could say Ray was crazy. He could accept that. You could label him insane. He knew that the bright, confusing carnival stage in his mind was purely his own, so he might not argue with you on that. But you had to say that Ray was a professional. You couldn't say he was anything less than that.

He was living, for now, in a rental apartment in a new development, attending to his computer consulting business out of the second bedroom. The business had proved completely mobile— he could run it out of anywhere. He liked the modernness, the facelessness, of this development. He liked it immediately when the broker showed it to him a few weeks ago. He liked all its subsystems—the plumbing, the drainage. The developer hadn't cut costs. Maybe he'd wanted a little suburban model, an example, a statement, a functional little utopia to leave to local posterity. The broker had thought Ray was quite eccentric, examining and admiring all those subsystems—and for a rental after all. But it was undeniably first-rate.

Because Ray had sighted the Camry just a street away from his rental apartment, he knew, clearly, they had staked out where he lived, so he assumed that the same team, or maybe even a second team, was situated somewhere watching the apartment itself.

And if they'd gone to all that trouble—and knowing they couldn't put a device into the apartment, figuring an experienced hand like Ray would find it—they probably had a surveillance scope on him, keeping a close eye on him moving around in here. That would be their best bet.

In his little kitchen, he read about the case in the morning paper, saw no mention of himself, but a couple of quotes from his lawyer, lecturing grandly about privacy rights and the presumption of innocence. You tell 'em, Feingard.

Ray worked at his computer on and off all day. He had several ongoing client projects—researching and planning and integrating new computer systems; refining and formalizing upgrade recommendations; mapping out new installations. Periodically he glanced out the window. There was no Camry or any other likely surveillance vehicle in view, but that didn't necessarily mean they couldn't see him. They could be in one of the apartments across the road. Anywhere.

That evening, after a frozen dinner in front of a television movie and an hour reading a Tom Clancy novel, he was tired. He went into his bedroom, stripped to his underwear, slipped on the wrinkled gray sweatshirt and gray sweatpants that he had slept in the last few nights.

In fact, it was two gray sweatshirts, two pairs of gray sweatpants, one inside the other, but slipped on together as if it was one.

He had put a third gray sweatshirt under the covers earlier.

Ray sat next to his bedside lamp, still turned off, leaned forward, and began to fuss closely with some paper clips and rubber bands and even a couple of radio batteries he'd previously stowed in the top drawer of the night table. He started to make an intricate little sculpture with them. The room was lit only dimly by the light from the hall, so it was hard for him to see what he was doing.

He counted slowly in his head, from one to ten.

At "ten," he switched on the bedside lamp right next to him.

After the dark, its 150-watt bulb would be blindingly bright, he knew, so Ray shut his eyes just before switching it on.

In a couple of seconds, he switched the lamp off again . . .

Mussed up the thick comforter on the bed and doubled up the pillow . . .

Curled to the floor . . .

Hustled low across the bedroom dark, down the narrow stairs, across the dark kitchen and into the garage . . .

Flicked the fourth fuse in the fuse box on the garage's back wall . . .

Twelve seconds, total.

Should be fine.

Ray knew the equipment. He knew its capabilities. Its limitations. No one knew the equipment like Ray.

"He's doing something with his hands," said Turner, the sloppy, heavyset one, holding the scope. "He's making something. I can't see."

"Well, Christ. Go closer. Zoom in," said Marcum, the lean one with close-cropped blond hair.

Turner zoomed in tight.

The light came on suddenly, blindingly bright. Literally blinding, being so close to it with the scope.

"Jesus!" Turner cried out, pulling the night-vision scope away from his eye, blinking it, rubbing the eye in pain. "Jesus, I can't see."

Marcum giggled. "You gotta be careful with that thing." He couldn't stop giggling. It was the most action they'd had.

"Jesus," said Turner again.

"Give me that," said Marcum, shaking his head now at his partner's wimpy incompetence, grabbing the fancy nightscope, looking into the high-tech eyepiece, needing a moment to zoom out, needing to give the equipment a moment to reorient to the once-again-dark apartment.

Once the scope was adjusted, Marcum saw the mussed-up comforter. He saw part of the gray sweatshirt the subject had just put on. He saw the plumped pillow over the subject's head. Marcum smiled. "He shut off the light, and now he's in bed. All right? The guy's in bed."

The capabilities. The limitations. No one knew the equipment like Ray.

Ray Fine pulled the grate off the drain at the back of his garage, slipped down easily and noiselessly into the development's admirable drainage system, and pulled the grate back in place over him.

A thick layer of brown pungent muck ran along the bottom of the wide drainage pipe, but it wasn't bad. He wasn't a big guy, and he'd been in tighter places than this. He doubled over and began crabbing forward.

It was laid out logically, with the clear topography of the development's land. He followed the flow of the water, letting it lead him through some rights and lefts, past other grates. The tiny pen flashlight was enough for him. Anything brighter was too risky, and he could negotiate a lot without it, just by feel. The pitch dark, the closeness, didn't bother Ray in the least. He had chased Marxist rebels through mountain tunnels not much wider than this. He was safe here, because he was alone here. He always liked being alone. He made his way along patiently and sensibly.

His underground travel ultimately led him to a grate a couple of blocks away. He looked up, checked all around its topside, before forcing the grate up, sliding it off, and hoisting himself up. He removed his top layer of gray sweats, now muddy, stuffing them into a plastic trash bag, where they'd mix with a hundred other plastic trash bags in a nearby dumpster.

He set out, free and unfollowed, into the night.

He wondered if Sam Stevens would be at all surprised to see him.

Thank you for your generous gift, Mr. Stevens. Your gift of freedom.

Here's an opportunity to increase your pledge.

24

The notion comes to Sam slowly. It circles him from far off at first, its outline barely visible, like a rider on the horizon, shapeless amid a cloud of dust—but it trots closer to consciousness until it is upon him, unexpected, looming.

He realizes: He is in a conversation with the sniper.

No words have been exchanged in this conversation. The two conversationalists are unknown to each other, after all. But it is a conversation nonetheless.

Because this is a sniper who—increasingly clearer the longer he evades capture—is plenty, harshly intelligent. Has the accurate, systematic intelligence of evil. Has abilities crisp enough to elude the experienced and coordinated efforts of local and national law enforcement.

Such a sniper undoubtedly knows, first of all, that it was someone else who killed Denise Stevens. The sniper sees each new victim mourned and bewailed on the television news, sees the details of each life enumerated in newspaper articles; he experiences whatever perverse elation he does from those reports, or else derives no such pleasure and simply uses the news as a source of information or a cataloguing system or a scorecard—but whichever, it is clear to him that Denise Stevens is not one of his.

Such a sniper undoubtedly knows the statistic as well as Sam—it's a family member, nine times out of ten. Such a sniper undoubtedly understands why the MO so closely matches his own. So close as to be potentially indistinguishable to the police.

He is in a conversation with this sniper, an accidental and sudden conversation. Who will the next words belong to? Who will speak next?

The sniper, given his pattern, is certainly due to strike again. To strike again soon.

Unless, because of the murder of Denise Stevens, the sniper won't. Unless the sniper now decides to wait, knowing that Denise Stevens's true killer is hoping, betting, that the sniper murders will continue—hoping that Denise Stevens can disappear further into the victims list, instead of standing at the top as the latest and newest.

Unless—knowing Denise Stevens wasn't him, wasn't his—the sniper decides to change his pattern. Change his venue. Leaving the old pattern and the old list, potentially, to the copycat.

A polite conversation, between murderers, thinks Sam.

After you.

No, please, after you.

Who has the greater need? Sam wonders vaguely, theoretically.

The sniper—to keep going with whatever dark bizarre heartless restlessness he began?

Or Sam, with the more mundane and practical need of hiding his own crime behind the bright blinding spectacular facade of a bigger one. Trying to tuck his own murder inside this spree.

When will the sniper strike again?

Will he?

What if he doesn't?

. . .

Sam lies sleepless in the town house's master bedroom—Denise's bedroom, for these last months, now returned to him, reclaimed by him, like a warrior of a conquering army. To the victor go the spoils. Her things are here—empty dishes, ashtrays, dirty underwear, unfolded laundry, fashion magazines, clothing catalogs—spread out across the bedroom over the last few months as if taking full possession of it, shunting his own belongings aside. He has considered not coming in here at all, closing it off, continuing to sleep on the foldout couch downstairs. But in the end, his decision is based on what sends the right signal to Tommy: to create a permanent shrine to tragedy and loss? Or to indicate a new start?

So he has moved back in.

Her scent is here—familiar, pervasive, in the closets, in the sheets, in the bathroom, wafting over everything like a ghost. Her scent is here—present, alive. But she is not. Her un-presence, her evaporation, is still somehow strangest of all.

Sam lies sleepless in their bed, for the moment free, but prisoner to thoughts and moods of dislocating power—startling new swirls of elation, tension, hope, doubt, circling him, lawless and untamed like bandits, looking for a new angle to burrow into, looking for a new piece of his sanity to steal. Thoughts and moods and circumstances that leave him—as they would anyone—restless and tossing and sleepless through the night.

At 2:00 A.M., Sam emerges from the town house's bedroom and pads silently across the living room to the kitchen for a glass of water. The ambient illumination from outside the town house windows—from the street lamps and the moon—is enough to navigate the town house, so he leaves the lights off, to not risk waking Tommy.

He pushes the lever on the refrigerator door down to put some shaved ice in his glass. He presses the button for water.

He turns, tiptoes back through the living room toward his bedroom.

He will, for the rest of his life, feel the gun barrel shoved under his ribs.

"*Ohhhh . . .*" The syllable spills out of him loosely, unformed, like vomit, uncontrollable.

"Quiet. Sit." Clear, flat, accentless, cold, mechanical.

His body assaults him. Heart pounding, head pulsing, thighs and knees shaking and giving way, stomach seizing.

But he is sitting. Sitting on the couch. The figure is seated in the upholstered chair opposite him. In the dark, he can see only the figure's outline, defined by the ambient light of the street and the moon coming through the window behind him. Denise's soft, warm, overly delicate white living room—utterly transformed in the dark.

Now—inexplicably, silently—the gun barrel is moved off Sam. The backlit figure sets the gun in his own lap.

Sam thinks he sees—he can't be sure—the figure's white hand idly stroking the barrel.

Sam wants to leap up off the sofa. Disappear backward into the darkness. But he is paralyzed there. He has no muscles to move with. He can barely focus on what the man is saying.

"Don't you recognize it?

Sam shakes his head blankly.

"It's yours."

"My . . ."

"Found it hidden in your garage. I knew you'd never bring a gun into the house with your son, Tommy, here with you. I know how your type thinks about guns. So where else would you keep it?"

Sam senses from the darkened figure across from him a slight downshifting. A settling in. "And since it's yours, you know it's not loaded. So relax. The shells are wherever you keep them." He pauses. "Those special shells."

Sam catches the implication of that. The implication of intuition, of understanding about the bullets, in that offhand remark.

Sam's own tension and tightness threaten to strangle him, to cut off his own blood supply. He squints to see. He can't see much. The outline of the man's face. The features a mere blue-gray blur in the dark.

Sam glances at the front door, at the kitchen door that leads to the garage.

"You can't keep a professional out of a condominium," the man says, seeing Sam look. Sam is seated facing the night's ambient light, so the visitor can see Sam's face and expressions, Sam realizes. Sam watches the man's dismissive, weary shake of the head. He hears the little snicker. As if the man recognizes the humor in his own choice of words.

Sam is calming down enough to think. He realizes the man may have been sitting here for hours. In the garage first, looking, and then simply sitting here, waiting. Sam realizes now that maybe it was a sound down here that woke him, not bad dreams.

"Who are you?" Sam manages hoarsely.

"Come on now, Sam. You know who I am." The voice as flat as prairie. As flat as humming machinery. Cold with practice and purpose.

Yes. Sam does know. He doesn't know if this is the suspect who was released or if this is someone who the police are as yet unaware of, but regardless, he does know who this is.

He even knows why the man is here: to show Sam he can be. To demonstrate to Sam he can be anywhere he wants, anytime he wants. To let Sam fully feel the invasion, the violation, the fear— in his own living room. He knows the man is sitting here, relaxed, to show that time, that physical space, are fluid, a sieve, that the man moves in and out of them at will. That he operates above and beyond conventional, even physical rules. That he can even see in the dark.

This is a man trained not just in killing, but in terror. In psychology.

Sam knows the man wants Sam to understand that, too.

Sam does understand. He understands it at every level. He understands that he is sitting there because someone who has just killed his wife can have someone suddenly sitting across from him in his own town house in the dark. Because all rules are gone, suspended. Because everything is fundamentally changed.

Sam senses, just now, that whatever happens, he is not about to be killed. Some subtler interaction is taking place, being arranged.

"How'd you know I'd come out here?" Sam asks.

"A man who's just killed his wife doesn't sleep too well for a while."

Sam feels the shiver run down him. It's as if the statement, the man's words, physically shake him.

Sam can see a little more now. This time there is no mistaking. He watches the oddly pale smooth hand run along the gun's butt, lovingly, sexually.

"Tango 51 with a U.S. Optics seventy-millimeter scope. Excellent choice, Sam. Excellent," says the man.

Sam shudders at the strange sense of community the voice is proffering.

"So. A sniper attack. Right down to the details. Even the shell casing matches, doesn't it, guessing by your time spent in Evidence, educating your television audience. Including, as it turns out, me," says the man. Sam can't see, but senses, the tight little smile. "I don't know how I feel about such a close match—if I'm flattered or insulted or a little unnerved or put off by it—but it's impressive attention to detail. You're a good student," the man says. "I know, because I saw the broadcasts. That's the thing about being a reporter, isn't it? We all see the broadcasts."

He pauses. He shifts tone. The irony is gone. The introduction is over. "I can't have them following me for the rest of my life, Sam. And let's face it, it's possible they'll put enough evidence together at some point to come after me. I can't have that either, Sam. You wouldn't want it. No one would." The man pauses. Sam feels the intensity in the dark. "It's like this, Sam: I need you to do it again."

Sam feels the darkness press in on him.

"I need you to do it again. To continue. And as you already realize, I'm sure, Sam, you don't have any choice in this."

Said almost gently. Genial, but beneath it, firm. Like a corporate boss's reluctant assignment to an employee. New project for you. Tough one.

But the gentle presentation doesn't hide the cruel syllogism, the mortal logic, that rolls over Sam like a bulldozer.

"If you continue to kill, Sam, then you continue to live. If you refuse, then you're next. Lucky for you, you won't waste precious time and energy wondering whether I'll actually do it. My record will make your decision easier."

The voice is calm, deliberate, hypnotic.

"You can't go to the police, or I'll let them know exactly how you murdered your wife. I can make it crystal clear that she wasn't mine. I'll give them the details they need to confirm it. By telephone or in person, if it comes to that. And for the police to end up with both of us, well I'm pretty sure that's an outcome you won't accept any more than I will. I think I know that about you. You're into managing outcomes. You've already killed to manage an outcome."

Sam is silent. Aware of nothing but the words emanating from the dark.

"Your only other choice would be to kill me, but we both know how that encounter would come out. It's obvious to you already, isn't it, that I'm a certain kind of professional. What kind isn't clear to you, exactly, but a certain kind, anyway.

"My way, you've got a chance. And you can't say no, you won't say no, because we both know you've got something to live for. You've got the reason you began . . . in there, asleep. . . ."

The anger stabs at Sam, momentarily punctures his fear. The

man's mention of Tommy. The *use* of Tommy. Sam can't stand it. Of course, the man knows that. That's exactly why he does it.

"Choose someone, Sam. Anyone. I won't be picky." The figure gestures to the gun. "I'm not asking the impossible. I'm not asking something you can't do. You've already done it. Here's the weapon you did it with. Here in your living room with us.

"And since you've done it, and you haven't been caught either, that's something we share, isn't it? I don't know if you're ready to admit it aloud or even to yourself yet. The exhilaration . . . the thrill . . . the high . . . But I know you felt it, in there with the sickness, with the self-loathing, with the disgust. It's funny, isn't it, how you're the only one who can know what I mean.

"And it meets your needs, too, Sam. Every new victim makes it look more like a serial sniper and less like a reporter killing his wife. Every new victim makes it look more like a maniac with no motive but terror. No agenda but evil. Can you keep getting away with it? Sure you can. Look at me. I'm living proof you can. It's like anything, Sam. The more you do it, the better you get. The better you get, the less likely to get caught. You get smoother, more practiced, less prone to foolish errors."

The voice has risen from its hypnotic tones into a kind of conventional salesmanship, pseudo-earnest, pseudo-slick, its slickness spoofy, given the context.

"More killings after your wife's—that's good for you. While the police are watching me in my boring apartment—an alibi for me. Good for both of us, you see?"

There is silence. A long silence, an aural blackness, pressing in on Sam.

"Why am I doing this to you, you wonder," the backlit figure says. "Is it only to make you look like the sniper? To transfer, to force all the risk onto you? Or maybe it's for something more sinister. For sport. To make it into a game. To make it less random. Is it that the sick sniper, being successful so far, now feels compelled to up the ante?"

Ray Fine sighs. "Thing is, Sam, it doesn't matter which of those reasons it is, does it? Makes no difference at all. You've still got to do it. You've still got no choice."

"Your deformed bullet helped free me, and I appreciate that, Sam, I do." The western American politeness and charm, dripping, ironic. "But it created an opportunity for me, didn't it, and I'd be crazy"—and here he smiles knowingly, teasingly—"not to grab it."

He pauses, picks up the gun, points it at Sam. Casually. Not casually.

"It's utterly simple, Sam. You have to kill again or I kill you. And you know your chances are a lot better against an unsuspecting random victim than against me."

He lowers the barrel slowly, as if reluctantly.

"And it has to happen fast, Sam. We need to keep them jumping. Don't want them too focused on the murder of Denise Stevens, do we? Don't want them hanging around outside my apartment forever, either. Now, I don't want you torturing yourself, staying up nights, overthinking this, so I think it's best for you and me if I give you a deadline." He lifts the gun again—as if he misses the feel of it in his hands, the feel of it aimed—and seems to run the barrel over Sam's body vaguely, in some private pattern. "You've got thirty-six hours, Sam."

Sam hears the number—its specificity, its tone of finality—but at the moment is unable to fathom any meaning beyond it. It is a kind of wall, unbreachable. *Thirty-six hours.*

"You can do it, Sam, you can do it."

Suddenly there is a pale wedge of light high across the far wall of the living area.

Sam freezes.

"Dad?" The little voice calls out tentatively.

"Why are you up, Tommy?" Sam says sharply—more irritably, accusingly, than he would have liked.

"I thought I heard something," says Tommy defensively.

"I'll be there in a minute," says Sam more soothingly, placatingly, this time. "Give me a minute." He doesn't know if Tommy has heard the other voice or can see the other figure from his angle. Ray Fine remains silent in the shadows, unshifting, unbreathing.

"Okay, Daddy." Tommy closes the hall door. The wedge of light recedes, then disappears.

"Ten years old, right?" says the steady, cold, ironic voice when the wedge of light is gone, and they are in the dark again. "You've got a son. How nice for you, Sam, that you've got a son."

Sam understands the implications immediately.

You have something to lose. And I don't. And that's a big difference, Sam Stevens. A big difference between fellow killers.

"Go reassure your son, Sam. It's late. Your boy misses you. You've been so distracted lately," says the voice matter-of-factly, calmly, its malevolence utterly hidden yet drenching it.

In the dim half light, the rifle is suddenly tossed to him. Sam manages to snap it out of the darkness—a misshapen, smooth-pelted one-eyed beast, hanging in the air. He would fire it. At this moment, he would fire and keep firing and not even consider the consequences. Fire to eliminate not just the figure but the thoughts, the words in the dark. But the shells are in the bedroom. Kept safely separate from the gun. Predictable behavior for someone like Sam with a ten-year-old son—just what the visitor had, in fact, guessed.

"See you soon, Sam."

As Sam feels the weapon in his hands, warm now from the other hands—the first time, he notices, that he has ever felt its stock already warm—the figure rises, moves silently, confidently, out of the living room, through the kitchen, and out into the garage to disappear, Sam knows, skillfully and utterly, into the night.

. . .

A conversation in the close, damp dark. As if to reinforce, to take the full measure and benefit, of the sense of unreality. Its nightmare quality. As if there was not even a figure on the couch, but merely an insistent voice in Sam's head.

He stumbles into the kitchen, sits motionless, silent, at the little kitchen table, trying to absorb it.

Conversation with a Killer.

This killer, loose.

This killer, demanding. Insistent. Cruelly clear.

Conversation with a Killer.

First in a series?

Or last?

Ray Fine makes his way back through the silent, calm suburban darkness, silent, calm himself. Bathed in the rich sense memory of a hundred night operations. Of thick, whispering jungle night. A lifetime of night.

Look what I do for you, Joe.

You behave now, Joe.

The Joe they don't know.

25

Sam Stevens. Hero. Martyr. Locus of sympathy. Of honor. Of tragedy. Of sorrow.

During the workday, covering events as always.

How can he do it? some of the reporters whisper.

Hey, how can he *not* do it? others answer, proud.

He lies there in the dark, intensely reoccupying the moment of her murder. Experiencing it at a new level of memory. A new kind of memory. Experiencing it in all five senses—in every way but literally—again.

It had been brutal—terrifying, retch-inducing. How could it still be so startling, though planned in minute detail? But there was one thing just as startling: It had been simpler than he'd thought. And seeing how insightful, how right, death-row Darryl had been, he knew Darryl was probably right about the corollary:

It gets easier.

. . .

Think the unthinkable. A logical nullity. The empty set. You can't really think the unthinkable.

Unless you are forced to, Sam realizes.

Thinking the unthinkable can also mean, he realizes, simply accepting the inevitable.

It was the best way to demonstrate that a killer was still out there, plying terror, and to make Denise Stevens's murder—amid local catastrophe—seem ever more likely random, ever less like the handiwork of a craven husband trying to hide it.

It was the only way he'd have peace.

The only way he'd have a life with Tommy.

It was the only way Ray Fine would let him live.

Thirty-six hours.

And it wasn't just Ray Fine's deadline that dictated the urgency, after all. Every hour that passed was another hour for Wyatt's department to investigate, to get closer, to inadvertently hear something, to stumble or blunder across a witness. A town house neighbor who heard Sam and Denise fighting. A neighbor near the cabin who heard Sam firing. A drunken patron sitting in the Dominique's parking lot that night. A frightened 2:00 A.M. witness in the park across from the coffee shop finally coming forward. Every hour that passed was another hour for Wyatt to find something unexpected and concrete. The faster there was a fresher trail—the trail of a serial sniper whose rampage continued—the faster a shallow offshoot trail might go cold. If another murder took place—and another?, and another?—the trail might conceivably even lead back to the real killer. The man occupying the living room shadows.

It was the unthinkable. But when he pulled the trigger on Denise, he had entered the sunless land of the unthinkable, and now was occupying it, a full-time resident in its crazy topographies and terrain.

The dark mathematics pressed in on him, theory, action, emotion, woven inextricably: The more he killed, the better his chances, because the more it would look like the sniper—the clever, uncaught sniper—and not him.

The more he killed, the worse his chances, because the risk became greater for making a mistake, the risk of the trail leading in some unpredictable but inexorable way, back to himself.

But the more he killed, the more practiced he'd become, decreasing the chance for a foolish mistake.

And how long would it have to go on? How long until he was free? Freedom had dangled itself tantalizing, pretty, briefly here and there, but clearly it inhabited only mist and dust. Would Sam have to continue indefinitely? A weird, dark, Sisyphean task. The darkest.

Sam had the sense that the silhouette in the shadows knew that Sam would come to this conclusion for himself, that it wasn't just what Ray Fine was demanding; it was Sam's best chance. And that Sam would come to see it that way.

You can do it, Sam, you can do it, the figure had exhorted into the dark. And, of course, Sam had recognized it for the little bit of cheap cheerleading it was.

But the fact is, he can. That's what's weirdest, oddest, darkest of all. Ray Fine knows—and Sam knows—Sam can.

The next existential question, jigging awkwardly at the back of his brain, now moves front and center: Who would it be?

It is one thing to eliminate the person who has ruined your life, who has made your own life and your son's life miserable and threatens to damage permanently the psychological life of your precious child; the person who has summoned a rage in you that has simmered minute by minute, year by year.

It is quite another thing to shoot a stranger—someone who's done nothing, someone who is a mere device toward your freedom.

A random stranger.

Someone whose life has never intersected with yours, except in its final moment.

How would he decide?

Who shall live, who shall die.

Like a god.

Like a devil.

An amoral, bestial, and therefore authentic one.

And in this weird, free-floating contemplation in his own bedroom's dark, he feels it starting to happen: feels walls beginning to crumble; acid seeping under them; borders shifting, threatening to give way. *Inside the Mind of a Serial Killer.* The randomness of the imagined victim is not actually random, he sees, the selection is unconscious maybe, or barely conscious, but it's a selection nonetheless. A child? Someone "before" life? Does that make it better or worse? Someone elderly? Someone who has had their life, someone he can tell himself he is putting out of their painful misery?

Or whoever comes closest to that lamppost? Or to that willow tree? Or whoever appears first in the rifle sight as he raises it on the park?

Or another pretty young mother? Establish a theme?

Or some other ten-year-old boy?

How will he choose? Or better, how will he find a way *not* to choose, so as not to drive himself insane?

The thoughts immured inside him with no outlet. If they drove him crazy, he'd have to go quietly crazy on his own, because there was no sharing this. No sharing it at all.

26

I t is a few minutes before dawn.

Wyatt lies in bed, unable to sleep decently for weeks now, unable to get more than one or two restless hours a night. He expects that now. He doesn't even try to fight the pattern anymore. His wife lies next to him, curled into sleep, unencumbered, unworried, secure in the knowledge that he will do all the worrying for her as he has for the thirty-plus years of their marriage.

He watches the rise and fall of her breathing, hearing in it the unvarying engine of their domestic lives. They've inhabited a marital state of companionship and predictability for so long, it's the only state he can recall between them. His life companion— jaw now slack, face crushed comically yet serenely into her pillow. He, on the other hand, has been thrust into change, onto center stage, into critical self-awareness. The utter predictability has been utterly disrupted. He wonders for how long. He wonders if forever.

He looks down at the lumpen mass of himself with amusement, with wistfulness, with sorrow, with a sense of time's mercilessness.

What he sees bears little resemblance to the hard, taut, coiled, sprung vessel of vitality he can acutely remember. The lean, lithe fastballer with the big, fluid windup who couldn't be touched on a day when he was catching the outside corners of the plate, throwing heat that was regarded as a gift from the baseball gods. College hero. Strikeout record holder. God, he loved how the world looked, how it felt, from the pitcher's mound. Loved every moment of it, no matter what the count on the batter.

It is a sorry shell he sees now. A sorry casing.

But it is breathing, after all. It is functional, alive, nominally agile, providing his worries, his theories, his emotions, and his rudimentary pleasures of warmth, affection, and appreciation of flavors and scents—when he remembers to notice and enjoy them—a host. A home.

A host and home to rudimentary pleasures that nearly a dozen women, men, and children have been unceremoniously evicted from.

His undercovers, Turner and Marcum, have reported to him on Ray Fine. Ray Fine rarely leaves his apartment, they say. Ray Fine sits in front of the television, in front of his computer, orders in pizza and Chinese and even junk food, does a rigorous and unwavering set of exercises. Is highly organized, regimented, if not particularly sanitary.

Phone calls to a sister in New Mexico, to a father in a nursing home. That's all.

Wyatt knows his men are missing something. He knows—just knows—it is a routine laid out by Ray for the benefit of those watching. For the benefit of Wyatt's department. To inspire complacence. Or disinterest. He knows—just knows—something else is going on with Ray Fine, but has no way to know what.

It is a few minutes before dawn.

Sam waits in a small stand of trash-littered woods across from a MiniMart.

His car is fifty yards through the woods at the other side of the stand of woods, parked at the end of a short access road whose opposite end dumps out a half mile away into the soon-to-be-heavy, early-morning commuter traffic of a local highway.

He has left a note for Tommy, mentioning an emergency at work—some breaking news that he has to go in to cover.

There *will* be breaking news.

Something is about to happen.

You're a big boy Tommy. You're making me so proud by becoming so self-reliant, and I know you can get yourself up and get your own breakfast, and by then Patricia the sitter will be there to take you to school.

Sam carefully inspects, one last time, the steel semijacketed hollowpoint bullet.

He presses it into the chamber firmly and clamps the bolt.

He shoulders the rifle, looks through its scope sight, as if into the lens of a television camera, as if preparing for a TV show, as if in the familiarly tense and heightened moments of countdown, before "going live."

Before going dead.

Yes, yes, television . . .

Inside the Mind of a Serial Killer . . .

A woman, bundled against the morning cold in a muffler and red ski hat, gets out of her blue Honda Civic, goes over to the self-serve pump in front of the MiniMart.

Through the rifle sight, he can see her squint to make out the pump's LCD panel.

That bright red hat.

It is a sign.

He needs a sign like that. It is all he can see, all he can recognize at this moment, on this morning. He has, he does, no other thinking. His thinking is otherwise switched off, shut down. He is completely functional in the lower processes—movement, muscle, physical action—but is incapable of any higher ones. It is the only way he can be here: by being absent, by *not* being here.

But that bright red hat.

It pushes through the haze of his shutdown, the mist of his unbeing. Snaps him for a moment into presence.

That bright red hat. It is clearly meant for him.

It explains things to him. It is obviously a target.

Thank you.

He steadies, squints, and squeezes his thank-you.

The crack is crisp in the early morning air. Bracing. Eager. Efficient.

The red hat disappears instantly behind the car.

No clerk emerges from the store this time. Maybe terrified to be a second target. Or else the clerk—beneath his headphones or talking on the phone—might not even know yet.

A bright blue pickup truck pulls in for gas. The burly driver gets out, strides toward the MiniMart, but in a moment stops short, looking over to the pump.

Sam trots in a crouch the fifty yards to his car, stashes the rifle quickly beneath the carpet of his trunk, gets in, turns the key, heads down the empty access road, and pulls out smoothly and unremarkably into the already-gathering morning traffic.

Darryl Jenkins was wrong. Sam is puking and retching and shaking all the way through the woods, all the way to the car. His bowels are loose and threatening, his bladder is pressing, his mind is careening.

Darryl Jenkins is very wrong. The second is far worse.

Get control. Get control.

He shrieks, he cries, he shakes as he drives. He tries to slow down and deepen his shallow, panicked breathing.

Get control. Think of Tommy. Tommy. Tommy.

In a few minutes, he is calmer. He looks at the seat. He hasn't puked in the car. He has contained it.

He turns on the radio to hear the first report from the studio. No one yet on the scene.

His cell phone rings a few minutes later.

"Sam?"

"I heard. I'm already on my way."

"Jesus," says his producer. "You're on the case."

Yes. I'm all over it.

27

Arlene Simmons.
 Forty-eight.
 Single.

Executive secretary.

Getting in early for the boss. Vacation in Europe with a girlfriend the following week.

Never married. Never dated. Alone, but competent, self-sufficient.

Number eleven.

At the MiniMart an hour later, the producer, cameraman, and local crime reporter Sam Stevens are allowed only within several yards of the police tape.

"We'll get as close as we can—we'll frame the MiniMart behind you, Sam. The locals'll know it. It'll scare the bejesus out of them," the producer says gleefully.

Sam sees the blood on the pavement.

"The clerk who found her might still be here," the producer says. "I'm gonna try to get hold of him . . ."

"That's all right," says Sam fragilely, queasily, his confident voice quivering a little. "Let's . . . let's do it without the clerk."

Too late. Too noncommittal. "I see him!" says the producer excitedly, noticing the black head bob in the storeroom doorway. He heads in to persuade the clerk. Such persuasion is his specialty, his skill in life, perfectly deployed in his current calling.

The clerk—a lean Ethiopian immigrant—is still upset, still wiping his forehead, rubbing his hands nervously, unable to shake the memory, unable to reduce it in the least.

"I wait to be sure I'm not killed, then I go out. She is over there. Blood everywhere. You can still see. She is on the ground. Her eyes are rolling. She is alive! But then, the next thing, they are wide, and she is gone."

Reporter Sam Stevens is visibly shaken by the vividness of the telling. He is dizzy from the emotion. He is looking at the spot on the ground in front of the pumps. He can hardly think what to ask.

The young producer is now especially pleased to have wrangled the clerk and secretly elated that the camera is still on Sam, distraught, nonplussed—the reporter who lost his wife, so close to the scene of the next victim. It will make riveting television. "You okay, Sam?" he asks, but only because he should; he doesn't really care, as long as the camera is rolling, and it is.

The lean Ethiopian clerk looks at Sam, narrowing his eyes, and suddenly his eyes go wide. "I know you," he says—staccato, victorious, with a rising excitement.

Sam feels himself pierced, jolted, collapsing under the weight.

"I know you," the clerk says again, with now, absurdly, a hint of joy, the pure joy of recognition.

Sam pictures the streetlighting of two hours ago, just before dawn. The lights bathing his car. Bathing him. He imagines that his sense of darkness was somehow only in his own head.

"You the reporter from television!" exclaims the clerk.

. . .

"Anything?" Billy Wyatt asks glumly, arriving at the MiniMart twenty minutes after the shooting. "Anything at all?"

The first deputy on the scene shakes his head. Then raises an eyebrow and smiles privately, archly.

"What?" asks Wyatt.

"A little fresh vomit halfway into that stand of trees over there. We figure just kids drinking earlier. It's apparently a popular spot for them."

"But you're checking its contents."

"Yes, we are."

"Kids drinking or an attack of conscience," Wyatt mutters.

"What's that, sir?"

Wyatt shakes his head. "Nothing. Alcohol or soda pop, fast food or fresh vegetables, you bring it to me, soon's we know."

"Yes, sir."

28

The reporters had all become amateur Wyatt watchers, and like any reporters captive to a briefing room would, they had turned their observations into sport. There was a betting pool on the progress of the case. Individual reporters would brazenly and good-naturedly predict turns in the narrative, get challenged on their predictions, and either collect a few bucks and the gloating satisfaction of being right, or lose a few bucks and suffer the appropriate ribbing. The dollar amounts were small. The main prize was bragging rights. The main stakes were reputations.

Several of the national reporters had been predicting the timing of when the Feds would take over the case. A rumor had been circulating about Wyatt and inappropriate behavior and mishandling of the suspect while in custody. It was only a matter of time for Wyatt and resolving whether Wyatt's department would continue to handle the investigation at all without him.

Sam, as good a Wyatt watcher as anyone, could read just from Wyatt's downcast expression this morning, by his nervous opening and closing of his palms, by how his huge head hung lower than usual, that this might very well be the morning the Feds stepped up to the lectern beside him. They had had a presence here—advisory only—but Sam sensed that about to change.

He should have bet.

"The latest victim was a woman named Arlene Simmons. She was forty-eight years old, single, resided over in the Crown Apartments . . ." Wyatt begins, and suddenly stops. He hangs his head for a long, silent moment, then raises it and looks around the room.

"I have not been asked off the case," Wyatt says suddenly and firmly. "I have felt increasing pressure, Lord knows, but just for the record, nobody has said anything, and nobody has insisted, and I have wanted to see this through for my department and for my community." He takes a breath. "But folks, people are dying." He looks up, starting around the room to each face individually, cordially, but eyes moist, as he continues. "So I'm taking myself off the case. The Federal Bureau of Investigation will oversee the investigation from here on in. Folks, a big case is different, and this is what they do. They have experience managing the information, the communications, the . . . the political issues"—he narrows his eyes on the last phrase—"that I don't. I and my department will assist in any way asked of us, but it's now theirs to handle and solve, and I know they will."

There is no commotion, no uproar, only silence.

The man in the blue suit, white shirt, and dark tie—impeccable, small, fit, as if in mocking physical contrast to Wyatt—the man who has been sitting in the folding chair patient, mum, for two weeks, now approaches the lectern.

Colorlessly, businesslike, curtly, he addresses them. "I'm Special Agent Brady. This morning's homicide victim expired between oh-four-hundred and oh-six-hundred hours. The victim was named Arlene Simmons. Forty-eight. Single. On her way to work. That's all. I mean it, ladies and gentlemen, that's all. These daily briefings are hereby suspended. Too open, too transparent, considering the intelligence of who we seem to be dealing with. The information and detail emanating from here amounts to a daily briefing for the sniper. I'll update you when there's something to tell you. That's it for now."

He turns and heads for the waiting protective clutch of identically dressed agents. He is, apparently, already on to the more pressing issues of the investigation, already unaware of, unconcerned with, the lazy cynical throng left slack-jawed behind him.

The investigation had entered a new stage.

The game had changed.

Sam would have to change with it.

29

The interview requests start coming to Sam from every major network, and the compensation offers that accompany them take all forms. Cash signing bonuses, fat additions to and outright completions of Tommy's college fund, a generous contribution in his name to exactly the charities where Sam has always given.

The offers, the bonuses, are so similar to one another, auctionlike, it's obvious there are leaks from one network to another.

Publishers and literary agents find ways to reach him—through his producer, through his staff, through his station.

None of them are pushing him to speak now. They pretend to be grieving with him. They say he should take his time, think it over. But all seem confident that he will sit down with them at some point, and each is angling to be the one.

Quietly, on the side, there are informal job discussions, too. Natural, opportunistic. Moving up to bigger markets for bigger money. Hey, researching this story, we've watched your tapes, Sam, we've seen your stuff, and you could jump up in broadcast markets, we could help you.

A reporter whose wife was killed by the sniper. Random? Or a target? What does the reporter think? How does it feel to be on the other side? It is a hard story to resist. Sam understands the frenzy, the competition.

Tommy is going to be provided for. On the amounts being tossed around, Sam will be able to take some time off. If he invests it intelligently, he'll even be able to retire.

He and Tommy can be together forever.

Killing his wife was the smartest career decision of his life.

If he can remain undetected.

If he can keep the trail cold.

The stakes keep going higher.

"Did you hear yet?" his producer asks him two mornings later.

Sam looks puzzled.

"About Scott Bayer?" the producer asks.

Scott Bayer. The rogue cop assigned to Evidence.

Sam frowns in incomprehension, but he is alert.

"Killed himself last night."

Sam knows. He knows instantly, completely, unquestionably. Scott Bayer had discovered the switch.

Maybe the FBI agents were reexamining all the evidence, dismissing local police efforts and starting over, as they liked to do. Or maybe Scott had simply noticed the evidence bag was not sealed as formally or neatly as the others and had looked more closely and had seen the hand-hammered, unfired round and had realized immediately what had happened—how he had been so easily duped, he had been used, how it would eventually be discovered. His incompetence—or even charges of complicity or blame—would tar him again, would propel him into the headlines again, and he couldn't take it again.

A bright cop, sitting there uselessly. He might have seen, slowly or all at once, Sam's plan.

He might even have seen how his own eagerness to assist, to

be useful, to rehabilitate himself, to prove himself, had ultimately helped a serial sniper go free by helping a reporter murder his own wife in the style of the sniper, making it look like the real sniper was still on the loose.

Poor Scott Bayer—a just man in the realm of injustice.

Had Scott discovered it himself, or did anyone else know?

30

The time spent with Tommy grew sweeter, more meaningful, with each moment.

Every second seemed to count.

The park. The ball field.

In sunglasses and baseball caps, they could lose themselves in the anonymity of a baseball-game or football-game crowd.

The neighbors respected their privacy. Even enforced it, Sam learned, by angrily challenging and turning away the curious, by standing down and pushing back the staked-out media. From the outset, he and Denise had always been good neighbors—unfailingly courteous, offering a lift when someone's car wouldn't start, generous with local charity drives and causes that the neighboring moms and kids came by with—and in return they had always made clear how important their privacy was to them. Denise's behavior had become increasingly erratic, of course, but a reservoir of good feeling apparently remained, and now he was reaping the benefits of their original neighborly tactics.

The woman hired to watch Tommy did their grocery shopping for them. He ordered everything else they needed online.

The fragility of the time—the potential shortness of it, the disaster lurking, looming, the knock on the door that could rip him from his son forever—was enough to make every moment special, meaningful, to brighten and deepen it, whether a baseball catch or a bowl of cereal and toast together or a DVD shared in the dark, the two of them sprawled on the carpet in front of it with chips and dip and soft drinks—the guys.

Their secret—to be forever unmentioned, hanging in the air between them, a third presence, familiar as a friend—continued to pull them closer.

And that knock on the door.

Would it be the police?

Or Ray Fine, cloaked in night, sitting in his living room, not bothering to knock at all?

31

Sheriff Big Billy Wyatt is sitting in his office, starting through the stacked backlog of paperwork. Budgets. Allocations. Clearing it up, zeroing it out for the next fool, whoever that will be. He still has all the trappings. He has none of the power.

He is still sheriff, but that seems to be a technicality and formality the bureaucracy will get around to correcting eventually, moving slow as bureaucracies do.

He's like royalty—ceremonial only, and everyone in the station house knows it and recognizes it. They still call him "sheriff," but it's with a smile or a smirk. It's merely a soft honorific now, like "sir," or "Grandpa." Vestigial. A dusty artifact.

He begins sorting through the paperwork, turning his attention to matters that were set aside when the sniper case began, which now he can attend to, because he has been set aside, too. He starts to make his way through all the unreturned phone messages—none of them urgent, several of them apologetic about bothering him at all, with what he's got on his plate. But the plate is now empty. He is getting a sneak preview of the stale, dull, endlessly looping film of retirement.

In the world around him, the manhunt goes on intensely. For Billy Wyatt, the investigation is over.

"Billy? It's Neil Tarsin."

The inordinately painstaking county coroner. Serious, humorless, but diligent, and he and his grisly crew have never been touched by even a whiff of incompetence or the slightest smear of impropriety—although, God knows, whiffs and smears of everything else.

"Hello, Neil."

"Hello, Billy, I'm callin' about the sniper case. . . ." Tarsin says.

"Not on it, Neil. That's FBI now." Wyatt cuts him off curtly.

"I know, Billy. But, well, see . . . it might be the sniper case, or just foolishness on my part, so I'm not comfortable telling anyone but you."

Ah, so if it's just foolish, you bring it to me. Thanks. Nice of you. Billy frowns. "Go ahead."

"Billy, there's somethin' I been thinkin' about on my next-to-last autopsy, that I just can't stop thinkin' about."

Billy Wyatt's chest sinks. His head feels heavy. "Jesus, don't tell me somethin' got screwed up." *Don't tell me something was there that wasn't found before, or something that you thought was there wasn't, or something got mishandled, or mislabeled, or misreported. Don't tell me that after all your competent service to the community, after paying extra care and attention, given the extra scrutiny, this is the case you messed up. The high-profile one. The one that has already haunted and buried me and now will haunt and bury you, too.* Wyatt can see himself taking the blame, even when he's supposed to be out of the line of fire.

"No, no, the autopsy was by the numbers," says Neil, momentarily offended, shocked that Wyatt would even entertain it. "Autopsy was fine."

"Autopsy was fine, but something is bothering you about it," says Wyatt irritably. "That's a puzzle, Neil."

"Well, it was something just before the autopsy started."

"Yeah?"

"When the body was identified. By the husband, I guess he was."

Sam Stevens. Neil Tarsin obviously didn't watch much local television. Figures. "He ID'd the body. Next of kin, per state law. What about it?" Wyatt asks.

"I was watching him, you know, to make sure he didn't faint. I always watch 'em for that. I pulled the sheet off, and he looked at her. Her feet, her legs, her body . . . her face."

"So?"

Neil pauses. "I'm a little more bothered than usual by the whole thing anyway. Guy comin' to identify his wife. Not some lowlife. Workin' guy, like me or you. So I'm lying there awake that night thinkin' about it, and I look over at Estelle sleepin' next to me, imaginin' if it was my wife—"

"Real nice, Neil . . ."

"—and I imagine myself lookin' down at her when some other coroner pulls the sheet off, and Billy, when the sheet comes off and I want to know if it's really my wife lyin' there cold in front of me, I look at her *face* first, not her feet. It's like the guy knew about the shot to the skull. . . ."

Billy Wyatt slumps lower in his office chair with dejection, with dashed expectation. "But he did know, Neil." Jesus, the guy really didn't listen to the news. Wyatt had to hand it to Tarsin— his department, his results, were certainly not influenced by the media. "A shot to the skull is the MO, Neil. It's common knowledge—especially among the reporters."

"But that's not what I'm saying, Billy. See, he was holding his hand out to block seeing the wound . . . I'm not sure he even realized he was doing it . . . and Billy, the thing is, he knew ex- actly *where* to hold his hand, knew which *side* of the skull took the shot . . . it's like he knew exactly *where* the wound to the skull would be."

Wyatt's eyes widen as if to accomodate the light.

"I've been doin' this a long time, Billy. I've seen a lot of people identify their loved ones, trust me. . . ."

Wyatt is no longer listening. He is churning. He is seething. He is awake. He is back.

32

Nothing yet.

No dark, whispering visit. No further contact. No terrifying note or piece of mail. No 2:00 A.M. call. Sam has expected it at every moment. He doesn't know whether to try to bolt the town house doors, arm them with alarms, hire a guard, or whether to throw them open wide, aware that the other measures are undoubtedly useless. Sam doesn't know whether his visitor will appear in the next moment—or never.

The logic is now a harsh geometry in his mind. A geometry so crude, so spartan and reductive, a geometry of such severe, unbreachable angles, it blocks out everything else.

If I kill, I live.

If I refuse, I die.

And with it, all the corollaries . . . tumbling at him, forcing themselves on him like streetwalkers against the car windows.

We are both vulnerable—a stumbled-on clue could lead as easily to either one of us, you or me.

Your total is greater, but mine is fresher. Does it leave the odds even? Or one of us with better chances and one with worse?

If I wait, will you kill again out of whatever compulsion drove you in the first place?

Unless my being in the equation has fundamentally changed it for you.

The thoughts flow at him strangely, unmodulated. They burrow into him as facts—as fate—with more power and insistence than any of his thinking before.

Who's going to kill again—me, to make it look more and more like you?

Or you, because you can't help yourself?

You, in further celebration of the prospect of getting away with it?

He feels his own humanness shutting down, surely, uncontrollably, maybe protectively. He recognizes from his news investigations, from his featherweight pop study of it, that he is taking on the thoughts, the personality, the patterns of a killer, but although he can see that, he is not free to change, to pull away. He has entered a strangely lit, vibrant, shimmering half world—or maybe more accurately, a world and a half. A private world of his own devising. A private universe in which he and Ray Fine are the sole inhabitants. He and Ray. A universe of only two. A language of only two. A history of only two. A set of rules for only two. The rest of existence begins to recede. His own voice and Ray's voice become the only ones he hears. Melding. Merging. Insistent. Powerful and reverberative and knowing and glorious. The adrenaline fires through him constantly, plentifully, a drug through a drip.

If I kill, I live.

If I refuse, I die.

"Roll it again," says Wyatt.

He is watching Sam Stevens's interview with Scott Bayer in Evidence.

Scott Bayer, who just killed himself, apropos of nothing, according to his weeping widow.

No reason. No change at work or at home. Everything status quo.

Wyatt knew Scott Bayer. He knew how the system had railroaded him. He knew that Scott Bayer's heart was always in the right place, so Wyatt had engineered the Evidence job. Now he felt awful. Somehow complicit. Somehow guilty, though he couldn't say how.

Scott Bayer. Who killed himself.

Sam Stevens. Who interviewed Scott Bayer, asking about serial murder evidence.

Sam Stevens. Who, according to the coroner, seemed to know just where not to look.

It could just be fear on Stevens's part, of course, there in the police morgue, the subterranean human chop shop. Natural paroxysms of dread and longing. Fear of looking in her eyes once more. Fear of seeing her beauty once more—ruined, tortured.

But it might be Sam Stevens knowing what he'd see, and not wanting to see it. Neil Tarsin's stock in trade was acute observation; he was a man who thrived on accuracy.

Wyatt watches the Scott Bayer interview over and over.

". . . Meet Officer Scott Bayer." The camera swinging onto him, a deer in the broadcast headlights, struggling to recover his composure, to be the expert that the off-camera reporter is promising.

The interview shows Wyatt nothing.

"Get me the rest of Sam Stevens's broadcasts," Wyatt calls out to Jimmy, one of the deputies outside, saying it with an authority he no longer has, but in the moment still assumes and commands.

33

Agent Brady senses already that to capture the sniper, he may ultimately need another killing beyond Arlene Simmons—maybe even another two or three—but he would never say that aloud, of course.

Brady sees the murder of Arlene Simmons as the first murder of his investigation. A place for his own people to start fresh. Untainted. To do it right. Of course, he would never say that aloud, either.

His field agents are redoing all the interviews, going over almost everything, as if the local police had never been there.

All they seem to have collected additionally so far, though, is a generalized grousing from Wyatt's police department and the irritation of witnesses interviewed twice.

Ray Fine is still being watched—now by Brady's agents—but he still never leaves his house, it seems. Once in a while, he goes to the supermarket, but otherwise, he seems to run his computer-consulting business from his den. He goes to sleep early, his TV turning off first after some dumb game or reality show, then the kitchen lights after a late snack, then the bathroom lights, after brushing his teeth and using the toilet, and then, after reading a computer parts catalog or a brochure, his bedroom light. They can see it all, observing him with a high-powered scope from an apartment across the street. Man, does he sleep. Guy gets twelve, fourteen hours. What an existence. Guy may not be a killer, Agent Brady, sir, but boy, he's weird enough to be.

Agent Brady reads and hears the reports. He's got the logs from Wyatt's guys—Turner and Marcum—and the updates from his own agents, and there's no difference between them at all. Ray Fine's existence is bizarrely regimented and rigid and unvarying.

Of course, maybe Ray wasn't really alone in there at all. Maybe the conversation was wildly animated, wildly spirited, inside Ray Fine's head. Within a day of Brady's taking over, a psychiatrist—an oddly dressed character in ratty white blazer and unpressed Hawaiian shirt—had muscled his way onto Brady's schedule. Brady had given him just ten minutes, in which the guy had been passionate, nearly frantic, proposing that Ray Fine was suffering from a psychotic break—brought on by his background and history as a military operative—a version of multiple-personality disorder, which allowed him to hide his actions, even from himself. Brady had sensed immediately that the shrink and his theory had gotten nowhere with Wyatt, and he was using the change of command to try again. But from what Brady could see, it was the shrink who was unbalanced. Crazy-eyed. Dogmatic. An opportunist, Brady sensed, looking to advance his own career in psychiatric forensics in one dramatic giant leap. Brady recognized opportunists, cheerfully admitting to being one himself. Wyatt obviously hadn't bought the shrink's argument. Brady didn't, either.

But Wyatt had clearly been convinced there was something there with Ray Fine. And Brady—self-acknowledged opportunist—is perfectly happy to capitalize on the excellent instincts of a career cop who was discredited when he had actually been very close. Brady has done it before. He'll gladly do it again.

It is also possible that Ray Fine *is* bizarrely regimented, bizarrely rigid. Or else is simply toying with them, knowing that they are watching, is amusing himself with his own overanalyzed behavior. Testing himself, and testing them. Operatives like Ray Fine, with his kind of military background—untraceable records, ultra-rightist connections—were off-the-grid characters to begin with, and reveled in that identity for ego, for pride, for fun. Just the kind of adversary Wyatt might build up in his own imagination, Brady figured, for no reason beyond the mystery Ray Fine himself cultivated, no reason beyond his own otherness.

In which case, Brady would follow his own instincts.

Which were that Wyatt didn't have any.

Billy Wyatt shifts around in his chair irritably as he watches another taped interview.

Inside the Mind of A Serial Killer.

Darryl Jenkins, Philosopher Lowlife.

Jesus Christ.

He had put Darryl away. It had been on his watch. A classic thrill-killer, their own homegrown Manson, careless, wild, an animal, easy to find, clues as bright as sunshine, just had to ease him back into his cage before he got his big gorilla hands and arms on anyone else.

And here was Sam Stevens, turning him into a celebrity.

Sam Stevens, listening fascinated.

Only pretending to be fascinated, TV style?

Or truly as fascinated as he appeared to be?

". . . The first one is the hardest, of course . . . After that, it gets easier . . . You start payin' attention . . . You start to get good . . ."

Did Sam Stevens get too close? Close enough to get singed?

Wyatt had never seen any of these interviews. He and his deputies had been with the investigation and with the media all day. He had been exhausted. He had only wanted to go home and crawl into bed. He never turned on the television. If he had, he wouldn't have missed all this.

"Stop," he says to Jimmy, who is scanning the tapes for him.

The deputy releases the fast-forward button, looks up at Billy.

There on the screen, Billy sees, Sam Stevens is giving a talk on sniper weapons.

He's holding a Tango 51.

Borrowed or outright purchased from some gun shop by some eager assistant, Billy figures.

Billy Wyatt will lay even money the rifle was never returned.

His big heart stutters in his chest.

Jesus. Is it possible? Good Christ almighty.

34

Agent Brady.

Regime change.

The briefing room is empty. The beige tile floor is visible again. The snakes of wire have largely withdrawn to the eternal shade of countless motel rooms.

The contrast feels like a news blackout, a silence.

While the sniper story goes quiet for a day—eerily, tensely quiet—WWBS station management is not, for the moment, requiring Sam to do anything more. They recognize that his being on the sniper story is somehow necessary for him, part of the healing for him, and the fascination of his covering it means a serendipity of viewers tuning in for this perverse twist on it, for the talk value of his even being there at all, doing his reports. Management doesn't want to tamper with the golden goose, and they recognize the temptations that may come from his interviews with the national press, and they want him to stay, so they let him be home with his son, come and go as he wishes. They want to look good to him. They want to *be* good to him. He is both the reporter and the story, and they recognize that better than anyone else. They know Sam Stevens has news value.

. . .

He lies there at night, sleepless, shifting, staring up, unable to dismiss or blunt the realization: Something in him is fundamentally different.

He is trying not to be. He is trying to fit back into his old understandings, his old perceptions. To any degree possible, his old life. He has done a yeoman's job of it so far, but it's not going to stick. It's not going to take. It's falling away.

He doesn't know if it was killing Denise.

Or the red-hatted stranger.

He hates the police for the threat hanging over him.

He hates the police for not finding him.

He recognizes this is the same stuff you hear from all these guys. From all the Darryls of the world.

The addictiveness, the power, the god complex.

But the recognition doesn't release him from the sensations.

Something beyond the events themselves has happened to him. Something fundamental and irreversible and so powerful he feels it physically; he is constantly aware of it.

He has become too diligent a crime reporter. Too close to, too connected to events. Like a narc who becomes a coke addict. Like a vice cop who starts to pimp.

It isn't just that he has killed. Soldiers kill. Defenders of homes and ideals kill.

It isn't just that he has killed. It's that he's *become* a killer.

Constitutionally. It's some inchoate uncoupling from civilization. A disconnection from the physical world. He is entering— has entered—another place, and while he is maintaining the appearance of his connection to this one—maintaining it for his own sanity and well-being as well as broader appearance—he feels himself slipping—no, slipped—into this other one.

He feels it, he knows it: He could do it again.

He wants it to be stopped somehow.

He wants it to go on.

He has become the story.

The knock comes at dinnertime.

A knock he has expected, but is not ready for.

His heart is palpitating before he even turns toward the door.

He knows now to expect the unexpected. A polite knock where he has always figured on another sudden appearance in the living room. Daylight where he has always pictured night.

But this, it turns out, is more unexpected than that.

The two uniformed officers regard him expressionlessly—purposely guarded, it seems to Sam, slightly edgy. "We've got a search warrant," says one of them, holding it out—a door-to-door salesman with an offer.

Sam looks at the document. He knows what they look like. He's seen them before, held several up before the camera, taken his viewers through their legal points.

The other cop's hand clasps Sam's bicep, and familiarly—almost friendly—but firmly, too, he is directed to the easy chair in his living room and directed to stay there. There is the implication that the cops want silence, and Sam senses and obeys it.

Luckily Tommy is still at basketball practice. He doesn't have to see this. He doesn't have to feel this. Sam stays silent.

It is not Ray. But then again, it is not the cherry phalanx he had always seen in the back of his mind. Washing the town house exterior in red light. It's just two police cruisers. No lights. And four cops. Sober and reasonable and appropriate—not what he has expected of the frantic, edgy Webster police department.

Something is going on here. Something unconventional. Something furtive and halfway.

Two of the cops begin to search the upstairs of the town house. The other two search the kitchen and basement.

They pass intermittently, wordlessly, through the living room, where he remains obediently seated.

Two of them then head into the garage. They leave the door from the kitchen to the garage open to stay in touch with the officers still searching inside.

He can hear them opening the Corolla's doors.

He can hear them opening the Corolla's trunk.

He is preparing what he will say to Tommy. The good-bye, brief and heartfelt. He is practicing saying it in his head in order not to throw up, not to break down, not to collapse, unbreathing.

He knows. He has seen how methodically cops search. He has seen how they're trained to search, has done a report on their search techniques. He knows that one of the cops is going through the trunk, checking the fit and flush of the interior panels to see if they've been shifted or opened, feeling professionally around the interior wheel wells, lifting the trunk's carpeting, checking thoroughly down to the car's underbody. Sam closes his eyes. He breathes. He prepares himself.

The two cops reenter the house. "Nothing," they report to the other two. "Nothing at all."

Ray Fine has saved him. Taken the gun out of the trunk, where he knew Sam probably still had it, after the red-hatted woman.

Taken the gun where?

Saved him for what?

Only to do it again, thinks Sam—dazed, blank, barely sentient.

Sam looks up, and there is Billy Wyatt—immense, blank-eyed, standing over him in his living room, looking down at him, studying him, wordless.

Wyatt says nothing.

Simply turns and goes.

35

ay Fine has saved him. He's taken the gun and hidden it, perhaps as safely, as shrewdly, as thoroughly, as he has hidden his
own weapons.

Ray Fine has saved him. As surely as the murder of Denise
Stevens may have saved Ray Fine.

Is Ray Fine returning the favor?

Proposing some dark, unspoken kind of community? *I'll do for
you, while you do for me?*

Or is he doing this as a warning? As a proof. A proof of his
powers of anticipation, of his stunning intuition, of his mastery
of the black arts. A proof that Ray has more control over Sam's
life than Sam might think. Ray giveth, and Ray can taketh away.
Ray hath taken away to save you, but Ray can giveth to finish
you.

Or is he doing this (a glancing, final thought) so that Sam is
unarmed.

Because he's figured out how Sam got the rifle. And knows
that Sam—obviously watched, observed now—won't be able to
get another one.

What's going on here?

Maybe that's part of the point, too: simply to keep Sam off balance. Maybe that's even the main point.

To show Sam how naked Sam feels now without the gun. To show him how much he has changed already. An initiation prank, welcoming him to the club.

Or maybe to taunt him with the possibility that the gun, covered with Sam's fingerprints, could be delivered anonymously to the Webster County police. An anonymous gift. (His prints not yet on file, but readily matched by an eager sheriff to a hundred surfaces in the town house.)

Somewhere in him, Sam knows that another meeting with Ray is coming, a meeting he knows will provide no answers to any of these questions. Only more questions. Only more insane demands. Or maybe some final outcome that he has not yet seen or predicted. That he won't see coming until it is too late. A death in life, or death itself. That is the realm Ray plays in, after all.

All Sam can do is wait. Wait for Ray. Wait for Ray to come calling.

He feels disaster drifting toward him. Ray rigging the game. Ray proposing some crazy camaraderie—but not crazy at all.

Sam feels acutely powerless. Feels the steady diminution of his options. His choices are narrowing, closing in. He feels the constriction of options literally—in his chest, in his throat. He feels the crisis creeping toward him, relentless, inevitable.

If only *he* could exercise the control. Shift the balance of power. Call the meeting.

And then he has an idea. An insane, brilliant idea.

Maybe the kind of idea that can only occur to someone who has begun to function outside society. Who has tasted the strange fruit. Who has gone lawless.

36

"Sir, you better sit down for this," Brady is told by one of his field agents.

Brady sits, looks up expectantly, a dog waiting for a juicy bone, or a kick in the flank.

"Billy Wyatt just exercised a search warrant on reporter Sam Stevens."

"What?" Brady is on his feet, his jaw is shaking.

"He got some judge friend of his to sign it, and he went in with some of his officers."

The anger rises red, thoroughly flushing Brady's normally pale, placid complexion.

"They didn't find anything, did they?" declares Brady.

"No, sir."

"Local thug cop pushed aside, in over his head, trying any damn thing," says Brady.

"Yes, sir."

"It was obvious we were dealing with a rogue cop the minute he jumped on Ray Fine," Brady says. "Well, now that he's blundered again like that, it'll get a lot easier. What a hothead, incompetent jerk! I can't have him in the way anymore. He still wants to be a hero? Let's see if he feels like a hero after I'm done with him."

"Yes, sir."

"What judge was that? Let's set up a little chat with said judge. Let's ground the cops who went with him. That'll help remind them and him and everyone else who is in charge of this investigation. I want to see that warrant."

Brady has been eager for an arrest in the case, and now, he thinks with satisfaction beneath his rage, there will be one.

37

ocal reporter Sam Stevens sits at a conference table in the FBI's temporary command center, surrounded by several agents, awaiting the arrival of Carl Brady.

He feels the beige institutional walls around him breathing. He feels their pulse.

He is deep, deep in the belly of the beast.

As Sam expected, the FBI has taken over a corner of the third floor of the police building, and it has all the indications of its hasty assembly, its makeshift nature—file cabinets set haphazardly in the halls, open cartons of documents lining the corridors, banks of phones and cords on old school desks and card tables in small cubicles along the far side, and piles of shiny aluminum carrying cases that, Sam knows, variously contain crime-scene forensics kits, GPS and surveillance equipment, and disassembled high-powered weapons. Despite its makeshift nature, he experiences it as a tight little corner of ultra-efficiency, tucked into the ancient, scraped, and scarred municipal police headquarters.

Several of the agents have expressed their sympathies, not mumbling them uncomfortably, but forthrightly, matter-of-factly, as if either accustomed to dealing with the collateral damage in this kind of war, or else formally trained in condolences. He feels, too, some of the agents admiring him, identifying with him—as if they expect that they, too—if it meant finding the bastard, finishing the job—would be undeterred by the death of a spouse.

When Sam mentioned the matter to the agent answering the phone—mentioned that Ray Fine, the previously released suspect, had contacted him and requested an interview in private—he was put on hold for less than a minute before a different agent came back on—in fact, joined the first agent on a speakerphone—and asked Sam to come in. They told him that, as he might have guessed, they were keeping an eye on Ray Fine, so Ray Fine would have no idea Sam was here, they assured him. Though Sam knew there could easily be another reason, of course, an equal or maybe greater reason, why they wanted him to come in, why they welcomed this opportunity. Wyatt had just searched his town house. He couldn't actually be sure the FBI knew that—the process had seemed so abrupt, so oddly furtive and quiet, but if the search was indeed an unsanctioned, rogue event, as Sam suspected, Sam assumed that word of it would have gotten to Brady, and Brady would know that Wyatt had found nothing. Sam's coming in, Sam knew, provided a chance for Brady to measure Sam for himself, taking advantage of Sam's show of good faith in reporting the pending interview to them. It was a chance for Brady to bring Sam into a hostile environment. Sam had expected that. Sam was ready for that.

Sam had been instructed not to discuss it further with anyone and to get over to the command center right away.

Going to the police after Arlene Simmons has been killed.

It is, Sam hopes, the most unpredictable move on his part, one he hopes even Ray Fine will not foresee. One that even the in-

PARTING SHOT · 163

genious Ray Fine would not imagine or predict. Because he needs footing, he needs his own ballast, in this dark, terrifying, unprecedented game.

If you kill, you live.
If you refuse, you die.
But two can play, Ray. Two can play.

Brady finally sweeps in, brisk, focused, an epicenter, a locus, of investigative intensity as well as bureaucratic polish.

He takes the chair that is waiting for him, his voice familiarly confident and brusque and efficient. "Sam Stevens? Carl Brady. These are agents Munson, Havemeyer, and Cruz. First of all, my condolences. I am truly sorry about your loss."

"Thank you."

"So what's this about, Sam?" Not missing a beat. Not wasting a moment. "And what I mean by that is, what do you think it's *really* about?"

"He contacted me. Said he wanted to discuss something in private with me. Wanted a private conversation. Gave me no details as to subject."

"He contacted you? We've tapped his phone. I'd be told if there was a call to you." Brady examines Sam for a moment. "I'll assume it was over his cell. What do you think he wants to talk about?" says Brady.

"Honestly? I think he's going to lay out his lawsuit against Webster County. List his grievances and hope they make their way into a broadcast. I think he's just angling for a payday."

"And why are you telling me this?" says Brady brusquely. He's suspicious, faintly accusatory. Squinting his face in exaggerated annoyance. "You're here, what, out of the goodness of your heart? 'Cause you've got an exclusive, and you want to share it with the FBI?"

There is a beat of silence, of tension.

Carl Brady looks at Sam—bores in—and answers utterly accurately, utterly correctly.

"You're here because Ray Fine is terrifying. Special Forces. Weapons specialist. Off-the-grid character. You want us there. You want us watching."

"Well, but see, I *don't* want you watching. . . ."

"Oh, so you want your agents, you want your little army, but you don't," says Brady mockingly. "You know we'll be watching, even if you ask us not to," says Brady. "You knew that when you picked up the phone to call us."

Brady was smart and quick and poison-tipped. *Ray Fine is terrifying.* That, of course, is exactly why Sam is here. Seeing Brady like this, up close, in action—incisive, accurate, commanding—has Sam made a terrible tactical error coming here? Has he perfectly executed this new kind of crime, come so close to pulling it off, yet out of the hubris and omnipotent sensations of his success—and out of his increasingly functional insanity—has he finally made his fatal error? Because in this new kind of crime—of high-powered scopes, of distance, of silence, of a mere vision through a lens—perhaps the only way that someone can be caught is to catch himself. To say something human. To reveal something human. Perhaps this new kind of crime comes full circle, circumventing the advanced technology of cutting-edge forensics to reckon—like ten thousand years ago—with only human guilt and frailty and fallibility to ultimately be detected. Had he come so close only to screw it up now, in the simplest, dumbest, most human miscalculation? But he has no other choices. He can't go on killing people.

"It can't surprise you to know that Ray Fine remains a person of interest, Sam. Wyatt was still watching him, as you might guess. Although frankly, I don't think Wyatt and his crew had any idea what they were doing." A brazen statement to make to a local reporter—and Brady clearly knows it is. It is as if it is code—

clever code, in its implication, *we are off the record: I can say any-thing, you can say anything.*

Sam would have to agree with Brady's assessment. If Wyatt was having Ray watched, what was Ray Fine doing in Sam's living room at two in the morning? He had obviously been able to slip Wyatt's surveillance. A fresh little frisson of fear ran jangling down Sam's vertebrae. Ray Fine was obviously ingenious, supe-rior so far to all this state and federal clumsiness. Did it do any good to be here with Brady at all? Or would it ultimately do Sam only harm?

"Should he wear a wire?" one of the agents asks Brady.

"No wires," Sam says forcefully, almost panicky. "No pres-ence. If he sees or senses you guys, he'll obviously feel at risk, and he may not say what he has to say. If he sees you, I think *I'll* be at more risk, and I don't want that risk."

Brady leans back, smiles. "Pretty creepy, isn't he?" Brady says. "I've seen your pieces, Sam Stevens. I don't know if anyone else notices, because they're about events unfolding in the here and now, so they have drama and tension and excitement, but they're all setups, aren't they? All planned. Controlled. So you're always in charge. So nothing will go wrong. An order to the questions. Talking to a killer who's safely behind bars. Ambushing a cop who's afraid to say no to you. But here's something real, Sam. Here's something that has the possibility of violence, of action, of anything happening. And you're afraid of what this guy—what this off-the-grid weapons specialist sitting across from you—is going to say or do."

Brady leans back farther, clasps his hands behind his neck. "Let me tell you what a guy like Ray Fine is about, Sam." And Brady starts to pontificate. To impress his agents? To impress himself? To prepare Sam for his coming "interview"? Sam isn't sure. "Ray Fine is about threat, Sam. Ray Fine is about power. If it's not a lawsuit or complaint, then it's going to be some message he wants to convey through you. He knows you're the mouthpiece, the conduit, to the local populace. That's his leverage, that's who he knows he'll be speaking to at the same time he's speaking to the authorities," Brady says.

It's a little grandiose, a little paranoid, thinks Sam. Brady is saying, after all, *Ray Fine is really speaking to me.*

"You're at risk, Sam. But not as much as you think." Brady pauses. "If we're there at all, he won't be aware of it and neither will you. It's only for your personal safety."

Yeah, sure. "Of course. Thank you."

And then Brady turns to Havemeyer, Munson, and Cruz, and says, "Gentlemen, give me a minute alone with Mr. Stevens here."

Sam feels it coming as clearly as if it were stated: *I'm doing something for you, now you do something for me.*

In a moment, the conference room is empty, and it is just Brady and Sam.

Brady is suddenly intimate, suddenly personal. His hard features soften, go slack, like a glimpse of his face ten years from now. "I know why you're here, Sam," Brady says. "It's not every reporter who has a stake. Who's no longer just an observer. Who wants this thing solved as much as I do."

But Sam hears it differently—and more clearly, he is sure. *It's not every reporter who's as hungry for glory as you are. So I'll give you the private moment of authentic concern, Sam, the sympatico moment, to keep you on my side, to keep us aligned.* That is what Sam hears and understands. If Ray Fine *is* about threat, as Brady says, then Carl Brady is about appearances. To his staff. To his superiors. To the world.

"Wyatt thinks you killed your wife," says Brady suddenly, sharply, staring at him.

Sam can only shake his head—disbelief, resignation, the burden of the world upon him.

"Did you, Sam?"

Sam stares.

"All the planning. All the control. Denise Stevens's murder, if it is a copycat, was highly arranged. Planned by someone who couldn't handle her diversions, Sam? Marital conflict? Someone who needed control? All the control of a Sam Stevens broadcast? Eliminate the messy reality?"

Sam stares balefully, with silent fury, at Brady. With all the fury he felt toward Denise, resummoned, reignited by the moment. His response is barely audible, just above a whisper. "How dare you."

Brady studies him for a moment, then sits back as if—even with all his experience and command—recoiling from the hostility he just witnessed.

"It's your fears intersecting with your dreams, isn't it? You want to do the interview, but you don't know anything about this Ray Fine, after all. You figure the Webster police don't know what they're doing. You wonder who this guy really is that the police grabbed him and then let him go."

Sam looks at Brady.

"Or else your coming here is the ballsiest move a killer has ever made—and I've seen some pretty ballsy ones." Brady cocks his head at Sam. "We'll be watching, Sam, as I'm sure you knew. We'll be watching."

Sam nods. "Thank you."

He gets up to go.

It has been an enlightening conversation, if not an altogether reassuring one.

Sam Stevens exits, and, sitting alone for a moment, Brady smiles.

He had suspected it, but he is sure of it now.

He is pleased—elated, in fact—that he has had this chance to look directly at Sam Stevens. To have him alone. To ask a few questions. To posture as a bully. To surprise him. To see him react.

Brady watched a few of the stand-up pieces before Stevens

came in. Watching a few of them like that, he noticed how staged it all was—how planned, how controlled. He didn't have to see many of them to at least see that. He knew that's what he'd find in all of them.

That kind of planning, that need for control—it was the fear of confronting anything real. The terror of the here and now. A terror of conflict. He had seen it in plenty of reporters before. It was hardly unique. Might even be generational, a trait in reporters of the TV generation more comfortable with the filter of screens and video and images than the sloppiness of real life. They would construct the story, because they were afraid of the real story.

Sam Stevens was a planner. Sam Stevens needed control.

The murderer was a planner. The murderer was someone who needed—thrived on—control.

If only his work was that simple, thought Brady. Sometimes it was, but mostly it wasn't. Because that was the part he knew before Sam came in here. Before he sat across from Sam and looked in his eyes. Before he pushed Sam and saw him get angry and lash back.

The fact is, someone coming in only to pretend cooperation and teamwork, someone as planned and rehearsed as that, would not likely have revealed such sudden fury at Brady's accusation. Brady's tactical glibness had gone too far, but going too far was how you got what you couldn't get otherwise.

The little glimmer of the truth.

Brady has been doing this a long time. Maybe too long, he sometimes thinks. But the longer you do it, the better you get at it.

He doesn't know much—nobody does—but he's pretty sure of one thing.

Someone afraid to do a real interview is someone afraid to do a real killing.

Sam Stevens didn't murder his wife.

38

"hy shouldn't I throw your fat ass in jail?" Agent Brady roars at Wyatt, poking a finger angrily and repeatedly and for maximum annoyance into Billy Wyatt's beefy chest. "Why shouldn't I throw your fat ass in jail right now for derailing this investigation?"

Wyatt is silent. Chastened. Facing the music.

Wyatt notices, however, that Brady never asks why he did it, what he discovered at Sam Stevens's town house, what he knows. Brady seems to think it was only about embarrassing Brady, showing Brady up. Brady seems to make the implicit assumption that Wyatt has no information. Is incapable of uncovering anything useful.

Wyatt had been patient, inclusive, with Brady; he put him at the lectern alongside him. And now this.

It is suddenly clear to Wyatt: Brady thinks he is nothing but a buffoon.

Worse, for Brady—a spotlight-stealing buffoon.

Wyatt could tell him what he knew, what the coroner had said, what the taped segments indicated. But none of it was hard evidence, after all. His bid for hard evidence had derailed. Hell. Maybe he *is* a buffoon.

So Billy Wyatt is not going to say anything. He is going to keep this for himself. He is going to solve it. He is going to make sure there is justice. He doesn't entirely trust the system any more, starting to see it, to experience it, from the other side.

"You're looking at an obstruction of justice charge here," says Brady.

"So toss me in jail," Wyatt challenges.

"I'm thinkin' about it," says Brady. He looks at Wyatt, shakes his head.

Your suspect, Sam Stevens, just volunteered that Ray Fine has contacted him and wants to speak to him. Your suspect was just giving us a heads-up. Letting us be there, if we want to. Does that sound like someone with something to hide, Billy?

"Sorkin, Ryan," Brady barks into the desktop intercom and looks back at his paperwork, ignoring Wyatt, still standing there for the moment, till the two agents appear.

"Escort Mr. Wyatt here out of the building and out of my sight while I decide just what to do with him."

A loose cannon. Conducting a separate operation under my nose. You are messing with the wrong Fed, thinks Carl Brady.

39

I t is a bench at the edge of the park's lawn. Full views all the way around it.

Two federal agents are watching from several hundred yards away.

Ray picks them out immediately.

"Clever of you, Sam Stevens," says Ray. "Trying to take control of your own destiny. Choosing the time and place. Daylight. High visibility. Making sure you survive the conversation."

"They'll never know anything we say here," says Sam.

"Oh, but I don't know that—I don't know what you'll say to them."

"And *I* don't know what you'll say to them," counters Sam.

"That's why we can both be here, isn't it?" smiles Ray.

"You agreed to this get-together. Ultimately, it was your choice," says Sam.

"Oh, you knew we'd get together again, Sam. I was just waiting for the right time. My movement is a little . . . constricted. But you couldn't be patient."

"It was my turn to arrange the meeting," says Sam, "and I didn't want to be ambushed or surprised."

"Ah, so you're trying to even things out somehow, Sam—is that it? Or are you thinking that you've fulfilled your obligation and you want me to let you off the hook, hoping that seeing your goons over there will help sway me."

"I didn't know they'd be so obvious," Sam says archly—and frankly.

"Or is it that you want to prove your control of the situation, that you want me to see that you have more power than I think, more resources, more cleverness. If your motivation is some combination of those—and clearly it is—then you're making a big mistake, Sam. If that's how you're playing it," says Ray Fine, sinuously, coolly. "You don't have the power here. You can't even things out."

Sam is silent.

"I think it's more psychological than practical, this meeting for you, Sam. I think it's more a meeting with *you* than with me. To show yourself you have control."

Ray is utterly calm. He knows he is being watched, yet his manner is as casual as if this were truly just a morning of two friends in the park.

"You're not saying it—maybe you don't even realize it—but you want your gun back, don't you?" says Ray. "And you want to thank me for saving you. Saving you to continue," says Ray.

"I saved you, too," Sam says.

"You helped put me back out on the street. I wouldn't call that saving me," says Ray Fine darkly, grimly. "It's certainly not saving anyone else, is it?" Ray smiles thinly, looks vaguely out at the greenery. "It's an odd little club we make, isn't it? Very exclusive. A secret society. The Assassins Club. We need some obscure Latin name, don't we? *Mortis Congressus*. Together, we're a terror, aren't we, Sam?"

Sam is silent.

He was amazed, when he called to propose the meeting, that Ray so readily agreed. He had thought the call alone might rattle

Ray, coming on a line that Ray must know was bugged. "Okay, Ray, I will give you that interview . . ." But Ray had played along, not missing a beat. He could have said no to the meeting, of course. Said over the bugged phone that he'd changed his mind, but he agreed. It was Ray showing he was unshaken, unfazed, up to anything Sam could concoct, showing his own deft fearlessness. A shudder had gone through Sam.

"Of course, there are different levels of membership, aren't there, Sam? You're a new member. A pledge. You still have one foot in civil society, but you're gaining fast. I know it. I feel it. Let's be honest, Sam. You got me here mainly to say you can't do it. You can't do it again. And to show me, with your half-hidden clumsy little entourage, that, by God, you *won't* do it again. But the problem is, Sam, you've proved to me that you *can* do it. Don't you see? You've proved you *can*. And as soon as I can get your weapon back to you, you can get back at it again."

Ray Fine looks out, expressionless, begins to wrap it up, controlling it. Controlling it as Sam hoped he wouldn't.

"What are you going to tell them we talked about, Sam?"

"I'll tell them you're suing the city. You're furious about your treatment."

"Good one, Sam. That will probably hold them for now. And as for your gun, I'll get it back to you as soon as I can. When I can avoid them," says Ray. "Obviously, you're not expected to perform until you have it again."

"Why'd you save me? If that's what you were doing, I don't get it."

Ray looks up into the sunshine. Like any retiree on a park bench in the sun.

"I couldn't have it end so fast, Sam. I couldn't have it over so fast. Where's the fun in that?" says Ray. "Maybe I saved you for a rainy day," he adds flippantly.

He gets up.

"Someone has to be the killer," says Ray, stark reminder of the binary universe they inhabit together. "They won't stop looking for us until someone is."

"Why does it have to be one of us?" says Sam.

"Because it does. Because it is," says Ray. "And which one of us is it?" asks Ray with a smile. "That's what isn't clear yet, is it, Sam? That's what hasn't been decided yet."

Ray stretches. In full view and full disregard of the observers hundreds of yards off. Then he looks straight at Sam—for the first time out here, Sam suddenly realizes—and presents, in summary, in passing, what amounts to celebration and explanation and confession, all rolled revealingly into one. "It's so much better with the two of us, Sam. It's so much better than doing it alone." In the wrinkles around Ray's eyes, in the cock of his head, Sam reads some private version of affection. Ray shrugs, mock playfully. "I can't give you up, Sam." He squints out at the sunshine, breathes in the day for a moment. "It's a lot more interesting than either of us thought, isn't it, Sam? Makes it good to get up in the morning."

Ray smiles giddily and starts to stride away. "Say 'hi' to Tommy for me," he says over his shoulder.

Sam is safer without the gun, of course. They can't find it. Ray can't expect more from him. He has to sit still, defenseless, while the investigation leads to him or doesn't.

But Sam is surprised to feel how itchy he is to have his gun back.

Something Ray alluded to. Something Ray could tell about Sam. Even before Sam could.

40

Wyatt is confined to his house.

That's the compromise reached with the department's two staff lawyers, for Brady not to go forward with formal charges. That's where they'll leave it for now, so as not to expose or direct more media attention to the internal dysfunctions of the Bureau and the local police.

For Wyatt, the confinement brings new meaning to the term *forced retirement*.

Is he a blunderer? A big, over-the-hill blunderer? Has his true nature been hidden from him his whole life, and now—in jumping at Ray Fine, in raiding Sam Stevens' town house and finding nothing—has his true blunderer's nature been revealed? Has the sluggish, cumbersome figure he sees in the mirror finally shown its true nature?

He had gathered his little band of loyalists, led them on a mission like some starry-eyed patriot, implying heroism and glory and moral action and moral superiority, and they had nothing to show for it. Nothing but demotions and suspensions and careers ruined for their antiquated notions of loyalty and devotion and honor and commitment and friendship.

Sam and Denise Stevens owned a little cabin over in Perry, almost two hours west. Wyatt had wanted to send someone out to it, but Thomaston, the friendly judge, uncomfortable enough issuing the search warrant for the Stevenses' town house, had balked at issuing a second one for the cabin. Ultimately, he'd given Wyatt the choice. Wyatt had picked the town house.

Now, of course, Wyatt felt nothing but frustration, wondering if the evidence he needed was at the cabin out in Perry.

Had he chosen wrong? Had he simply picked the wrong door, literally and figuratively? Was it one more instance of blunder?

Wyatt paced his own kitchen like a caged animal. The legal department's agreement with Brady amounted to house arrest, after all. Some kind of ill-defined diplomatic semistate—in trouble but uncharged, disapproval but not official sanction, threat but perhaps empty threat only. After a career spent catching the bad guys, he was close to being treated as one. Brady wasn't calling him a criminal yet, but he was threatening him with the designation.

But worse than any of that, he was here, a prisoner in his home, and Ray Fine and Sam Stevens were out there.

Wyatt was reduced to listening to the radio news for any developments in the case, like any other citizen. He'd dialed his deputies and met with cheerfulness and loyalty in their greetings, but obvious ambivalence and discomfort when he pressed for any current details. It was clear they'd received instructions from Brady. They didn't want to lose their paychecks. Judge Thomaston wouldn't even come to the phone. Brady was thorough. It was almost as if he wanted to teach Wyatt a lesson in thoroughness, in how it was supposed to be done.

His wife, Margie, chatted amiably about their upcoming construction projects and their travel plans. Wyatt did his best to focus, but couldn't. He wandered through his living room, looked occasionally through the draperies out at the lane. He saw an unmarked sedan cruise past once, saw the same sedan parked down the lane for several hours, and then, a half hour after that, saw nothing.

He paced. He looked out again.

He wouldn't survive this—this disconnection, this prison. He wondered if Brady knew how impossible it would prove to Wyatt. If Brady knew that Wyatt would inevitably put himself in trouble again. Bigger trouble. Trouble that would take Wyatt out of Brady's way for good. Maybe Brady had pulled the unmarked sedan away just to give Wyatt the chance to do something stupid.

He'd made a mistake jumping across the table at Ray Fine.

He'd made a mistake raiding Sam Stevens's town house.

Just before dawn, while Margie slumbers beside him, Wyatt rises quietly, dresses in the hall, tosses some toiletries and underwear into a shopping bag, checks through the draperies once more to the empty street outside, jots a quick "Be right back" note and leaves it on the kitchen counter, impulsively adding an equally quick "I love you," goes quietly out the side door to the still-dark driveway, hops into his wife's old station wagon, and backs it out into the night.

A third blunder?

Third time's the charm.

Three strikes you're out.

41

Carl Brady leans back in the smart, crisp, businesslike, no-nonsense office work chair he has brought into Wyatt's office to replace the absurdly massive, worn-out, grand leather recliner that Wyatt had been using.

He knows it will take more than replacing the office furniture to get rid of the guy. Brady's little hatreds—uncontrollable, irrational, a lifelong trait—have been, he believes, an asset of understanding and connection in dealing with the criminal mind. His personal acquaintance with hate has provided him, he's always thought, a special aptitude for his job. But he's felt one of his familiar little hatreds for the immense and lumbering sheriff since his arrival here. The sloppy looseness, the incompetence, the irrational reservoir of local affection and patience with Wyatt—ex-local baseball star, longtime fair-haired boy. The style is so contrary to his own, it's only served to harden the hate. It should have been Brady's case to begin with. He should have had center stage from the start.

The phone rings with a call put through by Agent Cruz, who has been screening calls for Brady. He grabs the receiver. "Brady."

"Sir?" tremulously, timidly.

"Oh, Christ, Andy," says Brady into the receiver. He can tell already. "You lost him."

"Yes, sir," says Andy.

Brady had half-expected it.

And fully hoped it.

The temptation had proved too much for Big Billy Wyatt. Just as Brady figured.

And now he could go after him in earnest. The kid gloves were off.

42

Joe.

Oh, the forensic psychiatrists would have a field day with Joe.

Ray Fine has so much more to tell Sam, after all: that he needs Sam to take up arms again to save the city again from the crime wave, from the sorry-ass citizens in its grip who can't do anything to help themselves and so they need us, Sam. There's a killer out there, Sam, a maniac, and one of us has to be out there, Sam, one of us needs to be out there getting rid of the targets that the killer would otherwise go after. We're doing our civic duty, working alone, without recompense, don't you see, Sam? This burg owes us, goddamn it, Sam. We're saving their asses, sacrificing the weak, the outliers, to save the herd, and where's our thanks?

All good and crazy. And all of it a way not to mention Joe. Ray's crazy, sure, always has been crazy, but he understands lucidly.

The question Sam is clearly asking is, is Ray Fine crazy enough to keep killing? To keep putting himself in jeopardy? To take Sam out of jeopardy?

Whereas the question Ray Fine has is, can he get Sam Stevens crazy enough to completely take the job over?

To give old Ray a rest? To keep Joe—and Ray, too, for that matter—out of cells and away from shrinks and hospitals. He doesn't want any of that. He can feel it, sense it, hanging on the horizon like a pack of hungry wolves. No, he doesn't want any of that.

Crazy like a fox. The old expression was helpful, but fell way short. He knew the truth. He was far crazier than what the expression implied, but far more stealthy, predatory—foxlike, too.

You don't know Joe.

God, he wants to tell Sam, his weird new compadre, his new brother in arms. He wants to tell him partly because the Joe thing is, he knows, best and craziest of all; makes all the rest of it look downright rational by comparison; it's the thing that makes him look and seem the most clearly and certifiably insane and gives him therefore the most power over the situation and over Sam.

But that is the one craziness he knows he can't mention, the one craziness not in his psychological war arsenal. Because that is the one craziness that is true. And it's confusing enough, difficult enough to manage as it is.

He likes this Sam. Jesus, going to the FBI to try to protect himself. To try to alter the game, level the playing field. How crazy is that? He feels Sam's insanity catching his own. A match for his own. He could be a friend to this guy. The Assassins Club. Ray says it facetiously, of course, but there really is a communion there.

He feels himself swerve so close sometimes. So dangerously close to telling him.

Oh, what the forensic psychiatrists would say about Joe. About Ray and Joe. They'd have themselves a field day. They'd have themselves an academic conference.

He himself doesn't really know where Ray ends and Joe begins.

You don't know Joe.

I don't know Joe.

Nobody knows Joe.
Joe the asshole. Joe the jerk. Joe the angel. Joe the saint.
Say it ain't so, Joe.
Oh, he wishes. He wishes it weren't so.

43

His habits and refinements of stealth had been adopted over decades of off-the-books superpatriot operations, "black" projects for the darkest corners of the American military, on-site "consulting" to various ultra-right and ultra-left causes in flash points around the world. Occupational necessity had taught Ray the techniques of erasing his official existence, of dusting clean his electronic and bureaucratic footprint, but he has taken pride in raising those skills to an art.

It was purely out of those habits and skills—and for the ability to be quickly and efficiently armed deep in any territory—that Ray Fine oversaw a sizable arsenal that nevertheless existed nowhere at all. It was an existential thrill for him, the arsenal's absence. Because it was always moving, always in motion, always in elaborate but conventional transit around the nation and across the world.

The elaborate, orchestrated movement was largely unnecessary. He could have the weapons—many of them, anyway—legally in his home. It was his right as an American citizen. But this system kept him light, kept him in tune, kept him at the ready to deliver any armament he needed to any region of the world he needed it, even on short notice, with border police and airport security and local authorities posing much less barrier to him—mostly, none at all.

He always knew where everything was; he had the tracking numbers—not written down, of course, but in his head. To send packages around these great United States, at least, didn't require much ID, God knows, and he did so under a variety of identities. He maintained, along with the list of his names, a list of addresses—a few at Mail Boxes Etc. and similiar independent mail stores, adequate for FedEx, UPS, and the other shipping systems. If he couldn't receive a package at a certain address, he knew where it went—to which holding facilities, for how long, and how you could, without even speaking to anyone (by using e-mail and Touch-Tone telephone commands) forward the package on to a new address, until it was so far away from its original shipping address, through so many other identifications and journeys, that no one would know who it came from.

There were certain packing techniques he'd learned and perfected years ago working security and operations for South American smugglers: hiding components inside toys and stuffed animals; disguising them as building supplies; even having them make cameo appearances in tool sets. Ray knew what materials to wrap them in, what arrangements to make to fool the scanners and X-rays, which luckily were still the exception in domestic intra-U.S. shipping.

Keeping track of which guns were where. Which guns could be picked up and retrieved when. It was a puzzle—one he excelled at and enjoyed. Remembering tracking numbers was no harder than remembering phone numbers—easier, actually, because there was a fond, physical association to each weapon, a shared history with each one. And there'd been no mistake yet. The package delivery business was extremely reliable.

It had been a good system. But then Joe had gotten involved. Joe had gathered the essence of the system from Ray—well, to be truthful, Ray had conveyed the essence of the system to Joe, and Joe had gotten hold of numbers that Ray had kept only in his head—well, perhaps Ray had communicated the numbers, and Joe had begun his current reign of havoc. Because it was a porous love between Ray and Joe. It was tricky, complex, between Ray and Joe. Ray had certain power over Joe. Joe had certain power over Ray. Like any relationship, Ray thought. Joe, of course, knew the guns were ex-military, knew Ray had eliminated the serial numbers on their stocks and barrels and in electronic records of them, making them essentially cease to exist. Then Joe, smart Joe, had gotten ahold of one of them.

Sam's rifle had briefly joined the stealthy merry-go-round. Circling and moving along with the other weapons, staying safely away from the investigation. God knows it was a far safer place than anything Sam might think of. And Ray couldn't leave a task that important to a beginner like Sam.

It was a Tango 51, which had been used for Sam's TV demo. Ray had been impressed seeing the rifle in Sam's hands in the original broadcast. Somebody knew what they were doing. Then again, expert advice—he supposed it wasn't that hard to come by.

Ray dials the FedEx 800 number, enters a tracking code, and confirms that the package he has in mind is waiting for a gentleman named Errol Sands at a holding facility about two hours from here.

He gets out his Errol Sands wallet, inspects it closely but pleased, like an artist admiring a finished canvas before exposing it to the opinions of the public.

He sits down at the computer, throws his Errol Sands identity onto the site the American shipping companies subscribe to for verifying identities.

Outside the apartment, the car is still there.

The FedEx regional center is a twenty-four-hour facility. He'll wait till nightfall and head out once more through the over-built drainage system; it's becoming his new front door.

44

S am Stevens tosses it teasingly, tantalizingly, onto the end of his *Sniper Update*. "Incidentally, I met today with Ray Fine, the original suspect, who was released from police custody for lack of evidence. As you can imagine, he expressed his unhappiness to me in terms that, let us say, fall well below broadcast standards. . . ."

The implied promise to his viewers of an actual interview to come.

He knows Ray will see the broadcast and won't be particularly pleased, but he knows Ray will understand that Sam had no choice. The broadcast is the only way to assure Brady that Sam is leveling with him, confirming the contents of his meeting with Ray Fine by reporting it on the news to his viewers.

It is a way of confirming for Ray that he told the authorities about the meeting, just as he told Ray he would.

It is also a way of reminding Ray about the one power Sam holds over him—the power of television, the power of the nightly news.

It is Sam's only bargaining chip, and it feels thinner and more fragile now, but Sam knows that the power of television is still—is always—there.

. . .

Brady is expecting a fuller report than the mere mention of it on the evening news, of course. A fuller report, an advance preview, was clearly part of the pact. So Sam calls Brady first.

Sam is put through to Brady directly and lays it out plainly and matter-of-factly, and somewhat disappointed, as a reporter would be. "Like I thought. He talked about a lawsuit. About police who were no better than criminals. Most of his bile was reserved for Sheriff Wyatt," Sam reports. "He wants to settle. Make a quick buck off the city or the state, figures they don't want this in the public eye. I think talking to me is just his way of threatening the authorities, making his gripe known. Bringing his complaints to the nightly news is his way of giving the threat more bite."

Sam listens to his own pause for a moment, weighing what he is about to say one last time, and then—a guess, a choice, a choice without choice—he throws it out. "Agent Brady."

"Yes."

"He implied . . . he implied he had something more to tell me. Something significant. It's just my reporter's instinct. Nothing more than a hunch. But I feel obligated to mention it."

Brady is silent, first. Then, cautiously, "Well, you stay in touch with this guy. Let him know it's an open line to you."

"Will do."

Thinking that Ray is only after money might not have been enough to hold Brady's interest. But they'll at least keep an eye on Ray now, Sam figures—given Sam's "more to tell," his vague reporter's "hunch," which he just dangled in front of them. Maybe they'll only be watching from a distance. But it's at least a thin measure of protection, of safety, in his dealing with Ray Fine.

I feel obligated to mention it. Brady snorts with annoyance. Since when did a reporter feel obligated to mention anything to the

FBI? How can Sam think Brady won't see right through that phony spirit of cooperation?

Sam Stevens is just trying to buy some more safety, Brady knows. Enlist a personal army without paying a dime. Well, reporters don't get personal armies, thinks Brady with annoyance. Reporters get what Carl Brady decides to give or not give.

He is irritated by this request meant to string him along. Brady has a sour taste in his mouth. Why should he do some reporter a favor? The guy is already getting more than his fair share of compassion and attention from the world. Sam has gone too far.

Sorry pal, you're on your own.

45

Ray Fine's parting mention of Tommy was, Sam knows, only part of Ray's persona, part of his habit, his stance of terror.

Sam is locking the doors. Checking the windows. He has instructed the woman taking care of Tommy to be careful. He has debated arming her with a gun—a registered, legal one—but concludes that her having a gun holds more threat of accident or escalation than being without one.

These are, he knows, probably useless steps. Steps that Ray would laugh at. But if it won't actually deter Ray Fine, it does, at least, make Sam feel better to try.

Sam knows how difficult it must have been for Ray to get here that first night. There must have been detectives watching. Dropping in on Sam like that, Ray had to shake or fool his observers to do so. Now, there was FBI. So another visit from Ray Fine at this point—if it were to happen at all—would not be a visit to take lightly.

Sam gets home at nine and dismisses the housekeeper. He puts Tommy to bed and stays up watching TV.

He sees his own broadcast segment at 11:00 P.M., which had run first at 6:00 P.M.

He hasn't watched himself on television since Denise's murder. He's startled by what he sees.

Startled that he looks precisely the same. Standing up, doing his segment, with his same induplicable mixture of earnestness and irony and bluster and directness and coyness. Interchangeable with broadcasts from months ago. Like nothing has happened. Like nothing has changed.

At midnight, unable to sleep, Sam heads to the kitchen to get a glass of water.

He is there.

Sitting in the same white chair, like a fellow occupant of the town house, a longtime roommate, his shadow carved into the dark.

"Hi, Sam," says Ray. The Tango 51 is sprawled across his knees, like a flirtatious lover across his lap. "I couldn't keep you two from each other," he says, stroking the weapon.

Sam is silent, trying to adjust once again to the idea of seeing Ray here, sitting casually in his living room at midnight.

"Saw your broadcast," says Ray. "Suing the city. Good one. As if that's how I get even. I tend to be a little more proactive than that."

"You know I said that to keep suspicion off you."

"To keep suspicion off *you*," says Ray.

"Off us," says Sam.

Ray fondles the rifle. Sam can't tell what part of that fondling is authentic and what part is only for Sam's benefit.

What are you doing here, Ray? But Sam already knows. Already sees.

"I brought her back to you, because I know she's your girl now, and I want you two to be together. Your wife is gone, and now she's your girl, and I didn't want you to be separated. I protected your relationship, didn't I, and now I'm bringing you two together again." Ray smiles.

Sam looks silently at Ray.

Ray suddenly tosses the gun to Sam.

Sam has no choice but to catch it to avoid the racket of it knocking over the lamps and waking Tommy and bringing his son stumbling sleepy-eyed and puzzled into the living room.

To avoid Tommy's meeting Ray. As if meeting Ray is somehow meeting Sam's dark half. Stumbling into Sam's other world.

"I think it's time for you two to go out dancing again," says Ray.

Sam's heart pounds. "You do, huh."

"I want you two lovebirds to get out there and have a good time," says Ray. "And I know you will."

"How do you know that, Ray?"

Ray's face darkens. "I saved you once, hiding your girl for you, didn't I? I loved saving a cold-blooded killer." He smiles. "I loved it so much I want the chance to save you again."

"Well, it's not so simple anymore," says Sam, cautiously. "In fact, it's pretty much impossible, as you must realize. Because Brady is watching now."

"Oh, I don't know if they're watching as closely as you think," says Ray with a rictus smile. "If they were, how could I be here?"

Because you're different, thinks Sam. *Because you are some other kind of creature. Operating by some other physics, by some other process, by rules beyond rules. In some unique zone of movement and terror.*

"You're a smart guy," says Ray, with snide mock confidence. "You'll figure out a way."

Unquestionably, Ray was crazy. A killer like Ray Fine was always, at some level, crazy. But this was a crazy man who was also coldly, calculatingly sane in his craziness, and it was hard to tell where the dividing line ran—or if it even ran at all.

There was another element, too, now, another black syllogism: A killer was always crazy at some level. Sam had now killed.

So had Sam therefore slipped—easily, unaware, unobserved by anyone including himself—into a killer's crazy realm? Could he even trust his own perceptions, his own judgments about any of this anymore? How far had he traveled? Had he already traveled over some imperceptible line?

"But see, I really don't want to anymore, Ray," says Sam—an appropriately arch, crazy yet sane response, he thinks. Referring to murder, after all, with a childish whine.

"Well, of course, you don't want to. Nobody really wants to. It's work. It's a task. But you have to. That's the crux of it. You have to."

"Because I owe you?" asks Sam.

"Because otherwise, I'll take your boy," says Ray, as if it is obvious. As if he is surprised Sam is even asking. "That's what I'm doing sitting here, obviously. Giving back your cool, sweet girlfriend here, and making it clear how easily I can come anytime and take your son."

I could shoot you now, thinks Sam, holding the rifle. But the gun is unloaded, of course. *I could shoot you now.* The thought is unfiltered, unmodulated, passionless and direct, Sam notices. Apparently he has crossed some line. He feels literally dizzy, unsteady, from the realization. He looks down at the rifle in his hands, and for an instant he doesn't even recognize what it is.

"Anyway, I think your son knows a little more than you think. Living in this house with his mom and dad. Knowing who goes out and who comes in when. Maybe I need to take him to help him remember how it happened, so he sounds nice and clear in front of a grand jury. You don't want him to embarrass the family with incoherent mumbling. You want him to be nice and clear."

Sam is cornered. At the mercy of someone crazier.

The darkness of the shadowed living room is close on him, close on them both.

The weight of it pushes down on him:

Why, Ray, why? he wants to ask. This is the moment to. With the silence of midnight, the intimacy of the dark. He knows this is his chance to be a reporter. A real reporter. *Why, Ray, why? What's driving you?* But he knows he won't get an answer. That Ray can't answer. Not really. Not accurately. If Sam can't answer it in himself, how can Ray?

Oh, he feels himself swerve so close. So dangerously close.

To saying it to Sam, his kinsman, his brother in arms, in that intimate midnight dark.

He longs to tell him. He feels he could trust him. The one person in the world who could understand. The one person in the world he could trust.

I have a son, too, Sam.

He's not like your son, though. He's a different kind of child.

But he's with me, inside me, always.

And I don't know where one of us begins and one of us ends.

I guess that's how it is with children, isn't it, Sam?

We don't talk. Not really. We never could talk. But we always feel each other. We're always aware of each other.

I have a son, too, Sam.

Joe. My little Joey.

He's with me always.

You know how it is, Sam.

He was always a quiet boy. A good boy. Even while I was away on missions, brutal missions, amid death and destruction and chaos, he was always a good boy.

But oh, he's been kicking up a fuss lately.

He needs me. My little Joey needs me. And I need him.

You know how it is, Sam.

It seems to Ray that Sam really does know how it is.

46

Wyatt drives through the early morning.

He has the address of the cabin.

He is not exactly a fugitive. But he is not exactly a representative of law enforcement, either. He occupies some tenuous place in between. What, then? Concerned citizen?

Of course, he is not exactly that, either. He has not been a mere citizen in close to forty years—not since the military, not since the academy, probably not ever. He has had a defender mentality, a protector mentality, since he was a child, and it is as if this series of killings—each new one coiling tighter around his chest, his throat, like a boa constrictor doing its methodical work—has been mounted specifically to negate, to unseat, that "defender" vision of himself. These weeks have been no less than an arrow to his heart. A personal assault. As if he has been singled out to be tested. He knows why he jumped across the table at Ray Fine. Because he has taken it, he has felt it, as a personal attack.

That had been the first of his mistakes. It was as if his life's personal mistakes had been waiting, collecting, building up, and the events of the past weeks had unleashed and spilled them all in an embarrassing clattering crash. He wonders if the crime's deeper effect on him has led to his misjudgments.

Leaping across the table at Ray. The raid on the reporter's house. The foolishly confident, arrogant, small-town, small-time things he'd said in the press conferences that brought smirks from the national reporters.

And now this. Sneaking out of his own home. A reckless trip to the Stevens cabin. Merely another mistake? Though this is a mistake that he knows from the outset is a mistake. A mistake that is not fooling him or catching him off guard. This is an endeavor that has the deck stacked against it already. Whose chance of success is slim, but is the only chance he has of progress, of vindication, of sleeping at night.

Wyatt drives through the early morning toward the cabin, wondering what he will find there. If he will find anything. It may be a fool's errand, it may be brilliant insight; at the moment he doesn't much care. He has motion, forward motion, and that is all he wants and needs right now.

The drive away from it all—despite the surreptitiousness, despite the pressure—is a moving out to a point of perspective. The simpler vistas, the swathes of fields, open his mind to a sense of reflection and distance he hasn't had the luxury of in months—months in the fishbowl, in the pressure cooker.

Why do they all have it in for him? When did they all decide to have it in for him? He doesn't know. He knows that in these cases, sometimes the media roots for you, and sometimes they root against you, and probably to some degree their decision reflects what they think will draw the better audience. But he senses it is more than that, too. More than that has turned them against him. His size? An ex-sports star's recent heft that, he knows, now helps him seem a caricature of the southern sheriff. How he hitches his belt. A nervous habit from adolescence, that they see as caricature, too, caricature of southern ignorance and southern buffoonery. No one explored his personal life. No one bothered with the full picture. His pleasure reading of American and European history. His diligent keeping up at the frontiers of forensic science, like an M.D. That doesn't fit the caricature, the look. And there is his gait, too. Which looks, he knows, cocky and confident and arrogant, but is just the way he walks, helping his knees and hips to compensate for the weight. It seemed they were casting agents, the press, and they'd sized him up for the role when he'd walked in the room, and it didn't matter much what was on his résumé; that was that.

Growing up, he had always been loved. The world had been a place of camaraderie and fun for him, and he had loved it, and it had loved him back. All of it. Uncritically, universally. A sense of camaraderie and place and belonging (to ball teams, to their fans in the stands, to the close-knit, cheering community) that had seemed to carry—uncritically, universally—into adulthood.

And suddenly, without warning, just weeks ago, the world had suddenly turned on him. At the lectern for briefings, quite literally facing the world, the world was uncritically, universally hostile. All his life he could do no wrong. Suddenly, he could do no right. Unfortunately, he was being asked to adjust to that shift in front of the world, and he couldn't make that adjustment.

He is heading to the cabin alone. His loyal cadre can't be coaxed again; they have all paid too-high prices for their loyalty already. Even if one or two were still willing, it's not fair to them.

He is heading to the cabin alone. On his own. As if to escape the city, as if to relax, as if to get away for the weekend.

In less than two hours Wyatt is there. There is no address on the rickety wooden mailbox at the end of the long driveway—which in fact is hardly any driveway at all, just parallel dirt tracks at a break in the dense brush—but he ascertains this is the place by the street addresses before and after it.

The closest neighbor is a couple of minutes' drive. It is rural chic. Upscale by being downscale. The land is scrubby, unattractive, unremarkable. And there is not a soul out here. Privacy with a capital *P.*

He drives past the driveway once, then once more, and finally pulls his car off the two-lane road at a dirt turnout up about a quarter mile.

Wyatt cuts the engine, gets out, looks up at the sun and at the surrounding scrub and up and down the empty road—questioning his own sanity one last time, appearing to query nature itself for an appraisal of his mental soundness. He swears vaguely and noncommittally at the task ahead and strikes off into the woods.

There's probably no one there—there probably hasn't been in weeks—but he can't just pull up to the house like he's invited. Like he's here for the weekend.

He trudges through the woods, breaks a sweat, and soon comes, with the directional instinct of the farm boy he once was, to the clearing where the cabin stands. He sees that he could easily have missed it and circled uselessly for hours. The natural paths have led right to it. He is lucky. Sort of lucky, anyway.

He stands and assesses it from the edge of the woods. The cabin's modesty impresses him. One story tall, faded white paint, a green bulkhead door to a basement on the side. The cabin's purchase must date from a time when neither of them had much money, or maybe it had belonged to one or the other of them before they met. It had obviously been their reclusive escape; they were not out here to impress anyone, since neighbors were pretty much nonexistent. Why hadn't he killed her here, where no one would know what had happened? Bury her out here, where no one could find her? Because that would mean always living under a cloud of suspicion. Because that wasn't taking ingenious advantage of the moment. That didn't hold the possibility of total vindication, total freedom.

There is no sign of movement or presence that Wyatt's aging but still-alert eyes can see. No recent or obvious tire tracks. No interior lights on. No sign of life. Wyatt figures he will walk carefully around the property's outside before venturing in.

He begins to tread the woods in a wide perimeter around the cabin, unsure what he is looking for.

He is soon standing at the charred black ring of a controlled outdoor fire, which maybe Stevens had used to burn brush. It's the first sign of Stevens's presence as he has circled the property. The presence of a person.

He bends down and looks. He notices the black char of the logs isn't streaked yet by rain, that none of the char on the burned logs has chaffed off yet through the wind and weather and wear. The fire, therefore, is fairly recent. He raises his eyebrows as if to fully receive that bit of information.

He stands up, pokes his boot into the char, circles the black ashes around a little, as if in some arcane, primitive ceremony.

Then he sees it. At the far corner of the black ring, maybe six, seven feet in front of his boot. A little piece of a burned foreign material on the ground, drawing his attention to it by its texture and not its burnt coal-black color.

He steps over and stoops to pick it up. He looks closely. It is smooth, unrecognizable. But it's something that burned in Sam Stevens's fire that wasn't wood.

He pulls it gently, and it stretches a little before it snaps in two, releasing a vestige of its familiar scent in the process.

Latex.

Latex, in a brush fire.

Latex, to a cop like Wyatt, means gloves. As in protection. As in care.

He puts the strip of burnt latex in his pocket.

He looks again at the black char. It's an enormous black pile of it. He closely examines different sections, different samples. All of it recently burned. All of it undisturbed yet by wind and weather. It had to have been a tree.

He therefore looks for drag marks toward the charred circle. He finds them. He follows them.

The drag marks—sometimes faint, but still there—lead him farther into the woods. The woods are dense, but their brush gives him more clues about the tree's path. He traces it to where the drag marks disappear.

He is expecting a stump, of course, maybe waist- or knee-high, but he sees nothing. The fallen leaves are thick on the floor of the woods, a crunching carpet of brown beneath his black shoes. He walks a little more.

He stumbles and almost falls.

He looks down, stunned and angry, and sees why.

There *was* a stump—but it's been cut down to the level of the forest floor.

Out here in the middle of nowhere, Wyatt realizes, you'd only cut it down that far to hide it. In fact, it is covered by an inordinate pile of fallen leaves. Clearly gathered up for the purpose of hiding it.

Latex gloves. This low-cut tree stump. Sam Stevens was being careful.

Wyatt gets down on his knees to examine the stump, but, of course, there is nothing left to examine.

He gets up, stands there for a moment.

You would cut down a tree that you were afraid would reveal something.

He walks to the trees directly behind the stump.

The morning light is bright.

He wanders among the trees, aimless, unsure.

There.

Just one.

A little divot.

What the woodpeckers used to make in the woods around his boyhood farm.

That's what someone else might take it for.

But he remembers those woodpecker holes—the worked-over nature of them, when you looked close.

And he is not just a farm boy. He is also a sheriff. A sheriff with thirty years' experience.

This is not the handiwork of a woodpecker.

This, friends, is a bullet hole.

A bullet hole without the bullet.

Target practice, he thinks sullenly.

The intended target—immense and ancient, tall and rough-skinned and graceful, regal and silent—now burned to black.

The intended target—Denise Stevens—ashes, too, buried beneath the ground at a crowded but silent ceremony.

He looks at the trees around him.

He wonders—he knows—what the burned tree would have revealed.

Billy Wyatt steps up onto the porch—really only two-by-fours built into a riser, a few feet off the ground. It couldn't be more primitive.

It looks like the original door.

He tries the door handle.

The door opens easily. The entryway is dark, expectedly cabinlike. Wyatt's eyes struggle to adjust to the interior dark after the brightness outside.

The blunt drama of the next few seconds would echo in him incessantly in the weeks to follow. The thick forearm across his chest, the pulsing hot breath in his ear, the grunting as Wyatt elbowed the figure hard, instinctively, panicked, unthinking, and shoved his huge fist up into the jaw of the second man, the man's sharp, curdling yelp of pain. The few seconds of wild tussle, during which no word was said—too intense, too busy for any words—and then the floorboards against Wyatt's now-bloodied cheek and nose. He could smell his own blood, hear and feel simultaneously the clip of the cuffs—the distinctive, satisfying clip and click he had heard often from the other side—and one of their voices firm just above him, in his right ear: "FBI, you asshole."

He had thought of course—vaguely, for a moment—that he was swinging out at Sam Stevens foolishly defending his home. Wyatt had quickly, at some level, processed the presence of a second man, but that did not slow him down. He was lashing out at his frustration, he was defending not himself, but something more ineffable—his point of view, his right to have one; he was swinging blindly against the unfairness, at what had happened to him, swinging out at his own world crumbling. And at some level, he knew it was just his unthinking, headlong idiocy, manifesting itself again, making itself so obvious to him he could no longer deny it to himself.

It was seconds. Seconds whose grunts and thumps of encounter would echo long after, echo in the corridors of the justice system, like any petty criminal's.

Wyatt was unspooling the mistakes, leaving a string trail of them.

Cuffs on, he is pulled to his feet, then pushed down into a chair.

One of the agents, still catching his breath, huffing heavily in recovery, punches the keys of his cell phone—obviously to report this to Brady. The agent puts the phone to his ear and in a moment frowns. As Wyatt suspected, they are out of cell range.

"Assaulting field agents," says the other one, rubbing his own wounds, still angry, fuming at the unpredicted level of resistance. "Not a real good idea."

Just the trouble Brady had been hoping for, thinks Wyatt. Just the kind Brady had been angling for, sending these two guys out here.

Wyatt foresees it immediately. The field agents will not say that they ambushed him. They will report the events purely in their favor—"assaulted," "out of control," "first use of force was his." Wyatt had read enough reports. Brady might even know his eager charges were slanting events, but he wouldn't care. Wyatt—already warned, already by agreement confined to his own home—had assaulted law officers. That's all that will matter.

His eyes have by now adjusted to the cabin's dim light. Planted in the chair, Wyatt looks longingly down the cabin's dark hall.

Despite what has just happened, he feels a moment of hope. They were here ahead of him, after all. Carl Brady is clearly hungry and aggressive—and if for glory, then so be it, if that would break the case.

Of course, if they have found anything already, they aren't about to share it with Wyatt now.

Wyatt senses they are here without a warrant. That concerns him more than a little. Jesus—don't jeopardize the potential usefulness of any evidence. Or does Brady have more sophisticated ways of dealing with that? Something Wyatt doesn't understand?

Wyatt squints down the hall with such open longing that one of the agents apparently understands. "Still want to look around, huh? Still want to find something and solve it, huh?"

He regards Wyatt disdainfully as he licks the wound to his mouth. He shakes his head. "What do you think? A crime reporter is going to leave a bunch of clues around his country cabin?" The agent snickers. "A guy who has watched police departments operate all his professional life is going to leave a trail that leads right to him?"

Wyatt first feels a strange sense of relief. They are as interested in Stevens as Wyatt is—obviously based on completely different reasons, since Wyatt has never shared anything—certainly never shared what Neil, the coroner, had noticed. Maybe Brady sees what Wyatt does in the broadcast tapes. Maybe if Wyatt and Brady pool their information . . .

"Searching Sam Stevens's cabin isn't going to net you Sam Stevens or anyone or anything." says the agent, dismissively.

Which Wyatt at first takes to mean, *you're dealing with something much more sophisticated. You can't apply your dinosaur methods. Your dinosaur mentality.*

Fine. Then take over. I don't care who breaks it, as long as we break it.

But Wyatt slowly realizes that the agent has said it only in mockery. Mocking Wyatt's wild naïve notions and bullheaded fervor. *What do you think? A crime reporter is going to leave a bunch of clues around his country cabin?*

Wyatt can tell, by the unbroken sticks he saw, by the untrampeled paths, the two agents haven't even bothered to look around the grounds. They haven't even bothered, Wyatt realizes, to look through the cabin.

Wyatt suddenly understands.

They haven't come out here to look through Sam Stevens' cabin at all.

They have come out here only to get Wyatt.

Brady isn't about thoroughness.

Brady is about politics. Brady is about one-upmanship. Brady is about laying traps. Getting Wyatt finally out of the way.

This isn't about nailing Sam Stevens. This is about nailing Billy Wyatt.

They haven't come here to look. They have come simply to catch Wyatt looking.

It is as if this was all staged not just to get him, but on top of that, as a specific insult to him. An insult to his investigative instincts, to his police intelligence.

And most of all—are the agent's snide implications right?

Is Wyatt a dinosaur, operating out of his time—oversized,

clumsy, upsetting and overturning the mechanisms of a more so-phisticated age?

Before escorting Wyatt back to Command (Wyatt will ride handcuffed with the big one, he is told, the other will drive Wy-att's car), the younger FBI agent sweeps up the cabin's dark hall-way one last time.

The sleeve of the agent's trench coat brushes a narrow hallway table, and something small is swept off it onto the floor and shat-ters quietly.

The agent—his heavy black shoes tramping loudly across the cabin's wooden floor—doesn't even notice. But Wyatt, sitting obediently silent now, facing the little table, sees it fall and break.

Wyatt's body, in the wake of its last encounter, feels particu-larly worn down and vulnerable. But his eyes are still pretty good. He can see it's a little piece of flat, rectangular glass, whose translucence might make it invisible from directly above, but from this angle it's attracting the little bit of light that crosses the dark hallway. He squints, blinks to see more clearly, concentrat-ing on the unbroken portion. About the width of a thumb. With the squared-off, finished edges of the glass in a picture frame, but way too narrow a piece for that. A flat, rectangular, narrow piece of glass . . .

He tries to imagine Sam Stevens out here. Sam Stevens, care-fully planning . . .

Suddenly, he's pretty sure he's got it.

A microscope slide. To compare. To prepare. What else would it be?

47

Brady liked the day's events on two counts.

First, Wyatt would now be finally and truly out of the way.

Second, Wyatt would see how Brady was ahead of him, thinking a little faster, a little sharper, a little shrewder.

And that if there was anything to Sam Stevens's involvement, Brady would be on it far ahead of Wyatt.

But, of course, there wasn't anything to it. Too bad.

Wyatt was hustled from Command over to Central Booking and processed briskly, practically carried through the building (by several of his former officers, who refused to make eye contact), so it could all happen unimpeded before the media found out.

But word traveled fast. The rapist in the cell next to Darryl Jenkins called out to him smugly. "Hey, Charlie Manson, you hear who was in booking today?"

Darryl Jenkins sat up. "Who?"

The convict paused for rhetorical effect, then plunged

ahead, unable to contain his excitement, his still-intact sense of wonder.

"Sheriff Big Billy Wyatt. Your old pal."

Wow, thought Darryl. Then grinned slowly, deliberately.

This guy Stevens was awfully good.

48

A line of holding cells along a dark hallway.

In the first cell, a homeless man whose fresh white bandages contrast markedly with his stained and grimy clothes.

In the second cell, another homeless man, also with fresh bandages, treating wounds suffered fighting the first man.

In the third cell, two prostitutes.

In the fourth, an abusive and still-drunk husband in his dirt-streaked Brooks Brothers suit and tie.

In the last cell, at the end of the row (the corner cell conferring no greater size or status, only greater darkness), the outgoing sheriff of Webster County.

The municipal holding facility was legendary—not for anything sinister, but as a matter of history and of amusement. It was a jail that dated originally from the Civil War era, had been upgraded only minimally, and was more suited to a museum tour than to its current use. The city had approved funds for a much-needed renovation two years ago, but the work hadn't yet begun. Cops joked that prisoners could break out easily, if they were only smart enough, but were generally so dumb, that—miraculously—no one had slipped out of it yet. The scant security measures were, of course, retrofitted. It was unreliable, but forbidding looking. Maybe it succeeded on looks alone.

Wyatt has been in here a hundred times—to see a suspect, to discuss a case, to interview a witness, to broker a deal—but he has never experienced it from this side, of course. Through the bars. He would never have imagined it could look so different, given just a few feet of shifted perspective. It's therefore a place he knows well and a place he doesn't know at all.

He listens to the echoes against the unadorned brick and dark stone. He hears the involuntary moans, the loud withering sighs, the desultory rootless mumblings, the occasional outraged scream. Low-grade torment, ramping up, settling down, in a physical half light of confusion.

Several hours later, at the sound of a distant clanking and echoing voices, he looks up, and there is Brady, striding down the hallway toward him, standing in front of him in a moment, only the bars between them.

"Should we have it opened?" one of the agents accompanying Brady asks—as if Wyatt is merely an exhibit, as if he isn't even there.

"No," says Brady, curtly. As in, *let's keep the bars between us. Let's remember who's on which side.*

And, *I'm not going to be here very long.*

Brady looks in at Wyatt, shakes his head, but he is suppressing a smile. A smile he seems happy for Wyatt to see.

"I couldn't have you messing with potential evidence. You've messed up enough already."

Said expressly to drive Wyatt crazy with frustration. Both of them know Brady hasn't bothered to search Stevens's cabin at all.

As if to pretend Wyatt's incarceration is legitimate. As if to explain his own actions legitimately. *I'm protecting you, Wyatt, from your own further incompetence. That's why my men were out there—specifically to protect you from your own further incompetence.*

"I'll keep you here as long as I need to," says Brady. "You come at me with your primitive little department, your little-league lawyers, your puffed-up local friends, I'll find ways to keep you here, long as I need to." In the tone of a parent, putting a child's foolish speculation to rest before it even starts.

Wyatt says nothing. He is surprised to find himself wearing the silent insouciance of every jailed criminal he's ever dealt with, but he understands it immediately. It is a way of protecting, of retaining, some border amid the powerlessness, some measure of self.

While his exterior is all insouciance, inside he is alive, electric—wondering, planning, how to get himself back to that cabin out in Perry.

49

It is an hour before dawn.

The end of his day.

Arthur Stanley drinks a cup of black coffee standing by his tow truck, the Black Pearl. He has responded to calls all night. His contract with the city is steady, but it's night shift. Night shift for eighteen years now. It's work for which he's never thanked— not by the city, for keeping their streets clear for the morning, certainly not by the customers, only a few of whom he ever sees, trotting after him with murderous rage in their eyes.

He knows he is hated. He tries to shut that out, but can't. He is a man who seeks to be loved, yet look—look where he is working, what he is doing.

It's no life, but it's a living. And the steadiest work imaginable. He'd fed a family, put three kids through college, by God.

Arthur Stanley takes one last sip of the coffee—not particularly good coffee, he thinks irritably—and he turns, and feels something tap behind him, pinch him, before the pain fills him, invades every crevice and pore, overwhelms him. He watches the utterly familiar side panel of his trusty Black Pearl now slide up past his eyes, past his face, and with acute and final awareness he says the number to himself—*twelve*—before his utterly familiar world of night for the first and last time goes pure black.

Ray smiles. He can't help himself. You shouldn't ever smile, he knows, in the face of something like this, despite the irrepressible charge of it, the undeniable, insistent, surfacing thrill. He's never smiled before in the face of such grisly work. It's serious work, after all, a serious calling, but well, Ray finds himself grinning this time. He can't believe it. He can't—but he can. He called it. He called it perfectly. Does he know his guy, or what?

The deadline this time was twenty-four hours. A shorter deadline, the implication clear—that Ray would shorten it a little more each time. Tighten it. Up the ante. Keep the game interesting. But Sam had clearly seen the implication, and was obviously trying to talk back to it, to trump it somehow. Because—Jesus—Sam hadn't even taken an hour. Obviously hadn't set up or planned or brooded or suffered or turned it over in his mind—or at least meant it to appear that way. That was Sam's point, obviously. *His* implication was clear.

Ray understands the tactic perfectly. To outcrazy Ray himself. To turn the terror back on Ray. Ray even feels it a little, and that's how he recognizes it for the tactic it is. But he cuts it off, simply by knowing that's the tactic. An ingenious idea. But it's not going to work, Sam. You are still the amateur, Sam—the passionate amateur. And I am still the professional.

Ray still has to admit, it does make him feel a little off balance. A little unnerved. Would Sam go ahead without explicit directions? Would he go ahead, deadline or no? Is he trying to show that he would easily turn the gun on Ray? That's obviously what he wants Ray to think. The question is, how much truth is in that? Getting out from under Ray's threat? Proving he is crazier? Proving he is his own person? What's the point here, exactly? But that's what Sam wants Ray to wonder. Ray knows that. All these questions. That's the tactic. A good one. But not good enough.

And if that's the tactic, Ray has to smile.

Sam lowers the gun, stares at it for a moment. Mystified, enlightened. Filled with dread and omnipotence. Remorse and amazement.

It is only then, staring at the gun—somehow a result of the startling hyperclarity, the corruscating hyperreality, all the synapses still crackling—that it hits him:

It's not his gun.

He knows instantly. He feels it instantly. Realizes it in a time shorter than any conscious thought about it, as if pulling the trigger has jarred his consciousness, has brought a crack of clarity.

It's obviously Ray's rifle. The same model. Tossed to Sam, now fired by Sam, both actions putting Sam's own prints all over it.

Tango 51 with a U.S. Optics seventy-millimeter scope. Excellent choice, Sam. Excellent. He hears Ray saying it again, and this time Sam understands.

He'd worked so carefully to make his round match the sniper's. And look what had happened. Look at the extent and perfection of that match. Look at the price he would pay for that match.

Identical weapons. As if to say—mockingly, metaphorically—how the people who fired them had become identical. Interchangeable. Inseparable.

And now the sniper's gun in his hands. (Unless it isn't, of course. Unless it's actually Sam's gun, and Sam's untrustworthy imagination, his paranoia, the stress, causing the subtle but cascading collapse of his powers of analysis and observation, his growing separation from reality . . .)

But no. It's Ray's gun. In Sam's hands.

As if Ray was never even here. Only a ghost in the town house living room. Only flickering light.

Like television.

50

He's Back.
Sniper Strikes Again.
His Silence Was Golden. Now It's Gone.

The headlines fill the front pages, bleed across the newspaper stock, black and thick.

The news stations trip over one another, pushing and shoving and panting with the latest details—a goal-line pileup of the airwaves.

It has worked, Ray sees. It has worked brilliantly. Flawlessly.

Ray figures they'll pick up Sam at some point. They'll close in on him eventually. That crazy discredited sheriff already has it, Ray figures, although apparently no one's listening to him.

The FBI guy, too, will figure it out soon enough, Ray is sure.

And if for some reason he doesn't, Ray can help him. An anonymous tip about where to look for the gun. About reexamining all the bullets in Evidence. The FBI will get it, eventually. They're stupid, but not that stupid. Not stupid forever.

Though Ray realizes—the realization draping him like a new morning, like sun crossing his face, like pure power in pure oxygen—it could go on indefinitely.

If there was no mistake, if each of them continued with the same care, if nothing else changed on either side of the equation—the crime side or the investigative side—it could go on forever.

It began to have the strange mathematical magic, the odd, dizzying mental effects, of infinity in his mind.

It could simply go on without resolution.

He kind of liked this Sam. This Sam, who was making it work. Liked him enough to weigh, briefly, the idea of no resolution.

But it needed resolution. Without resolution, it felt mismanaged, unintended. Crazy. A different kind of crazy.

And now, at last, there was enough there for resolution.

And Joe, you'll be free. Like it never happened. But you'll have to behave, Joe. You're so lucky. Lucky Joe. But you'll have to be good, Joe. You'll have to be a good boy from now on.

What is it, Joe?
  Is there a problem?
  What's the problem, Joe?

But Ray already senses the problem.

If Sam simply continues until he's caught—with or without Ray's direction or encouragement—Sam Stevens will go down in history. And Ray Fine will remain unknown. A cipher. A mistake. A footnote.

And that's fine with Ray.

The plan has worked brilliantly, flawlessly, and Ray sits in his rental apartment, the unacknowledged mastermind.

That's also fine with Ray.

But is it fine with Joe?

When Joe gets involved, that's where the trouble starts.

It was as if Joe could read, could anticipate, exactly these thoughts of Ray's. Could penetrate the edges of Ray's mind like a permeable membrane. Although Ray knew that was silly. Ray was Ray, and Joe was Joe.

Joe. Uncontrollable Joe. Crazy within crazy. A vortex within the vortex. An explosion at the center of the explosion.

He can already hear Joe saying it.

He can already hear Joe's complaint.

That the reporter is taking Joe's victims.

Taking Joe's moment.

Taking Joe's place.

It's an unintended consequence of Ray's generosity. Of Ray inviting Sam into the club. The Assassin's Club. *Mortis Congressus.* But clubs had leaders. Clubs had someone in charge. A club needed hierarchy, structure, organization, a plan. It is a club, yes, but Ray sees now, it is a club that can't have any members. Because every member is his own club. With his own rules.

And Ray himself recognizes that if it goes on indefinitely, then there's no way to know who's best. And after all, there can only be one best.

Two killers. It implied competition. It was open-ended. It readily invited the questions of who is the real one, the original, and who is the copycat? Who is the amateur, who is the professional? Who is the apprentice, and who is the master? Which one's superior? How do they rank? How do they compare? Put the stats side by side. It's the first question a reporter would ask, it's the first question anyone would ask.

(He could even see explaining all that to Sam. Sam would understand—understand once more, understand even better, how crazy Ray really was. How crazy, how sane.)

But Joe is making Ray rethink it. Joe has a knack for that.

And Ray can see it, he supposes, from Joe's crazy point of view.

How they will credit it all to Sam.

The perverse ingenuity of Sam's wanting to cover the story himself. To revel in it, Ray knows. Like a firebug who sets the fire to make the rescues. Like a vice cop who plants the crack to make the collar. That will be the ready explanation.

Right down to doing his own wife to thrust himself even more front and center.

Ray can see it's what the law—certainly the media—would gladly believe.

The story of the decade. The century.

Sam Stevens will be pondered, analyzed, despised, admired, for years.

The antihero who still has *hero* in the name. Still occupies the lit stage.

But that is my stage, where I belong—and not him.

The stage I built. For good or ill. Whatever the consequences.

The stage I built. With my craft. My art.

The stage I must occupy—and not him.

Ray can hear Joe saying it. Can hear him so clearly.

He's cursed with Joe's voice, rattling around in his head.

Does Joe even really believe it? Ray wonders. Joe's so hard to get a handle on. Joe's so confusing. Ray's not real sure what Joe thinks anymore. Joe's been so crazy lately. Acting up. He's acted up before. But not like this. Never anything like this.

Requiring more of Ray. More effort. More ingenuity. Raising the bar on Ray. Requiring Ray to do even more to hide Joe. To save Joe. To shield Joe from the world.

Joe, I can't believe you're saying this. Why are you doing this? I've solved it for you.

I don't care, he hears Joe saying. *I want what I've done. I want what's mine.*

You want to make it harder for me, is what you want.

(It reverberates with all Ray's fuckups, all his mistakes. It hums in him with his own errors, his own powerlessness, his own self-destructiveness and self-immolation. But he doesn't see any of that. He pushes it down, manages to hold it away from his own consciousness.)

So what do you want me to do, Joe? Shut it down? End it?

All right. I'll do it for you, Joe. But this is the last time, Joe. This is the last request. This is the last thing. This ends it.

So now he'll take care of it. He'll close the circle, shut down the system. He'll tie up the overstuffed, messy, heaving bag of destruction, let it suffocate itself, choke on itself, neatly and hermetically and efficiently finish itself off. He'll not only end the game, but he'll dictate exactly the terms of the ending. He'll eliminate the competition, make it look like a suicide, a husband's overwhelming guilt at having gone off the deep end, having got too close to the story, having dipped into, gotten caught in, the madness of murder. Or maybe he'll make it look like an accident. Or maybe he won't even bother—and the police would find a silent, professional vigilantism—and speak out against it and welcome it and fear it all the same.

But I'll get him off the stage, Joe. I'll take him off your stage.

Ray is not to blame. He has never been to blame. It has always been someone else's doing. And it has always required cleanup. Cover-up. That's been his work, always. Cleanup. Cleanup shift.

Joe, you're a jerk.

But only the last in a long line of jerks, thinks Ray gloomily.

51

Sam and Tommy head for the cabin.

Tommy hasn't been there in years. When the marriage started coming apart, they stopped going out there as a family. Sam would use the cabin to get away from her, and she would occasionally use it to get away from him—it was a use never discussed but thoroughly understood—and Tommy was left out of the equation, never played a part in the gloomy brooding solo trips out here. So in a way, coming out here with Tommy is reclaiming it for Tommy. Reclaiming it for their family. The family of the two of them.

Sam is trying to see possibility. Sam is trying to hang on to what he has with Tommy. Trying to push aside for the moment the arcane depravity, the fluid, unpredictable motivations of Ray Fine, his dark doppelgänger. To push aside thoughts of Brady, probably onto him now, trailing him now. It is a circle, a rope, slowly, methodically drawing tighter—drawn tighter by both Ray and Brady, working together, each unseen by the other.

Sam also knows the trip out here is a last chance to stabilize himself, to grab some purchase, some balance and ballast from the past. He is drowning. He is going under. He is in extreme danger—the most danger, from himself.

He doesn't know if it is his desperation or his will to survive that is bringing him here.

Is he coming out here to die?

Is he coming out here to live?

Sam will give Tommy some memory of the place, before the police storm it. Before the sirens. Before it is lost, overrun. Before they come and round up Sam. Before Ray tips them off, calls them in. Game over.

Or doesn't turn him in. Chooses, simply, to continue. Ramps it up another excruciating notch. Game extended.

Ray is insane. There is no question that Ray is insane. But now—as he drives his son to the cabin, looking, to all appearances, like any father driving his son to their country home, looking, to all appearances, conventional, loving, tender, bonding, as if building memories—Sam is asking himself:

Am I just as insane as Ray?

No more? No less?

Their body counts indicate merely a difference in quantity, not quality. Their ingenious avoidance of consequences—both of them operating outside the necessary guilt or morality—is the same.

After the first one, it's just another. It could be a hundred more. You've severed your connection. You're living in darkness. So what difference does the exact number make? That's the smallest element, the smallest variable of it. That's just the number on the price tag. You've already made the purchase.

Is he any more sane than Ray? Why? Because his own actions have a purpose, and Ray's do not? That only says that Sam is purposefully insane.

If he is functionally insane as Ray—no more, no less—then he sees how he can still operate within parameters of judgment and care and precision, just like Ray apparently does.

Which is an indication—a warning—about the extra care that Sam must take in dealing with Ray. Ray's insanity has caused no compromise in Ray's moment-to-moment judgment and precision, just as Sam's own insanity has not affected his moment-to-moment judgment or precision either.

So Sam's insanity serves him well as useful warning about the strength of Ray's.

But who is Sam kidding? Sam is simply trying to stay one step ahead of Ray. Of Brady. Of everyone. Of anyone. It's survival. Nothing less. Nothing more.

They pull up the dirt driveway. Tommy's eyes gleam at the sight of the cabin, and Sam sees not only that Tommy seems to recall it at some level, but that somehow it has meaning to him—happy, pleasant, exciting meaning—and Sam will try to preserve that and build on it.

Tommy grabs his bag without being asked. He is going to be cooperative, he seems to want this to go as well as Sam does. With his bag, he lopes to the front door, looks up at it inquisitively.

"Go ahead in. It's open," says Sam. Always open. All yours.

He has tears in his eyes, watching Tommy go in. Watching Tommy lightly, eagerly, innocently enter what once was a portal of their happy dreams. Watching Tommy enter the cabin he had always imagined they would raise Tommy in together, letting Tommy roam the woods, be a boy.

He has bought more time. It defies logic, of course. To kill someone normally means to shorten your time. Here, it lengthens his time. He has had to do it, to appease Ray. To feed Ray. To live up to the vague, free-floating, black bargain. And with the eager-looking swiftness of it, the velocity of it, trying to destabilize Ray a little, make him guess a little, to the degree that was at all possible.

He has bought more time. The cost is brutal, an algebra of the unthinkable. He will be punished the same, pay the same price, no matter what the body count. So is there a difference? Yes, all the difference. Because he needs the time. He feels the end pressing in inevitably, utterly, relentlessly, and he needs the time.

He still vomits, though he is numb. He still lies there, unable to sleep. He is inhabiting the unthinkable. It is now the only existence he knows.

He had to do it. One last one. To give him time. To give him the chance to engineer a high-wire, white-knuckle victory. He is looking for hours, minutes now. Every minute precious. Every minute near his last.

52

"Hello there, Sam. And this must be Tommy." Sunglassed, grinning, in a beat-up black leather jacket, plaid shirt, and jeans, Ray steps into the cabin uninvited. "Nice to finally really meet you, Tommy."

It has been easy, so laughably simple, to find the Stevenses' cabin, not even knowing the town or state. It had even occurred to Ray—seeing the town house, knowing Sam's visible job and station in life, knowing that Sam somehow, somewhere, must have gotten comfortable with the gun—that there must probably be some place like this. It was easy, so easy, to search county records and real-estate transactions online, patiently, using only last names and bank records, tax rolls and public registries, and various other databases.

Ray was pleased when he first saw the cabin. Ramshackle, backwoods, it was a beautiful sight—out in the middle of nowhere. Plenty of time, plenty of opportunity, to stage events the way he wants. To alter and tailor those events however he chooses.

. . .

The problem with random, Ray has felt for weeks, is it's only that: random.

It's a lower skill set, and therefore obviously less satisfying than what Ray was trained for: a target. A target is purposeful, planned. Random doesn't adequately demonstrate the careful planning, the sense of mission, that Ray is all about. That makes him tick. A target, a mission: That is much truer to his training. Truer to his profession. Truer to his inner being.

Joe likes random, of course. Joe chooses random. But not Ray.

And letting the target know he's a target? Entering his home, chatting with him, all but pointing your finger at him?

Well, that's a higher level. That's the highest level. All the civility, formality, collegiality, elegance, of a duel.

That's the highest level of the craft there is, thinks Ray.

Because the world needs to understand. If not now, then to understand someday.

There's Joe.

And there's Ray.

The tense expression on Sam's face upon Ray's smiling entrance is worth the price of admission, thinks Ray. It is so obvious what Sam is processing behind that expression: their distance from neighbors, the boy's presence an extra burden and element, the proven unpredictability of his uninvited guest, the lengths Ray must have gone to—or didn't have to—to find Sam out here, all of it dancing behind Sam's alarmed eyes. Sam's voice struggling to stay even, no longer successfully casual and nonchalant.

Tommy looks up at Ray, mildly curious, figuring, Sam can tell, that Ray is an unpredictable colleague from work or a friend from his past, but someone his dad will deal with summarily, and everything will return to fine.

"Tommy, say hello to my friend Ray," Sam says finally. *See? I've never told him anything, Ray. He doesn't know you, he doesn't have any idea. And I'm calling you "friend," Ray, because that's what we are, right?*

"Nice to meet you, Tommy. I'm sorry about what happened to your mom. I hope they find the guy who did it," Ray says purposely, inappropriately cheerful, annoying in order to set all parties on edge.

He barges right in, as if to demonstrate in advance, in the opening step of the dance, that there's no stopping him.

Perhaps there is some harsh, crude justice to Ray's sudden appearance here, thinks Sam. The house where Sam planned and practiced his own liberation—thanks to its isolation, its ramshackle casualness—is now the site of his doom for the same reasons.

Is this merely what I deserve? What I have brought on myself?

He doesn't know why Ray is here. If Ray were going to kill them, would he come in first? Introduce himself? Spend time like this?

Yes.

Sam understands why.

Because Sam has messed with the previous Ray. Inserted himself into the equation and caused Ray the silent killer to rethink everything. Rethink his universe. He has unleashed a new Ray.

It is what Sam feared.

It is what Sam wanted.

Emotion is now collapsed, melded, unsortable, in Sam Stevens's jagged post-mortal world. Wanted, feared. Dreaded, invited. There is no difference anymore.

And calling Big Billy Wyatt? *Save me. Save me from Ray Fine.*

Calling Brady? *He's here. I'm telling you, it's him, and he's here.*

Calling them to save him would only bring the knowledge of his own role, and his own eventual destruction.

There is a few minutes' exchange of platitudes—Sam's heart pounding fiercely, his legs wobbly, his mouth dry, the words passing between them distant, barely heard or processed by Sam. Until Ray says—like a neighbor just dropping by before continuing on his errands—"Well, nice to see you Sam. And real nice to meet you, Tommy."

Preparing a polite exit. Disappearing as suddenly as he appeared.

As if to give Sam a sporting chance. As if to level the playing field—or, at least, to pretend to himself that he's leveling it. The true effect, of course, is to maximize Sam's terror.

Ray Fine's easy salesman smile. His cheerful departure, which Ray makes sure to execute in Tommy's presence, Sam notices. "See you soon, Sam. See you soon."

Sheriff Wyatt, help me. Agent Brady, save me.

It is an evanescent fantasy, anyway. Cell phones don't work out here.

Sam knew anyway, as soon as he saw Ray's smiling face in the door, that the landline—primitive, exposed—had already been cut.

53

Sam sees it clear as night, clean as rain, sharp as a pin.

The thought falls onto him as inescapable, factual—spreads evenly across him, without sentiment, without affect, adamantine and inarguable, as if etched in granite, with no connotation attached beyond its absolute meaning:

He is going to die.

And its corollary, its slight expansion—its absolute, unsentimental, mute cousin—is seated immovably next to it, its accompanying pillar:

He deserves to die.

This is the form that justice will assume in his special case. A justice no one will know but him. (And probably he won't know it either, he assumes. Probably so swift he will never be aware of it. So no one will. Only the earth beneath him. Only the stars above him. And Ray.)

Inadvertent justice, of course. Because it is utterly accidental and coincidental that he is the focus of a madman's fascination, a madman's ego and rage. He has had the misfortune to make his way into the orbit of the madman's insane system, where justice—biblical justice—will ensue. An eye for an eye. A life for a life.

And the madman? Why will he live? Maybe that is a justice, too. To live mad is a punishment as well. Although to live mad believing one is a king, a hero, a conqueror—is that justice, too?

He should be terrified, he knows. He should feel only terror, yet he finds a part of him—an awakened, ignited, red-burning part of him originating deep down—is looking forward to whatever is coming. Is excited by it. It is the thrill, the addictive thrill of the illicit. It is a cocktail of guilt, excitement, power, rebellion, retribution, independence, lawlessness—a potion that for whatever reason unleashes exhilaration, sends it coursing through his body, through his senses. It is unpredictably powerful, a power, a sway, no one could prepare for.

He is shocked to feel it, and yet the intensity of it—the strange *pleasure* of it—is undeniable. He wants it. Whether it is some measure of guilt—wanting Ray to inflict justice, however inadvertently—or wanting simply to survive, or wanting simply, rawly, to triumph, to prove himself and prove Ray wrong and win the perverted black game—well, that is a cocktail whose ingredients he can't separate from one another, can't taste distinctly. All he knows is that in some way he welcomes this. Not merely as resolution. No, as something more.

He is surprised to notice—as he begins to think the moves through, work out his playbook—that he wishes the boy were not with him. The boy complicates things, makes Sam more vulnerable. He wishes Tommy weren't here. He doesn't mean moving Tommy to a safer place. He means wishing Tommy simply weren't in the picture.

Sam has changed. Changed radically enough that they don't even qualify as personal changes, which implies subtle shifts and progressions, but as something entirely new. A new person looking out.

Sam feels it coming. Feels its force of inevitability.

He feels it coming, because he knows Ray now. Because he is a little of Ray now. More than a little. He shares something with

Ray, after all, that few in the world will ever share. They are both killers. More than that, both are killers at large. Both free, at the moment, to kill again.

It puts him closer to Ray. Close enough to sense him. Close enough even to predict him.

He is ready.

He can't tell if his next thought comes out of his craziness or is a final vestige of his sanity.

He can't tell if it arises from the worst part of him or the best.

The thought reflects the omnipotence that he has discovered, in his interviews, that killers seem to share. The only thing they seem to share. This growing, kingly, amoral, contra-civil world regard.

He knows it is omnipotence, but he is not free to change or correct the feeling in himself:

He is going to die.

But he fully intends to survive.

54

Wyatt was kept in a separate holding cell. A county sheriff wouldn't last ten minutes with the burglars and thugs and punks and junkies thrown together in the communal lockup, awaiting their preliminary hearings. Such a prize would be too much to resist, no matter how fairly he might have treated several of them in the past, no matter what decency he may have shown them. Such a display of fairness and decency might, in fact, make them even angrier. They resented mercy in any form—took it for softness.

Brady would probably have liked to put him in lockup with the others, but he couldn't get away with that. And Brady could cobble together pretexts to hold Wyatt for a day or two, could make enough political noise and put up enough bluster and fuss and outrage at the attack on his men, but he would have to release Wyatt eventually. A day or two. Brady knew that, and he knew that Wyatt knew that. The question was what could two days bring? Two days. The clock was ticking.

The truth was, Wyatt welcomed the isolation. A chance to reflect. To reexamine. A chance to hide.

After the chaos of the last weeks, the stillness, the changeless-
ness, was welcome—and eerie.

He had been at the center of a maelstrom, and he was suddenly at the center of a pause—yesterday's newspaper, sitting in
the dark.

He had failed in the klieg glare of the lights. He was glad to be
out of the glare, here in the shadows.

He felt a kind of resignation grow over his fury, taking hold
hour by hour.

He felt himself beginning to accept it: Brady—with his broad
experience, his bureaucratic maneuvering, his toughness, his political astuteness—had won out.

He felt himself beginning to accept it: Big Billy Wyatt was
done with it. Done with it, and done.

He was taking his breakfast alone when the guard—humorless,
sullen, rotated frequently—informed him curtly, "Visitor."

An elegantly attired African-American man approached the cell.
The man had the formal posture and purposeful stride and air of a
professional attending to some business matter, so Wyatt assumed
this was a lawyer somehow involved with the sniper case—a lawyer
whose name he must have seen but had never put a face to. The silk
muffler, the tailored overcoat, the spit-shined charcoal wingtips.
The man wore his own apparent success, and wore it well.

"Do you know who I am?" the man said authoritatively, confirming Wyatt's take on him.

"Afraid I don't," Wyatt answered honestly.

Wyatt expected from a man dressed like this, a snort of repug-
nance, of incredulity, at this lack of regard, especially amid these
demeaning surroundings.

But instead, the man only smiled gently, with acceptance;
even, it seemed, with instant forgiveness.

"I tried to get together with you when you were leading the investigation. Couldn't get near you. Now, of course, it's much easier to get some time with you." More gently, he tried again. "Do you know who I am?"

Wyatt shook his head.

"Care to venture a guess?" Said like a schoolteacher coaxing an answer out of a pupil.

Wyatt shook his head.

"I'm number one," said the man, smiling gently—without irony, apparently.

Number one. An oblique if not crazy response. Wyatt was glad the bars were between them.

"Nice to meet you, Number One." Adding, drenched with irony, "I'm no longer number one, as you can probably see."

The African-American man looked at Wyatt silently, as if waiting calmly for Wyatt to understand.

And sure enough, in a moment, Wyatt did.

"You're Mr. Lahan," said Wyatt.

"Yes, that's right. Amos Lahan."

Elinor Lahan. When it had been one murder. Standard tragedy. Proportional sorrow. When it had been a county killing. A murder to be solved. Procedures to begin. Before the deluge.

"Jesus, I'm sorry." *Sorry about not understanding. Sorry about your loss. Sorry about being a fool. Sorry about letting you down. Sorry about being in here. Sorry about everything.*

"That's all right," said Amos Lahan. "You didn't do it."

"That's right," said Wyatt glumly. "I didn't do it."

Didn't solve it. Didn't do it at all.

A moment passed while they looked at each other.

"Must be plenty strange being inside here," said Lahan gently.

Wyatt smiled acknowledgment. Yes. Plenty strange.

"I'm sure you shouldn't be," said Lahan confidently.

"What makes you so sure?"

" 'Cause I've watched you for weeks. I feel like I know you."

Well-dressed, thinks Wyatt. Elegantly spoken. Yet look what he believes.

"With all due respect, sir, that's television you're watching. News conferences," said Wyatt.

"I know it's television. I know it's news conferences. I thoroughly understand how staged each event is. Nevertheless, I still see you. We all do." He smiles.

Wyatt's patience is tried—split between sympathy for this man and his loss, and exasperation. He doesn't have to entertain every visitor, after all. That's a redeeming feature of incarceration—you can be left alone—and he wasn't about to give that up. "What are you doing here, Mr. Lahan?" he asks curtly.

"I wanted you to see me," said Lahan. "We all see you. But you never see us."

Wyatt was silent. They looked at each other. What Lahan said was true. And there was something that shifted and plunged in Wyatt, caused a pinching in his core, in seeing Amos Lahan. A plunging, a pinching so unsettling Wyatt tried consciously to resist it.

"But that's not the main reason I'm here," said Amos Lahan. "I'm here for a more pressing reason, as an emissary for the other families."

Wyatt could see that. The well-dressed, elegantly spoken Lahan. The perfect, obvious choice for emissary. A spokesman. Of course. They were organized. Getting their lawsuits ready. Interviewing their legal teams. They'd have Wyatt back in jail in no time. They'd have the county on its knees.

"Go ahead. What is that more pressing reason?"

"We want you to solve it."

Wyatt could only smile. "How the hell do you expect me to do that from here?"

"You're a decent man. A good man. Obviously, you won't be in here for very long," said Amos Lahan. "And this other man, Brady, he's not going to solve it."

"What, you can see that by looking at him on TV, too?"

Lahan regarded Wyatt. "Yes. I can. You laugh, you say it snidely, but I can see it. He's not interested in solving it. He's doing other things. Which leaves only you. But you *are* going to solve it. Personally speaking, I know it. I feel it so confidently, I didn't even think that I needed to come down here and plead, but the other families insisted. We considered coming down here individually, one after another. A constant parade of sorrow and grief, since you are now a captive audience. They wanted to pummel your heart." A quick wry smile. "But I assured them your heart was already pummeled. So we agreed to just my visit. Just this one. To let you know we're still counting on you."

You're all crazy, Wyatt felt. Your loss has made you crazy.

"And are you visiting Brady, too? Telling him you're counting on him?" Wyatt said cynically. It didn't cost the families anything to do that. It upped the ante, kept the pressure on. He'd seen it before—the families found themselves not just at the center of events for the first time in their lives, but suddenly with power, clout, a voice, suddenly a force with consequence. A voice to be respected, answered, coddled. A voting block.

"Of course we did," said Lahan cheerfully. "But that is only lip service, believe me. You're the one who will solve it."

Lahan suddenly pulled his trench coat tight, buttoned it against the ancient jail's cold. "I don't want to take undue advantage of your captive status," he said. "I only wanted to fulfill my promise and my role as promised to the other families. So I'll leave you alone. I know we'll visit again under much better circumstances."

"When I'm out of here."

"No, no—when you solve it."

"Oh, yes, when I solve it."

"You will. I'd even bet you, but it's against my faith," Lahan smiled.

Ah, a Muslim. This elegantly dressed, elegantly spoken, moderate, Americanized Muslim. A man who immediately projected forthrightness and honor and civility, even from within these fetid bowels of the criminal justice system, and certainly on the outside. A doctor? Lawyer? Clergyman?

"What do you do, Mr. Lahan?" Wyatt asked.

Lahan smiled, understanding the question, but answering otherwise. "Whatever I have to, Sheriff Wyatt. Whatever I should. Just as you always have, Sheriff Wyatt." He bowed slightly, turned, and strode off, regal and self-contained.

Wyatt lay on his cot, thinking about the families—just as Lahan and his families fully intended, he knew. Lahan didn't insult him by cataloging, by specifying, the woes, the pain, the suffering of each. He seemed to sense that he didn't have to.

That proud, precise little dandy. Damn him.

He was making it stay alive as ever in Wyatt.

Even here, as deep into this dim and ancient fortress of a jail as you could go, Wyatt lay staring into the fire of his imagination, looking futilely into it for shapes, for clues.

55

Ray Fine draws a map of Sam's cabin.

He draws each side and each elevation, sketching in, most specifically, the doors and windows. He is able to map the location of each room inside thanks to his quick glances into them.

He draws a map of the yard. Draws in the protective tree line that stands fifty to seventy-five yards from the cabin on all four sides. Even sketches in several of the trees that are strategically placed in open areas of crabgrass between the tree line and the cabin. Finally, he pencils in the sun's trajectory across the sky to note where and when it will be in the eyes of someone firing from the tree line . . . and in the eyes of someone firing from the cabin.

He is pleased to find that he remembers everything. It isn't so much that he has an extraordinary memory, although he does. It isn't even that his concentration has been focused and intense at that moment, although it is. It's that he has trained for this. This is precisely the kind of preparation they would do for missions, for night raids. This was where he excelled. It was the other stuff—the politics, the sucking-up, the snap moral judgments—where it broke down for him, where he didn't measure up.

He removes the new Kevlar vest from its package, fits it to his torso. Adjusts the straps snugly, comfortably, carefully, around his shoulders and waist. You never know—Sam Stevens might get off a lucky shot.

He opens the second package. The one he has just picked up from Mail Boxes Etc.

He draws it out slowly, carefully, welcomes it home from its aimless hobo travels. He reassembles it familiarly. Examines all the sights. Recalibrates it.

This is what he's been waiting to do, he realizes. It feels so comfortable, this preparation. It all feels so right. Not the random strikes, the lashing out of a madman, of an insane person, which any half-wit could pull off. This is what he's been trained to do—in jungles, in deserts. This is a proper enemy, with a proven record, with multiple kills of his own.

He assumes—he hopes—that Sam Stevens will mount some sort of defense, some sort of effort to elevate this above pure slaughter—to at least, at worst, a low-level game. He is giving Sam time to prepare. It won't be a complete surprise.

And if Sam can't mount a defense, well, so be it. A mission is a mission. If your enemy is ill-equipped or ill-prepared, that's not your fault.

All along, Sam has had a purpose. Ray could see that purpose, it was obvious. Ray, too, had a purpose, a purpose equal to Sam's really, but Sam couldn't see it; Sam couldn't know it. Sam must think it is only random, only crazy. Can Sam see past the craziness, see the sense of purpose in Ray? Maybe Sam has grown to sense it from Ray's behavior. Maybe Sam has begun to sense it even from his own behavior. Ray hoped so. He desperately wants Sam to know, to understand, that he is dealing with a person of purpose. He wants Sam to really understand that—before Sam dies.

But deciding once and for all who is superior, who will reign, who will collect the credit, collect the chips—that can be seen as purpose, too. That's what Sam will see. That's what anyone will see.

We make our own bed, Ray thinks.

Isn't that right, Joe?

56

Thirty years in law enforcement, and you think you've seen and heard it all.

But then the big case comes along, the once-in-a-lifetime case, and you realize how much you haven't seen, how much you don't know. How much of the world is shimmering just beyond your comprehension, perpetually twinkling, perpetually stunning, forever out of reach. You think you've learned something—that as a result of being at the crucible of hopes dashed and chances taken, of standing next to the cauldron of dreams and passions and seeing your fellow man at his worst and best, you've learned something, that you have something to offer—but it turns out you've learned nothing. Nothing of how the world works.

He had seen it on the floor of the cell, in the corner, an hour after Lahan had left. His body pulsed with the shock, but alongside that pulse, that jolt, his police mind processed it immediately. His visitor: Amos Lahan. His elegant visitor had slid it in gently, slickly, beneath the toe of his elegant wingtip, without saying a word, cautiously assuming they were being observed. His elegant visitor obviously knew someone, persuaded someone—someone sympathetic to the cause, someone who knew Wyatt, someone who knew justice. Or he'd made the necessary payments with funds from the families. Or maybe whoever it was hadn't needed much persuading—maybe hated Brady's arrogance, the FBI's grand insolence, making the whole department look inept, insulting them in front of a national audience, and could any worse insult really arise from what was about to happen? Maybe someone right here, who would simply look down, turn away, at the appropriate moment.

Or maybe someone who thought he could have it both ways—give him the key, knowing Wyatt would only be seized again shortly afterward.

The renovation plans included cell doors and locks controlled by computer codes. Some were reassured by that; for others it spelled less security—hackers, software, more to go wrong. But for now, it was the previous generation of technology. Almost quaint. Keys with an embedded magnetic stripe. Secure, actually. Except if someone handed one to a prisoner.

He saw it on the floor of his holding cell and knew immediately, and while he couldn't quite believe it, he didn't doubt it either.

He remembers those elegant wingtips.

"What do you do, Mr. Lahan?"

"Whatever I have to."

Thirty years of crime and motive and the drama of his fellow man observed close up, and he still doesn't know anything. He is surrounded by forces, factions, longstanding relationships, unstated agreements, debts owed and debts paid, and he understands nothing of them.

The world is mysterious. Everything is unknown.

Except for this:

He has a key.

57

In the cabin's bedroom, with the door shut, Sam examines the rifle. Looks through its site, aims at the bathroom doorknob, catching the foreshortened reflection in the doorknob's exaggerated, distorted version of the gun and himself.

Is it his gun? Is it Ray's? He doesn't actually know. He'll never know.

He attempts to hold the weapon steady as he aims it. The rifle shakes, shivers as he tries. Maybe it is simply too heavy. Maybe he is too tired this late. Maybe guilt and nerves, as much as exhaustion, can shake and shudder the weapon like that.

He goes over a checklist in his mind. Doors. Windows. He has already done what he can.

He debates it one more time. Getting to a neighbor's phone, calling Brady in. Revealing it all. Letting him know everything. But that is a capitulation to life in prison at best, a life filled with puzzled, hateful, baleful stares, a life of monthly visits from his son, a lifetime of ceaseless shame and humiliation for the boy he loves.

Sam realizes that if Brady isn't here already, then for whatever reason, Brady isn't watching, and Brady isn't coming.

Now Sam must make the final step in his preparations. The one he has dreaded, that he has resisted and avoided up to now.

He opens the bedroom door.

"Tommy?"

"Yeah, Dad."

"Can you come here? I need to talk to you."

Tommy, sweet Tommy, appears obediently at his father's bedroom door.

He looks at the gun. He has never seen a real gun, in fact, and this one is held by his father.

Sam looks at his sweet, perfect boy, tells him only what he needs to know, gives him his instructions in a tone that makes it obvious to Tommy that they're the most important instructions in his ten years of life.

As he does so, he looks at his boy's face. He is, he realizes, memorizing it. Taking it in, he knows, in a way he never has before; knowing he may not have the chance for such memorization again. Its smooth contours, its pliant skin, at the edge of adolescence, before the onslaught of manhood, before the abusing, scarring furrows and marks of adult life and responsibility carve their way into its smoothness. Sam experiences, in the midst of his close, clinical examination of his son's unlined cheeks and brow, a sudden, unexpected rush of feeling, loose and ill-defined. Humanness, he'd have to call it, connection . . . washing over him now; lurking there all the time.

He is filled with the weight of the task at hand, and of its limited outcomes. Yet at the same time, he is buoyed by an absurd sense of lightness—and limitlessness—as he regards his son.

He converses silently, briefly, offhand, with a force he particularly doubts at this moment, but helplessly addresses nonetheless. . . .

Forgive me, Lord. Forgive me, Tommy. Forgive me.

58

The first shot punctures the cabin's picture window and whizzes between them as they sit having breakfast. An unidentifiable disturbance, unseen but felt, until it splinters into the Sheetrock across the room.

The abruptness of it. That's all Sam can think. The dazzling abruptness of it . . .

A warning shot—just as Sam had predicted. Intended to be understood as a shot that could kill, but chose for the moment not to.

Proof of Sam's interpretation of it comes a moment later. "Good morning," called out with mock cheer from across the yard, once Sam and Tommy have gone prone to the floor, pulses pounding, Sam willing to offer his life to cancel—to take back—the moment.

Sam doesn't look at his son. He doesn't dare to. He doesn't dare risk seeing the boy's stunned paralyzed expression. His abject fear.

"Stay down, Tommy. Just like we talked about."

This is exactly the start Sam had anticipated. That is good. Maybe his other insights, his other judgments, will be as prescient, as useful, as keen.

He swallows hard. He calms himself for a moment, steadies

himself a degree. He manages to bring up enough saliva into his mouth to say it.

"Good morning, Ray," he calls out, returning the greeting. "Nice day, if it don't rain." To wrest back the verbal lead, the verbal advantage. To imply that he is ready.

He does his best to focus, to ignore his terror. To simply begin to execute the plan.

"I'm not going to shoot you, Ray," he calls out to Ray Fine.

I'm not going to give you the satisfaction.

I'm not going to play a game with you.

I'm not going to be a more engaging victim. I'm going to be the same as any other. No more satisfying, no more interesting, than that.

You'll have to take me in cold blood.

Is that what you want?

"I'm not going to shoot." Sam calls it out again across the yard. It sounds like a taunt, he notices, his words hanging there above the scrub in the still air.

Surrender, as a taunt.

A unique defense. But then, a unique situation.

Maybe it wouldn't matter to Ray Fine. Maybe Ray would kill him anyway.

Maybe Ray would never take him at his word. Ray would question, certainly, whether Sam can abandon the defense of his own boy like that, even if he can abandon the defense of himself. Sam questions that, too—when the time came, could he really abandon trying to defend his child? Could a father do that? Yet look what this father has done so far.

A second shot whirrs through the broken glass. Lands against the far wall, precisely where the first one did. That was the point, Sam knew. To demonstrate the accuracy. To taunt with it. To convey that it was just a matter of time. Hours. Minutes. Whatever Ray chooses.

59

L ying on his cot, Wyatt found he could name each victim in order, could picture each easily, knew their ages and occupations
and addresses. It wasn't such an extraordinary feat of memory,
after all. He had been intensely occupied by each of them, individually, for days at a time. Still, it was remarkable to realize how,
amid all the tumult and distraction and pressure of these weeks,
he had such full, supple, ample recall of all this information. He
realized that he was probably the only one with this ability, with
this command. The individual families were wrapped in their individual griefs, the clerks and other police and bureaucrats assigned to the case could probably produce all the information
readily from their briefcases, but probably only he, Wyatt, could
summon them all from memory. He was like a tribal elder, a sage
charged with keeping the tribe's collective memory, who passes it
on in the oral tradition.

Elinor Lahan. Eddy Jefferson. Lorna Macomber. Stanislaw
Zinski. Niles James.

Sheryl Behar. Adam Katz. Estelle Saunders. Damien Agnew.
Denise Stevens. Arlene Simmons. Arthur Stanley.

Wyatt lay there in the dark, drifting uneasily, fitfully, in and out of sleep, dreaming of the victims—sometimes in fragments, sometimes in elaborate plots. Sometimes in awesome, heroic glory, in triumphal settings, sometimes in mute, abject, discordant corners. Elaborate dreams that wove around a lifetime, that upon waking, he had knew had lasted only moments. He awoke in a sweat, fell back asleep still sweating, feverish, tossing, but a fever fed only by memory, and not sickness. Not a literal sickness, anyway.

In the supernal clarity of predawn, he stated the fact to himself—not aloud, although the thought had a permanence that could have been said aloud: *It will never leave me alone.*

It is the quietest time. It is the moment he has waited for.

He turns the key carefully in the lock. Waits a moment to make sure there is no stirring from close by, no response from further away. He pushes open the door—like a prim garden gate to a waiting path—and strides out through the cooperating darkness, floating through a world of troubled sleep. Unnoticed. Unremarked upon. A ghost. A wraith. A half presence. The thick, low stone arches and squat, massive support columns of the subterranean, barely lit, Civil War vintage structure, provide folds of shadow as he moves through it. Moving through the past . . . through history . . . a man out of place, a man out of time . . .

Still in his street clothes, fortunately, he walks out into the hall of the ancient prison, past the hired night guards. He pushes open the institutional door at the end of the hall, steps out into the dawn. It doesn't require even a nod, an exchanged look. Nothing.

It is a world of phantoms, after all. Where a phantom, a ghost, has methodically reduced the local populace one at a time.

It is a world of strangeness, after all. Where the sheriff is held behind bars. Where a key appears on his cell's floor.

Wyatt makes his way briskly down a couple of side streets, until finally he finds what he was looking for—a nondescript older sedan parked illegally overnight, a vehicle that dates from before car alarms, a car that Wyatt still understands. He bunches up his shirt in front of his fist, punches in the side window to reach the inside lock, yanks the door open, reaches beneath the steering column to hot-wire it.

He creeps out into the quiet street.

He is soon on the highway, headed into the countryside.

He prays he is not too late.

60

What follows the first two shots is silence. The tense, active silence of a fully inhabited terror. Sam is inside the terror. Functioning inside its sheer unbreachable walls, because he has no choice; he has to.

He knows the shots came from a couple of hundred yards away—not by the shots themselves, but by the taunting call of the "good morning" that follows it. He knows that the accuracy of those two shots from that far off—the distance made clear by Ray's "good morning"—is meant to inspire fear in him. What fun is it for Ray if Sam isn't fearful? But it gives him a gauge of time, at least, while Ray is—for the moment, anyway—farther out on the perimeter.

Wordlessly, obediently, wide-eyed with fear, Tommy goes low, prone, crawls to the doubly shielded spot behind the kitchen counter, just as they rehearsed. Sam scurries to the stairs that lead to the crawlspace under the cabin, and, staying low, crabs down the stairs into the low dirt-floored crawlspace, making his way, crouched, over to the narrow venting window.

He doesn't want to get caught down here, but it's a safer place to look out and assess from.

The window shatters in front of him, splinters shockingly, glitteringly, wildly, as he approaches it.

Sam gasps. Sucks in his breath. Feels his heart pound.

He knows Ray couldn't physically see him. It's just a guess on Ray's part. An educated, trained guess at what Sam's next step will be. Meant as a further point of proof to Sam, he is sure, that he is out-thought. Outclassed. Breathing his last breaths.

The first shots were introductory. This shot is mockery. Only Ray could coax different moods from bullets.

Ray is letting him live. Closing in. Maximizing the pain. Maximizing the game.

He'd have to be less predictable.

"I'm not going to shoot," Sam calls out again. "I'm not going to give you the satisfaction."

He reaches into his pocket. He begins to toss rifle shells out the shattered window, one by one, to prove it.

61

Ray moves through the morning's bright silence toward the cabin, taking a tree trunk for cover along his way, tucking his elbows expertly, keeping his posture aligned, turning his head to minimize exposure and risk in a way that is instinctive for him. It is as familiar as sport for him; it is deep in his muscle memory, requires no thought, no cogitation. It is taking a Laotian supply hut, a Serbian outbuilding, a Colombian hideout, a warlord's hut in Somalia. It is automatic.

Saying you won't shoot is one thing. Not tossing your gun out is another. *Come on, Sam. I wasn't born yesterday.*

In a moment, Ray is examining the front porch a few critical yards ahead of him.

62

e is prepared. He is surprised, beneath the panic, to feel the sense of preparation in him. He is prepared for anything.

He is unprepared.

It is his primal, recurring nightmare from childhood. Wholly conventional. The stuff of millions of anxious dreams. An intruder entering the house. The footsteps across the kitchen floor. The telltale groaning of the stairs. The faceless intruder putting a gun to his parents' heads, and once he has pulled the trigger, finding the child, putting the still-warm steel barrel to the back of Sam's skull. That primal nightmare is more terrifying by its utter familiarity, by its previously summoned detail, by the intimacy of a thousand previous occurrences in Sam's childhood imagination, as it now comes real.

What stops anyone from coming in? Not locks. Not doors. They can always get past those. What stops them? Civilization. Laws. Conventions. Agreements they haven't agreed to. What's to stop the evil from ignoring those agreements? Nothing.

"I'm not going to shoot," Sam calls out again.

He waits. He waits for Ray Fine.

63

Ray thought it through carefully the night before. The windows are too high off the ground. The bulkhead door is too loud and too heavy and maybe too rusty even to open. Given the floor plan inside the little cabin, given prospective defensive positions available to Sam, the most viable entrance to the cabin is, counterintuitively, through the front door, Ray knows.

Ray runs crouched toward the front of the cabin and leaps up the front steps and onto the porch.

The wooden porch falls away under him, and he knows what Sam has done even before he hits the ground. Knows exactly how all the nails were pulled silently, steadfastly, all night long—only a couple left to support the porch until the first bit of weight was put on it.

Ray lands on his back, and the pain is immediate and fierce, but his eyes are open and alert, and in a moment, he is reaching for his gun, grasping for it where he let it go in the fall.

Pain. Invigoration. Exhilaration. See, Sam? It is a game.

64

S am hears the porch fall away with a crack and thud. He clicks off the Tango's safety, throws open the front door, drops to one knee on his home's threshold, aims down at Ray sprawled below him, and doesn't pull the trigger.

Can't.

Won't.

He will never know which of those it is.

Whatever it is that permitted him to squeeze the trigger with Denise in the sights is preventing him from squeezing it now.

He is as surprised by his not pulling the trigger as he was surprised by his first pull of it before. As surprised as ever at that sixteenth of an inch—navigated, then unnavigable. That sixteenth of an inch whose mechanical tension so aptly echoes the psychological. That sixteenth of an inch that completes a circuit—the physical analogue of a synapse firing. The circuit completed, or left incomplete.

He had crossed over some line. And has now—unpredictably, inopportunely—crossed back.

It is self-destructive. A death wish. To murder your wife and invite justice and retribution, to murder again to protect yourself, to give yourself time, and then not to murder the person who has promised to kill you.

Or, a life wish. So desperate to free yourself to life that you will kill your spouse. So desperate to free yourself from the imprisonment of killings that you will not, in the end, murder a murderer.

The thoughts will explode in him, beat at him mercilessly . . . but not now. Now, Ray Fine is in the crosshairs—his eyes wide, alert, staring at the Tango 51, reaching desperately for his own gun.

As Ray gets hold of his own weapon, Sam pulls back inside, slams the door, crouches—automatic, self-preservatory, stunned.

It is all a matter of three, four seconds. Laid out across the psychologies of a lifetime.

"God!" Sam cries out at his foolishness, his desperation, his indecision.

A shot pounds into the front door with a thud.

The next shot comes through it with a splintering sound.

I've got my weapon back, the shot says.

Your moment of mercy means nothing, the shot says.

I'm coming in, the shot says.

Ray's bullets are speaking once again.

"Dad?" the voice calls out, desperate, from behind a door down the hall—tentative, crying.

"You stay there!" Sam screams fiercely, animal, furious. Though he knows his son is only checking to see if his father is alive.

One more shot pounds the front door.

"I won't shoot you. I won't do it," Sam yells out.

And now, it appears, he really won't.

He pulls back into his own bedroom.

He pulls back into his childhood.

It is in the bedroom, after all, where his childhood nightmare of attack took place. The fantasy was always at night. This is bright morning—as if only to let him see it, as if only to show him it is no dream.

Inside the Mind of a Serial Killer.

Last in a Series.

The Final Episode.

65

If Sam had fired from such close range, Ray probably would have been hit.

But probably wouldn't have been seriously hurt.

Ray is wearing the vest under an untucked work shirt. He doubts Sam would have noticed that in the moment.

Sam didn't fire. Loss of nerve. The stunned moment of combat. Ray knows better than Sam does that it was likely only a momentary failure—a reaction to the power and charge of the moment—that wouldn't necessarily be repeated. A classic battlefield occurrence. Sam is undoubtedly beating himself up about it, but it doesn't mean it would happen again.

Ray fires again at the door, leaps out of the wreckage of the fallen porch, and only a second later is crouched felinely at a window, surveying the entry hall, clearing the area, advancing, relentlessly advancing.

The rusty brown car is a crummy little thing. The alignment is off. The steering wheel vibrates. The whole vehicle shimmies. The transmission moans and protests between gears. Wyatt doubts the car has been taken onto the highway in years. But the interstate traffic heading out into the country isn't very heavy at this time of the morning, and Wyatt can't risk going too fast anyway. He's afraid to pull into the passing lane. With his missing vent window, he's afraid to invite any attention at all.

Brady will undoubtedly send agents directly to the cabin when Wyatt is discovered missing. But even if they use a chopper, Wyatt figures he has the head start he needs.

He is afraid to turn on the car radio. Afraid of the alarming report he might soon hear. About a former county sheriff escaping from a holding cell.

He needs to hurry to beat Brady. To search the cabin.

He is sure this time he'll find what he's looking for.

What he's looking for—and more.

He's a fugitive. A fugitive from justice? No, a fugitive from a lost world of justice, trying to restore, retain, some little bit of it. While he still has a chance.

And if Sam Stevens is there? Sam Stevens, holding the television-demo Tango 51 that Wyatt is certain was never returned to the gun shop? Wyatt is unarmed. He'll just have to deal with that when he gets there.

He is sure it's there somewhere.

He hopes it is there, of course. Evidence.

And he fears that it is, as well.

66

It all comes down to this, thinks Sam, sitting on the bed, listening to the whir. Looking at the objects beside him one last time.
It all comes down to this.

Ray Fine stands crouched in the hallway of the crummy little cabin—unopposed, unchallenged, supreme, shattered glass and wood splinters at his feet—regarding the closed doors, listening, weighing the silence.

The doors are closed, but they nevertheless pose an invitation to him. It is on its way to being his house. If it were Somalia, Nigeria, Uganda, he would soon be able to radio *target secure*. If there was a radio. If there was a team to radio.

He looks for any shadows in the telltale strip of daylight between the floor and the bottoms of the doors. He listens for any creaking beyond the doors. It is all instinctive, all automatic. The kinds of actions he will become aware of only hours later, in retrospect, when it returns to him as memory—savory, pure, his.

His silent, expert attentiveness proves unnecessary.

"I'm not going to shoot you." Sam's by now familiar refrain comes from behind the door on the right. One of the two bedrooms, Ray knows. "I'm not going to shoot you."

It is plaintive, pained—short of pleading but not much short of it—and though it is muffled by the door, it is coming, Ray can tell, from just inside it.

He knows what the repeated phrase is meant to do. It is meant to drill the prospect, the possibility into him, that Sam actually won't. It is meant to relax him. To challenge him with it. To perplex him. Its repetition is meant to lull him. A lullaby. To close his eyes to reason. To melt into its promise. It is, Ray must admit, a somewhat more fascinating refrain now that Sam has aimed the rifle at him at the front door but failed to pull the trigger. Is it proof that he isn't going to shoot? Or proof that he is?

But Ray knows better than to trust it either way. Ray knows that the phrase has no meaning—except, of course, for the meaning of revealing where Sam Stevens is. In the bedroom on the right with the door closed.

"I'm not going to shoot you, Ray," says Sam from behind the door. "I'm telling you, I won't do it. I won't give you the satisfaction of my attempt."

The same theme. The same unvarying message. But the panic is rising in Sam's voice. Ray hears it, muffled by the door, but plain as morning, unstopped, undisguised by it. Panic, undisguisable.

"I won't do it Ray. I won't."

Then throw your gun out, Ray wants to say. But if he throws his gun out, then he is unarmed, like any of the other victims—no different—and what good is that? How would that look?

"I'm not going to shoot. I'm just not. I haven't, you notice, and I've had opportunities here. But I haven't because I won't."

Ray smiles. It's getting on his nerves. Just as Sam intends.

"I'm not going to shoot," says Sam again from behind the door. "I'm done with it. It's over for me. You win. Uncle. I'm not going to shoot."

But how do I know that, Sam?
Here's how I know.

Ray Fine fires into the middle of the door. The bullet punctures the thin wood easily.

What follows is everything he expects, everything familiar to him from the dark years and dark corners of his existence. For him it is the beat of second nature, of muscle memory, and still fills him with an emotion hard to quantify—a formal though intimate sense of regret combined with the primal joy of the kill.

The dull thump against the floor on the other side of the door.

The strip of daylight observed beneath the door, now blocked, filled in.

And the silence. The familiar, sad, exhilarating silence.

His weapon still poised and cocked, Ray steps closer carefully. There is no sound, no motion.

He listens for anything. Any sound.

Sam.

The boy.

Nothing.

In a moment, the blood begins to trickle, to seep under the door.

Ray straightens a little, in victory, in dark glory—his chest, his spine, fill with the victory, with the power.

He waits crouched, alert, another fifteen, twenty seconds. He weighs the quality of the ensuing silence, listens into its corners, hears nothing.

The body's dead weight is against the door.

So he forces the door open with his foot, in order to keep his gun at the ready.

Ray Fine—highly trained, alert, incisive—absorbs it all instantly. The sandbag with Sam's shirt buttoned over it. The camcorder on a tripod, its little red light still blinking. The reporter's audio recorder on the bed, a wire running from it to a stereo speaker sitting on the bed, aimed toward the door. The spilled bucket of dark liquid running across the floor.

Ray Fine manages to take it all in before the shot to his chest and vest knocks him backward off his feet, and he is staring at the cracked ceiling.

His head clears, and he knows immediately by the point and angle of impact against the vest that the shot has come from a corner with another closed door . . . a bathroom? A closet?

He is proved right. The bathroom door opens wider now. He can see a strip of Sam. The real Sam. The live Sam.

From his knocked-over position, Ray fires. He hears Sam scream.

But it is an awkward position for Ray to fire from, and he knows from the sound of Sam's scream that he is off target. That the job isn't finished. From this position, splayed on his back, the round has gone left or right.

After all his experience, his record of perfection, he has missed.

Sam will get off the next shot. The thought penetrates Ray like a bullet.

It is an honor to die in the line of duty. . . .
And Joe will live on, undiscovered.

An assault like this. A professional like Ray. Of course, Sam realizes. A bulletproof vest.

In contrast to Ray, Sam is in position. His arm is hit, but he is functioning. The adrenaline is flowing. He fires again immediately.

With a little experience, he's learned.

With a little confidence, he's gotten better.

The shot goes through the center of Ray's face and comes to rest deep in his crazy head.

. . .

"Dad?"

The word seems to rise through amber, disembodied. A plaintive, choked syllable from another dimension. A lone syllable floating to him from some other existence.

He cannot answer his boy yet. He tries to draw the breath to, but can't yet. He has to gather it up, has to remember to breathe, to not faint or expire.

"Dad?" The plaintive fear—the fear that is on the other side of the other bedroom's door, the fear that his father is gone, and a madman now turns toward him—is what lets Sam Stevens finally speak again.

"Yes. Yes, Tommy," and the pain sears through him just to say it.

Tommy is there in the next moment, looking not at Ray, but at his father's bloody shoulder. The blood is running down Sam's side, pooling already on the bathroom floor.

Sam feels its sting and throb more intensely now, the pain starting to thrum across his body.

"Get to a neighbor's house. Dial 911. Tell them to send an ambulance," he instructs, but barely above a whisper.

Sam Stevens smiles at his son.

The next moment, feels woozy.

A moment after that, passes out.

67

The first officer on the scene is Sheriff William Wyatt.

Before the ambulance. Before the sirens. Before the other officers. Before the cameras. Before the world.

He abandons his caution in approaching when he hears the boy's crying.

He clamors, unthinking, up the broken porch steps.

He sees the man dead in the hallway. Face blown off, but he still knows, by the wiry limbs, by the white neck.

Ray Fine. Faceless in death as he had been in life. Faceless, shadowless, recordless. A man who does not exist. A phantom of modernity. A stunt of erasure.

Wyatt only has a moment to register it as he tumbles headlong toward the crying in the bathroom.

"Move away, son. Let me help him."

The blood is all over the bathroom. So much blood, Wyatt can't ascertain where the injury is. Stevens is literally white. There. His arm. Wyatt tourniquets it with a bathroom towel.

Thirty years at the crucible of human experience. He has seen this amount of blood before.

Based on his thirty years' experience, he doubts Stevens will make it.

It was speculated later that Billy Wyatt—the first officer on the scene—may very well have saved Sam Stevens's life. It was so far out in the country. It took a long time for ambulances and police to arrive. Wyatt heading out there like he was probably saved Sam's life.

Wyatt and Sam would ponder that, of course.

Sam's breathing was labored.

He was concentrating on his breathing. That was good, thought Wyatt. A good sign.

Of course, he couldn't ask Sam anything right now.

It didn't matter, really. As he held Sam's head up and did his best to calm and console Sam's son, Wyatt looked around and took in the scene.

Whatever the reality might be, it was obvious how it looked.

It was obvious how it would go down.

It was obvious how it would play.

The truth had just retreated irredeemably, Billy Wyatt knew. The truth was gone forever. Swallowed up in myth, in story, in the news at six and eleven, in the talking heads turning it inside out, in the experts' smooth comments.

The truth.

Victim number thirteen.

Add it to the list.

Never to be seen or conversed with again.

68

A man who had defended his son. Who had defended his home. Who had finally stopped the serial sniper, the one who had tricked and evaded and walked blithely away from the incompetent police and their big, foolish, incompetent sheriff.

A man who had gotten retribution, vengeance, on the vile animal who had killed his wife.

The story leaped beyond mere sensation. It was an interstellar explosion. A galactic event. The sandbag wearing Sam's shirt was shown incessantly. The gun he had used in a demonstration, covering the sniper killings, and that he happened to have, fortunately, the day it happened. The showdown Sam Stevens had prepared for, firing the gun repeatedly into a dead tree on his property, learning to shoot, obviously preparing to defend his son and his home if it should come to that. Sam's plaintive voice recording, the one he'd fooled the sniper with—"I'm not going to shoot you, Ray"—was played over and over. And of course, most of all, the videotape that Sam had run. It was too much for network broadcast, which made it even more desirable, more sought-after. The grainy, terrifying tape—all the more terrifying for being a record of both ends of the event. Of bloody offense and bloodier defense. Of Ray firing through the door. Sam cutting down the sandbag. The sandbag falling. Ray pushing open the door, taking the shot in the chest—and then the face. A snuff film rendered legitimate, rendered heroic. Ruthless aggressor who is in minutes final victim. Tables turned. Justice delivered swiftly, ideally, within the perfect time frame of a two-minute stand-up segment. *Interview with a Serial Killer. Last in a Series. The Final Episode.*

It was a victory for families. A triumph of will. A tale of survival. It was a victory for victims, for the little guy. It was a standoff in the ultimate American Western tradition, in the American grain. It was an American story. It was an international story. It was a timeless story. It was a phenomenal story. It was a frenzy of books and movies and analysis. It was poetry for a time that hungered for poetry. It immediately transmogrified, melted into myth.

That infamous numeral, of course, only gave the story further traction. Offered headline writers and television graphic artists an extra handle they hardly needed. *Victim Thirteen. Lucky Thirteen.* Letting viewers and tabloid readers ruminate infinitely on the nature of luck and fate itself. Unlucky thirteen to suffer such a brutalizing ordeal. Lucky thirteen to survive it.

Sam Stevens gave two full months over to it. Hiring a state-approved tutor for eight weeks, he was able to take Tommy with him everywhere. Tommy was part of the story, the emotional payoff, the final hook: Come on out here, Tommy, let's meet Tommy, unleashed applause, standing ovation, here's the reason I did it, here's what gave me the courage, the will, my son Tommy, my sweet boy Tommy.

Crescendo of applause. Tommy's shy wave. Hugging his dad for protection, for assurance under the lights—only bringing a fresh higher wave of applause and adulation crashing around them.

· · ·

The unpaid shipping bills, the circling weapons that gradually stopped circling—they slowly revealed themselves in shipping terminals and warehouses across the country. With a little detective work, they were all traced back to Ray Fine. Eventually, the implicated weapon would certainly turn up. It was undoubtedly part of this ingenious and perverse system.

(Local FBI confirmed it. Sheepishly admitted that reporter Sam Stevens had been to see them with suspicions too vague to act on, but instincts vindicated and proven now. The FBI never admitted to the highly credible anonymous call they'd received, the detailed and absolutely credible tip that had pulled them literally in the other direction, that they eventually realized was arranged by Ray Fine. They never had to admit it. Ray was dead.) Brady returned to Washington. In the wake of this stunning resolution, outstanding charges against Wyatt were dropped. His career was finished anyway. And he did get there to save Sam Stevens, after all. Further charges could be construed as merely political and merely harassment anyway, so Brady moved on—and up.

For the two months that Sam and Tommy made the TV newsmagazine and talk-show circuit, Billy Wyatt steadfastly ducked all interview requests—the first officer on the scene, probably saved Sam Stevens from bleeding to death, knew Sam Stevens was in trouble, had the sense something terrible might happen. Billy Wyatt knew that it was the man he leaped at in the cell—finally caught, finally finished. They'd let the man go the first time, but Billy Wyatt had been right, after all.

He'd be the story, if it weren't for Sam.

Sam Stevens, former journalist, understood just how big the story was.

Maybe too big for him ever to be discovered. Maybe too big ever to be found out. The story might have too much momentum as it was, ever to make room for the truth. It might be too big for the truth.

He might have sidestepped the truth, by escaping, disappearing, into myth. J.F.K. O.J. Princess Diana. Occasionally it happened.

He gave it two months. Two months of hotel rooms and green rooms and makeup chairs and network negotiations and agents and managers and sums deposited into a variety of accounts, and then Sam Stevens said (quietly, and only once, because now everyone listened), I'm done. I want to be with my son. I want to go on with my life.

And by and large, everyone heard him. Let him.

He let the tutor go—a pretty but serious young woman who had traveled with them, sometimes by jet, from interview to interview.

He put Tommy in a fancy private day school, experienced and specializing in protecting celebrities' kids.

With the proceeds from the sale of the cabin and the money from the book advance and the studio deal, he bought a rambling, comfortable shingle-style house, surrounded by eight acres of property, on a lake near the school. Its huge wraparound porch, only feet from the water, brought the changing seasons, the parade of colors, the lake's currents and its stiff winds and gentle breezes and the surprising daily variety of the lake's beauty, up the broad plank steps and right to them.

He furnished the house in Adirondack style. Deerskin rugs over its beautiful cherrywood floors. Simple, substantial, authentic handcarved pieces—sturdy chests, an immense harvest table. Deep couches. Stick-style chairs. A man's place. A man's taste. As far from Denise's frilly curtains and creamy pastel colors and thick-pile comfort as he could get. Her furniture was gone. Every vestige of her banished. Not a cup or plate. Not an ashtray, not a picture. It was a new start for them. Literally, symbolically, completely.

· · ·

In the evenings, on the porch, after homework, the two of them would play a game of chess.

"So let's see what tricks you're learning at that chess club of yours," Sam says with an arch smile.

And Tommy's moves are good ones—schooled and smart.

Not a word as they concentrate. The only sound is the breeze off the lake, humming gently in the porch screens, rustling around their evening ritual. As if the lake, in its vast serenity, respected the requirements of the game.

"Jeez, you're a good player, Dad," says Tommy, finally breaking the silence, surprised by his father's prowess. "You make moves I never see coming."

Sam Stevens smiles mildly at his son.

They go on.
    Their new life.
    Their old life.
    A different life in between.

69

On a sunny summer morning several months later, Sam Stevens sits high in the bleachers watching Tommy's baseball game. It is a beautiful day. Tommy is playing well.

Sam is focused on the game, so focused he is only vaguely aware of the parent who sits down next to him, until he looks up at him.

"Sheriff Wyatt," Sam says with a cordiality warmed by the bright summer morning, greeting him with his old honorific.

"Sam," says Wyatt in return, keeping his eyes on the game, as if not wanting to miss a moment of it. "How's your boy doin'?"

"Doin' great," says Sam. And then, realizing Wyatt means not the game, but generally, without his mother, Sam says, "Adjusting fine, Billy. Doing much better than anyone could have expected." A pause. "He's gonna be okay."

"Good. Good to hear," says Wyatt. "I remember him, you know, when we interviewed him. Seems like a terrific kid. Loves his dad, I'll tell you that."

After scoring a couple of runs, Tommy's team flies and grounds out, and they take the field, Tommy beaming at first base.

"Ah, first baseman," observes Wyatt with evident admiration.

"He's a pretty good fielder," says Sam.

They watch the infield toss it around before the opposing batter steps up.

"I went through Evidence," Wyatt says, as the batter pumps the bat and crouches for the pitch. "I counted the bullets. I couldn't figure it out. So I got permission to look at them under a microscope. Nothing fancy. Old-fashioned school microscope. Just like yours."

Wyatt pauses, gestures loosely out to the field, to let Sam watch his son execute a play. Grounder to third, the long throw to first base. Tommy is tall, rangy, reliable, and confident on the playing field in a way he hadn't seemed to be on all the television shows, Wyatt notices. It seems that the athleticism, the outdoors, the motion, relaxes him. "One bullet had never been fired," says Wyatt. "I double-checked the police entry log. Everything comes over directly from Autopsy. Everything in order when entered. All rounds entered at Evidence, needless to say, had definitely been fired."

He looks out at the scoreboard, squints out into the beautiful day. "Reason I went over to Evidence at all, was I'd watched that piece you did with poor Scott Bayer. You remember him. The one who killed himself two weeks later." Wyatt continues, expressionless. "When you're a reporter, everyone can see your work."

"The police could easily have entered a bullet that hadn't been fired," says Sam flatly, somewhere between disinterest and politeness. "One thing you learn as a crime reporter . . . the police make mistakes all the time."

"Oh, that's certainly true," says Wyatt. "That's why the bullet itself wasn't the most interesting thing to me there in Evidence. The bag holding the bullet was more interesting. Had your fingerprints on it. Evidence right there in Evidence," says Wyatt, cocking his head as if abstractly amused.

"If you looked at the tape of the broadcast, you saw I handled a lot of those Baggies. No wonder my prints are on it."

Wyatt nods somberly; shakes his head nearly mournfully. "And then, of course, Brady's crowd started to look at everything again. Handling everything. Contaminating everything. What a mess. You almost got lucky there, Sam."

Almost got lucky?

"Wondered if I might get a fingerprint off the unfired bullet. 'Course I knew how careful you were, 'cause I found the burned latex gloves you used, even to practice."

Sam shifts a little in his seat.

"That unfired bullet didn't even have partials on it. That's obviously someone being real careful. And DNA? Sample was too contaminated by clothing fibers from your pants pocket. Too small a sample to clean. Casing of a bent-up bullet . . . not a great host site, as I'm sure you know." Wyatt shrugs.

He continues as if newly fascinated. "Found fresh vomit on the path in the woods across from Arlene Simmons the morning she was killed. We matched it to a meal in your trash, Sam. Guess your conscience got the better of you." Wyatt looks out at the ball game again. "Spaghetti and mushroom sauce. Maybe you remember. Maybe you don't. Of course, it's a meal ten thousand other people within driving distance ate that night. DNA was inconclusive, like it often is with vomit. But I bet you know that, too.

"And the two bullets taken from the corpse of Ray Fine were a match to the one removed from the body of Denise Stevens. But also a type and caliber match to the earlier victims, given the consistent deformation and shattering of the bullets against skull. And you could come up with alibis for most of those, I'm sure."

A short fly ball is popped up in the infield. Tommy gets under it and handles it confidently. He is having a terrific game.

"So it's all circumstantial. That's what you're telling me," says Sam.

Wyatt looks out silently, his big jaw set.

"I'm a crime reporter, Sheriff. I know what you're saying. You think I killed my wife. But you're telling me that it's all circumstantial, that it can never amount to a case. So I'm a little puzzled at what you're doing out here."

Wyatt shifts his bulk on the bleacher, as if settling in. "It would take quite a story to top the one about the reporter who brought a serial sniper to justice by defending his home and his son. Now the fact that that same reporter actually killed his wife and used the serial sniper he was covering to hide the crime—well, that might just do it." Wyatt smiles and shakes his head. "But the thing is, Sam"—he looks up at the open blue sky—"that's not the half of it."

Sam Stevens remains silent, pretending to watch the game. His eyes are glazed over and fixed resolutely forward, but Wyatt knows he is listening.

"Turns out there's a good reason we could never pin a single murder on Ray Fine," says Wyatt. "Ray Fine never killed anyone."

Wyatt sees Sam blink. Blink twice, three times, but sit, immobile.

"Sure, Special Forces alum. Sure, weapons and tactics expert. He had the knowledge. He had the means. But turns out, he didn't commit a single one of those murders."

Wyatt will tell him the rest. But he takes a moment now to look at Sam.

"I know he was coming to see you, Sam. I don't know exactly what he said to you, of course, but I'm going to assume something significant in the way of threat or blackmail or intimidation, based on who he was and who you probably thought he was. When you killed Ray and the case closed and Brady went back to Washington, the charges against me were dropped, and I was back in the loop, and that's when I heard about your interaction with Ray Fine. I don't know exactly what he said to you or what exactly happened between you two. But I'll bet it comes as something of a surprise to you that Ray Fine didn't kill anyone."

"Why?" Sam says quietly, evenly, staring out. Wyatt has never heard anyone utter a syllable of such abject bafflement and confusion and incipient despair. "Why? . . ."

Why come to me, then? Why threaten me?

"Because Ray Fine was covering up for someone. Trying to clean up after somebody." He pauses.

What? Jesus! Who?

"His son," says Wyatt, offhand, looking out. "Covering up for his son."

"You've got a son. How nice for you, Sam, that you've got a son." Words in the town house darkness.

"Got a kid. Never told you that, I'll bet. Wanted you to think he was acting alone, capable of anything, that you were at the disadvantage, not him. Kid's seventeen. And ol' Special Ops Ray taught his kid everything he knows, and it was all fun and bonding and father-son gun stuff American military style out there in the Arizona desert, nothing really wrong with it, I guess, until brooding, loner Ray and the wife divorce, and it's ugly, and the mother gets custody and she moves herself and the kid east for a fresh start, even changing their last name, which takes nothing these days, a quick appointment with a judge. Well the kid's whole world has come apart, and he starts to act out with some skills and tactics that other teenagers don't have and can't even imagine. Ray taught him everything he knows, and it comes back to haunt us all. A time bomb of Ray's own making, and now it's detonating. Doesn't take Ray long to put two and two together, and he hustles east to do what he can to stop him, I'm sure, and maybe he does stop him. The kid tells us he didn't actually shoot anyone after Ray got here"—Wyatt doesn't even look at Sam for that, simply continues—"but Ray isn't about to simply turn his own son in to the police and help end his own boy's life with a death sentence from the state. He's got the skills and experience to pull off something better than that.

"And suddenly there's you, Sam Stevens. He knows his son

didn't kill your wife, Sam—either by what his son tells him or by knowing where his son was when your wife was killed—and he's been watching your pieces on TV like everyone, sees you fire the gun and handle the ammunition and talk to the serial killers, and it all just confirms it for him, he sees you and suddenly he sees a chance for his son, and a plan, and if he's smart enough about it, now there's someone to take the fall.

"I'm sure he fooled you, just like he fooled me," says Wyatt. "It didn't take much, with his record and his manner, and let's face it, Sam, he was good at it. He was a professional. Figured if he could outmaneuver Middle Eastern and South American intelligence forces and cutthroat drug lords and triple-agent renegade colonels, he could easily handle a county sheriff and the sleepy local town police.

"We both got fooled into thinking he was the sniper. I almost killed him with my bare hands for it. And you went ahead and actually did it. But it was an act, Sam. A performance. He was doing a show. A stand-up piece. You know something about that, Sam. An act. A performance. Doing a show." Wyatt smiles grimly.

"How do I know any of this? Because the kid finally turned himself in. Walked into the police station, gave himself up. Because his father had been killed. Did it all to impress his dad. To win him back. To pull his family back together in the crisis. Typical teenage plan. Did it all perfectly, too. No mistakes. No trail. His dad taught him well. Stealth, erasure, perfection—family values, I guess. The air they breathed.

"Kid's name is Joe. Joseph Fine, he says. Wants his last name back, he says. I looked again at all of the murders—time, geography—and you know what? There was a pattern, after all. A pattern we all missed. No killings between eight in the morning and three in the afternoon weekdays. You know why? The kid was at school.

"And the steel semijackets? The subtle, ingenious choice of thinner and more shatter-prone steel as opposed to copper?" Wyatt snorts, shakes his head. "Not much science there. For a seventeen-year-old kid, they were cheaper.

"He just decided to talk. That's the thing with a lot of people, isn't it Sam? You know that better than anyone. Something horrible happens to them, and people just decide to talk.

"So you see, you actually broke the case, Sam. You killed Ray Fine, and in the end, that's what brought that boy in. You broke the case." He smiles almost imperceptibly. "Thank you, Sam."

There's a fly ball. It's handled by the center fielder with a textbook catch.

"Must have been real interesting for Ray when we inadvertently picked him up after that traffic stop. He probably would have been glad to be charged with the murders, probably would have been glad to accept being blamed for them, though he probably knew we'd never have enough to convict him or even hold him very long, since he hadn't actually committed them, unless we railroaded him or fabricated evidence, which I bet he was hoping we would. But he probably thought, with his experience and training and ability, that he could do better than that. That a guy who had slid in and out of countries his whole career could outwit some backwoods county. That his kid could get away with it outright." He looks hard at Sam. "That he could get away with it. That he and his son could be together.

"And I'll tell you what, Sam. If they couldn't be together, Ray was more than ready to die for his son. To take the fall, just a Special Ops weirdo gone awry, let the reporter be a hero so his son could go free. That's what the attack on you was about, Sam. Dying like he did was probably his backup plan. That's why we couldn't catch him, I guess—because he was crazy and sane.

"A son, Sam. Maybe that's how Ray knew what a son can mean to you. Maybe that's how he knew he could get you to do what you did. Because he knew what you'd done already. He loved his son, Sam. And he was willing to do anything for him. And obviously I don't have to explain that to you.

"You're the reporter closest to it, Sam. You're the reporter who's lived it," says Wyatt, sardonically, honestly. "So I thought you should have the story." He smiles grimly. "I'm givin' you the exclusive."

Wyatt stands up now, breathes out, feels a sense of release. "What a court case it'll be. Especially with all your stand-up pieces to liven it up. All your videotape of the bullets with poor Scott Bayer in Evidence. Your interviews with Darryl Jenkins. Your videotape of Ray Fine's killing."

Wyatt nods to two men in the bleachers above them who Sam had assumed were dads from the opposing team. The two men step down toward them, and one reads Sam his rights off a pocket card while the other puts the handcuffs on him.

The ball game has stopped.

Tommy looks from first base into the bleachers along with the rest of the players to see his father led down out of them.

"We'll take care of Tommy," Wyatt offers, walking alongside Sam to an unmarked sedan. Sam nods, satisfied, as if he knows and trusts that Wyatt will.

They stand looking at one another before Sam is guided into the sedan's rear seat.

"Guess you're back on TV," says Wyatt.

"Guess you are, too," says Sam.

Big Billy Wyatt watched the unmarked sedan and the support vehicle behind it start to pull away. The detective on the passenger side lowered his window. "Sure you don't want to come in for this, Billy?" he asked Wyatt.

Billy shook his head. *Naw. You boys go ahead.*

The detective appeared a little surprised. Then shrugged and rolled up the window.

It was a new era for the Webster County Police Department—and it was time to give way to it.

Big Billy just wants to savor the victory a little by himself, they were probably saying.

Savor the victory. Sure.

He watched the sedans pull away and began to stroll away from the ball field, alone.

He would get kudos, he knew. He would be seen as some combination of brilliant, dogged, independent, determined, mythic. He would finally have his moment, just as Sam Stevens had had his.

But he knew he wasn't such a brilliant detective, after all. He figured he was a mediocre detective, at best.

And when he said to Sam Stevens there in the bleachers, *the thing is, Sam, that's not the half of it*—well, it surely wasn't.

He wondered, in fact, if he had been able to follow the case through, to solve it in the end, to imagine and accept its startling and unpredictable turns, because of the turn—the brutal, mirror turn—that he had experienced himself. Because he now knew personally, powerfully, irremediably, how anything—anything—was possible.

He had met her there on the barstools at Dominique's—that crowded, dimly lit adult pickup joint of seething sex and craved connection. No one in an adult pickup bar knows what their local sheriff looks like, of course. He was completely anonymous then. Before the murders. Before the spotlight. Before the bedlam. Before the glare.

But she knew him. Two barstools down. "You're Billy Wyatt, aren't you?" And in response to his look—*how could you possibly know that?*—that slinky smile of hers. "My husband admires you." A coy pause. "Says you're a man's man." That slinking, urchin smile already challenging him with the implications beneath the words: *But are you really? Aren't you corruptible? Aren't we going to corrupt each other? Can't you tell already?*

"Who's your husband?"

"Sam Stevens. The reporter."

"Sure. Sam Stevens." And smiling back at her by now. *Because if you're in here on a barstool, obviously the Stevens marriage isn't so great.*

And obviously mine isn't, either.

"Big Billy Wyatt," she says, her voice full of flirtatious implication.

He can only smile.

"I'm Denise," she says.

And Billy Wyatt knew—within moments of feeling her kisses course through him (a sweet warmth down his spine, over his thighs, into his loins), within moments of being inside her (feeling her desperate, clawing abandon, her dark pleasure beneath him and then astride him), knew what he had forever mildly suspected (yes, the mediocre detective)—that he had not been alive before. That despite his connection to family, friends, community, despite his dutiful but genuine care for his sweet wife, Margie, his had been a half-life. He had been a groomsman, an attendant—in a continual state of waiting, unbeknownst to himself. Whatever would now follow, he knew, his life would divide forever at the hard and telling angle of these moments. There would always be before and after, from here on in. (That naked hunger. That naked affection. Moving, writhing, struggling with her bliss beneath him, and eventually, the smile. That wry, challenging smile different now, peaceful. In truth, two smiles of matched understanding; of renewed surprise at life, that two people, two histories so different, could connect like this, could share this.) She had brought back his best self, his buried self—athletic, youthful, optimistic, the star pitcher in command from the mound—brought it coursing back through him as powerfully as her kiss.

They would meet at her town house in the morning. A couple of times, lying there afterward in bed, they'd had a drink, smoked together, she'd puffed playfully on his cigar—like college kids, momentarily immortal, as if only happiness were ahead of them.

And then a case—a local murder, then, only days later, another—put him gradually into the spotlight, into the glare, and they'd had to be even more discreet. It made their rendezvous less frequent and consequently even more intense.

The serial sniper. Striking at random. And one of those random strikes took her. As if fate could not allow his happiness. As if fate could not allow his discovery of himself. Random? How dare anyone call it random. It was fate—laughing at him, howling at him, directing its full force and fury at him.

At first, he didn't know it was her, of course. *Another victim,* they informed him. *Number ten.*

And then, when he learned, he'd managed to remain steady in front of his deputies, before the chance to close his office door. Before his huge body gave way. Before crumpling to the floor. Before the heaving sobs escaped him in waves. Before the severing, the folding of his soul. Before pulling himself together, opening the door, soldiering on with the practiced deceit of the affair itself.

Before becoming a figure in some Greek tragedy. With an extra burden to bear upon the stage—in front of the cameras.

Attending her funeral, just as he had attended all the victims' funerals. So his presence was expected, unremarkable. His graveside pain—pain that he was forced to hide—a silent scream inside him, too much to stand.

Of course he had leaped across the table and tried to strangle Ray Fine in his holding cell. He could not even see straight, he was so blind with rage.

Of course, he realized—soon enough, no longer blind—what had really happened. Her bad marriage. Sam's failings. Difficulties connecting with her son. That was her small talk—mentioned in passing—brief, pointed, undwelled-upon, everything she was trying to momentarily push aside, after all. But it had not occurred to him—amid the pressures, the relentless rising body count, the all-consuming focus upon a serial sniper, a rampaging madman—that the petty squabbles and deceptions of Sam and Denise's marriage could rise to the level of murder. Maybe he simply could not bear to imagine that their affair could have any connection, could have played any role, in her death. Maybe he hadn't wanted to admit he could have failed her, that her confessions about her marriage amounted to a message: *Watch him. If anything happens to me, watch my husband.* Slowly Wyatt realized what the opportunity of a rampaging madman could mean for Sam Stevens, though the forensics still made no sense. It still seemed impossible that it could be Sam. Until the coroner's subtle observations of Sam at the morgue. Until Scott Bayer's suicide. Then the elements started to meld. It began to seem possible. It started to rise above the surface. Of course it was Sam.

It seems so personal for him, the reporters said about Big Billy Wyatt, with grudging admiration for the beleaguered, shell-shocked sheriff. But, of *course* he was dogged. Of *course* he clung—alone, eccentrically—to his investigation, when Brady, when everyone else, had dismissed and abandoned him. Wyatt knew the truth about Sam. It was only a matter of proving it—and here Sam Stevens turned out to be more than a match. Though the challenge was as much within Wyatt himself. To stay with it. To keep pushing. Even when he knew there was little point anymore—that there would be no life for him afterward. That he would only return to his previous half-existence. That his brief stab at happiness had been snuffed out forever.

He had teetered on the edge the whole time. And when he drove out to the cabin, it was to kill Sam Stevens. To kill him before Ray Fine did—or else, second-best, to see Sam dead. Justice had failed, so justice had to be done.

He realized—when he knew where she'd been killed, when he

reconstructed what must have happened—that Sam very likely had waited for her outside Dominique's that night. If only *that* had been the night they'd met. Maybe seeing them together would have shaken Sam enough to abandon his plan. Maybe Wyatt would have been the target and not her. Maybe it would have played out in some other way. In any other way than the way it did.

Big Billy Wyatt walks alone, moving farther away from the ball field. He squints in the bright summer sunlight. It's a morning of pure sun, he notices—no clouds, no shadows. If they suspend the game today because of what just happened to Tommy's dad, because they're all too rattled, he knows they'll pick it up tomorrow. He knows league play will go on. Watching Tommy and his teammates, he has realized how much he misses his ballplaying days. The green fields and fresh air. The camaraderie. The clear rules. And the score, posted simple and immutable at the end of the game. Yes, he misses playing ball.

He knows he will get kudos. The Webster County police will experience his victory as a return to the world they know. A world of order. The world of before.

Yes, he has solved it—although more accurately, more humbly, he has been present as it has solved itself.

And Billy Wyatt has discovered firsthand how far people will go. What people will do.

How far Ray would go for his boy, Joe.

How far Sam would go for Tommy.

How far you'll go for love.

Out on the horizon, Wyatt can see the unmarked sedan carrying Sam Stevens and the support vehicle behind it turning up onto the interstate, glinting in the midday sunshine, heading down to the Webster County jail.

It would probably make the television news by midafternoon.

Sam Stevens. Local television reporter. Talk-show hero.

Who killed his wife Denise Stevens.

Just for starters.

Sam Stevens was going to prison forever.

Where someday, some young, ambitious local television reporter would undoubtedly do a piece on him, it occurs to Wyatt.

Inside the Mind of Sam Stevens.

Wouldn't want to be there now, thinks Wyatt.